The First Time I Knocked

JO MACGREGOR

VIP Readers' Group: If you would like to receive my author's newsletter, with tips on great books, a behind-the-scenes look at my writing and publishing processes, and notice of new books, giveaways and special offers, then sign up at my website, www.joannemacgregor.com.

The First Time I Knocked first published in 2022 by Jo Macgregor
ISBN: 978-0-6397-3751-5 (paperback)
ISBN: 978-0-6397-3752-2 (eBook)

Disclaimer: This is a work of fiction. All the characters, institutions and events described in it are fictional and the products of the author's imagination.

Cover design by Jenny Zemanek at Seedlings Design Studio
Formatting by Polgarus Studio

"Where ask is have, where seek is find,
Where knock is open wide."
— Christopher Smart, *Song to David*

"Why are you knocking at every door?
Go, knock at the door of your own heart."
— Rumi

$$- 1 -$$

Every woman secretly hopes that her boyfriend's ex is ugly. Ryan's wasn't. Every woman secretly hopes her boyfriend hates his ex. Ryan didn't.

On that cool Vermont evening in early October, I was in the right place at the right time to witness both of these unwelcome truths. Outside, the trees wore their fall blaze of sunset colors — candy-apple red, egg-yolk yellow, Halloween orange. Inside Ryan Jackson's house, the colors were more muted, and we were in a mellow mood. I sat at one end of the long couch and he at the other, with my feet in his lap, while we watched the logs in the fireplace burn down to a steady glow and sipped at our glasses of red wine, unwinding from what had been a long week for both of us.

Ryan — police chief of Pitchford, Vermont, and the thirty-five-year-old, attractive, smart, and sane man who'd inexplicably chosen me as his plus-one — had been investigating a spate of fires that some arsonist kept starting around town. I'd been helping my parents clear out the basement at our old family house. Spending time with my mother always left me in the state of annoyed exhaustion that made me feel guilty for being such an impatient, difficult daughter. So it felt good to sit still and get my feet massaged. My eyes closed, and I was just drifting off when Ryan's phone rang.

He checked the screen, and his eyebrows rose. "Videocall. From Desirae."

Desirae Jackson was Ryan's ex-wife. They'd divorced five years ago, and Ryan had told me they usually only exchanged texts on birthdays and Christmas, which was the kind of distance I welcomed between them. I hitched what I hoped was a pleasant, unthreatened smile onto my face.

Keeping my ears tuned to their conversation, I forced myself to look away from the phone, staring at the fire, my toes, the couch. With its worn leather, sagging middle, and stains like Rorschach inkblots, that couch had seen some wear, probably even the kind of mileage that Ryan and Desirae had once put on it.

Pushing aside images of intertwined limbs and locked lips, I glanced over at Ryan. A mistake. Meeting my gaze, he told Desirae, "Hey, there's someone you should meet," and, ignoring my furious silent protests, he turned the phone to face me. "This is Garnet McGee, my girlfriend. Garnet, this is Desirae."

Desirae's blond hair was barely restrained in a messy bun, her eyes were bright, cornflower blue, and her friendly smile was as sweet as peach pie. I mistrusted her immediately.

"Hey, Garnet. Good to finally meet you!" she said.

Finally?

I exchanged a glance with Ryan. He'd mentioned me to her

before now? How had he described me — the basics as per a police rap sheet: twenty-nine years old, medium height, brown hair, heterochromatic eyes? Or had he also explained the more complicated bits: Master's in psychology but doesn't want to be a psychologist; reluctant returnee to small-town Vermont; the gal who'd dated the boy who was the brother of his first girlfriend? Or the truly wild parts: survivor of a near-death experience, inexpert and erratic psychic, amateur sleuth, compulsive nail-biter, occasional skin-picker, and longtime cynic?

"Yeah, good to meet you, too!" I said, aiming for the kind of extrovert friendliness that was utterly alien to me.

"Oops! Hang on a sec, the water's boiling over." The image on the phone spun, showing her hand laying a wooden spoon across the top of a pot.

"What's on the menu?" I asked, knowing I'd probably regret it. Ryan's ex was a trained chef who worked in a restaurant in Austin, Texas.

"Homemade pumpkin gnocchi with sage butter."

Yup, instant regret. My cooking repertoire extended to sandwiches and a chili hot enough to raise a sweat.

"Sounds delicious … Um, well, here's Ryan." I shoved the phone back into his hands, narrowing my eyes at his knowing smile. He probably knew exactly what I was feeling.

Uncertain as to whether I should stay on the couch or give them some privacy, I hesitated. My wine — almost on empty — decided it for me. I took both of our glasses to the kitchen to top them up, leaving Ryan to chat with Desirae. My ears, however, still strained to catch his every word.

"You did? That's amazing — congratulations!"

Maybe she'd met someone new and married him. A girl could hope.

But Ryan was speaking again. "Yeah? … Ah, man, I'm so sorry. I knew you were close. Have the local cops— … Oh … Uh-huh … Uh-huh … But he doesn't agree?"

I snuck a look at Ryan. He was sitting up straight, frowning in concentration, and running a hand through his thick black hair. I filled our glasses, knocked back a large sip of my Pinot Grigio, and topped it off again.

"I mean, I could," Ryan said, "but it might piss them off — an outsider coming in, sniffing around … What? Well, I could do *that*, I suppose … Actually, I might have an idea."

He looked up and caught me watching him. I spun around and made a business of tidying a kitchen counter. In the lounge, it sounded like Ryan was finishing up their conversation.

"Let me see what I can do. I'll get back to you tomorrow. … Okay, bye."

He came into the kitchen, and I handed him his wine. "What was Desirae's good news?" At his blank look, I added, "You congratulated her about something?"

"Oh, right. She won some kind of cheffy award. A really big deal, it seems."

"That's great." I turned back to the counter, allowing the smile to slide off my face.

Ryan put down his wine and hugged me from behind, nuzzling my neck. "You're tastier than homemade gnocchi any day."

"You say the most romantic things, Chief." I turned in his arms to reward him with a kiss.

After a long moment, he lifted his head. "How would you

like to get out of town for a weekend with me?"

"You want to go to Texas?" I looked up into his slate-gray eyes, which were filled with an enthusiasm I didn't share. The prospect of a weekend visiting Ryan's ex didn't exactly fill me with delight.

"No, not Texas. New Orleans."

"New Orleans? *Really?*"

I'd always wanted to visit the Big Easy, but I couldn't remember ever having mentioned it to him. Maybe I wasn't the only psychic in this relationship?

He grinned at my enthusiasm. "Really. We could escape the leaf peepers."

Locals had a love-hate relationship with the tourists who flooded New England every year to see the stunning fall foliage. On the one hand, they took all the parking spots, left litter behind, and had yet to master driving etiquette. On the other hand, they filled local coffers.

"Tempting," I said.

He took my hand and rubbed a thumb lightly over the backs of my fingers. "We could find a nice romantic hotel with a king-sized bed and spend a lot of time in it."

"*Very* tempting."

"And do I need to remind you that New Orleans is the home of Cajun and Creole cuisine? All very" — he brought my hand to his mouth and slowly kissed each fingertip — "spicy."

"Sold!"

Pulling me closer, he added, "Plus, it should be right up your alley."

"Oh yeah? How's that?"

"There's a murder that needs investigating."

– 2 –

The last murder I'd investigated had an outcome that was good, bad, and ugly. The good: I'd caught the killer. I knew I'd have to testify at the court case and wasn't looking forward to coming face to face with the murderer again, but nothing was happening soon. The date for the trial hadn't even been set yet.

The bad — or perhaps sad — part of the outcome was that nailing the serial killer hadn't brought back the young men who'd died at his hands. Of course, I'd known it wouldn't, but until you've hunted a killer, you think that finding him will somehow restore justice and make things better. Spoiler alert, it didn't. In my *what-was-it-all-for?* moments, I reminded myself that at least he wouldn't be ending any more lives, and that mattered; that counted for something.

The ugly? I'd dug deep into myself and my knowledge of psychology, and tortured a dangerous — but also damaged — man with words that scared and hurt him to his core. I'd been appalled to discover that deep within me lay a potential for cruelty and violence. According to the great Swiss psychologist, Carl Jung:

"Everyone carries a shadow, and the less it is embodied in the individual's conscious life, the blacker and denser it is."

It had been a shock to discover just how cruel mine could be, and almost five months later, I was still trying to process what had happened, what I'd done. I wasn't sure I wanted back into the psychic private eye game, not if it meant becoming a darker version of myself.

However, I did want to spend a long weekend with Ryan exploring New Orleans. And each other. Our relationship was going well. Better than well, really. He still laughed at my jokes, I still valued his opinion, and the sex was still good and sweaty. It helped that *my* ex, Colby Beaumont, was honoring his promise to stay out of it. I still felt his presence on my left-hand side when I sat alone down at the pond or went for a solo stroll in the woods, and sometimes I caught the scent of cola — his favorite flavor lip balm — in the sleepy moments when I woke up from an afternoon nap. But when I was with Ryan, he stayed away. Or was it simply that I was — finally — healing from my loss, that I was more attuned to the man who was here and now rather than the boy who'd once held my heart and my hopes in his golden hands? Either way, a couple of romantic days spent in a warmer climate indulging all my appetites sounded really appealing.

I didn't mention any of this the next day when I told my boss that I needed time off. Instead, I emphasized the investigation angle, even though it was Ryan's detecting expertise that had been requested, not mine.

"It's a family murder," I explained.

Henry Mason was a semiretired attorney, and I was the

part-time assistant who helped him out with admin on the few cases he still worked, while keeping a watchful eye on his health on behalf of his daughter who lived out of state. In exchange, I received wages so modest they verged on shy, but I also got to live rent free in a loft apartment above his garage.

"Murder?" He looked up from the purple and white petals of the orchid he was tending and lowered his grizzled eyebrows at me. "Going to stick your nose where it doesn't belong, eh?"

I sniffed. "If by that you mean: am I going to try to help out, then yes, Henry, I am."

With a curmudgeonly *humph*, he turned his attention back to the plant. It was one of the scores that watched me from every bench, table, and rack in his large, temperature-controlled greenhouse. I used to like orchids; I thought they were pretty, delicate little things. But the sheer overwhelm of this place — the riotous colors, the nausea-inducing stink of their sweetly rotten perfume — had turned me into a hater. Now they seemed like predatory jungle creatures, with their pale, twisted roots ever eager to escape the confines of their pots.

Frowning, Henry snipped a yellowed leaf off the specimen in front of him and cast a suspicious look in my direction. "*Someone* ... has over-watered this *phalaenopsis*."

"Don't look at me. I know better than to touch your babies," I retorted.

"Too much water kills as surely as too little."

"So you've told me. Many times."

"And this *Cymbidium* doesn't belong here."

"I didn't put it there, Henry. You must've."

He handed me the plant with its long spikes of pink flowers

— like gaping mouths with protruding spotted tongues — and pointed to a lower, shadier shelf. "They're endemic to the foothills of the Himalayas and like cool conditions."

"Fascinating. Anyway, as I was saying, Ryan has been asked to check things out on this murder case, to give his input and—"

"I *like* Chief Jackson," Henry said, somehow conveying by his tone of voice that he didn't feel the same way about me.

I didn't take offense; I was onto Henry Mason. Beneath his crusty manner, he had a marshmallow heart. True, it *was* buried pretty deep down, but I caught glimpses of it every now and then. But he positively thrived on giving me a hard time; it entertained him, particularly if he could bait me into an invigorating argument.

"I like Chief Jackson too. And it might interest you to learn that the chief thinks *I* may be able to provide some insight into the case," I said, proud that Ryan, at least, had some faith in my abilities.

"Or maybe he just wants some female company?" Henry packed peat moss and bark chips around the base of a plant with miniature flowers and gave it an approving nod.

"Either way, it's a vote for me."

I took the orchid from Henry's arthritic grasp and climbed onto a step stool to return the plant to its spot on a high shelf.

"Thank you," Henry said gruffly. He hated anything which made him feel helpless or dependent.

"I didn't do it for you. Your daughter would hand me my marching papers if I let her old man do it himself."

He perked up a little at that, though whether because I wasn't treating him like a helpless old man, or at the thought of my being sacked, I couldn't have said.

"Going to use your crazy ghost eyes?" he asked, peering first at my blue right eye and then at the left, which had turned brown after my near-death experience nine months previously.

"It's not my eyes that give me the visions," I told Henry, not for the first time.

"You sure about that? I've told you what they say about them."

"Yeah, yeah. Ghosts, fairies, witches."

He wiped his hands on a cloth. "But did you know that differently-colored eyes can be a symptom of diabetes or glaucoma?"

"Been reading up about it *again*?"

"Or Posner-Schlossman syndrome, or even" — he gave a gleeful cackle — "Von Recklinghausen disease."

I dusted my hands on my jeans. "You have a real bug up your butt about my eyes, Henry, you know that? It's verging on an obsession."

"All I know is I never met another *human* who looked like you."

"Well, it's good to know that I bring some novelty into your dotage." I shoved the step stool under the workbench and gave him a bright smile.

"But I've seen plenty of rabbits with them. And dogs — huskies and collies."

"You just keep the schtick coming, Henry."

"Sometimes rats get odd eyes, too, I hear."

"You'd better hope I'm not a rat by nature, then. There were *three* empty wine bottles in the trash last week."

That shut him up. If I told his daughter how frequently her father replaced the packages of kale juice and bran-and-broccoli muffins she sent him with cabernet and cookies, she'd insist he go live with her, and Henry valued his independence.

"Anyway," I said, "the point is, I'll be away the whole weekend. We're flying out on Thursday afternoon and coming back on Tuesday."

"I daresay I'll survive your absence. Of course, I'll have to dock your pay."

"No, you won't. It's a mere pittance already." Before he could argue the point, I said, "Want me to bring you anything back from New Orleans?"

His eyes lit up. "Roman candy, if you can find it."

"I don't know what that is, but I promise to look."

"Look twice," he said, winking first one then his other eye.

I rolled both of mine.

"And some pecan pralines," he added.

"Anything el—" I began but was interrupted by the ringing of my phone. It was my mother, and she sounded like she was in a flat panic.

"Come over now, Garnet. Quick! We have an emergency," she said, and hung up before I could ask any questions.

I ran to my car and sped over to my parents' house on the other side of Pitchford, pushing my old Honda over the limit, and cursing when I got stuck behind a tractor on the stretch of road that passed by Plover Pond. What was the emergency at home? My thoughts went first to my mother. In the previous year, she'd taken a tumble and broken her foot, and she'd also suffered a series of mini-strokes which had left her possibly even more addled than she ordinarily was. Had she fallen again? Had her blood pressure spiked?

But maybe, I thought as I turned into Abernaki Street, this time it was my father who was in trouble. He was sixty-four years old, and although he hadn't had any major health scares so far, there had to be a first time. Imagining him clutching his chest and toppling to the ground, I tore up the driveway — braking hard to avoid ramming the ancient black Buick already parked there — and sprinted to the front door.

My father answered my hammering, and he seemed perfectly fine. So if it wasn't him *in extremis*, that meant …

"Mom!" I yelled.

Stepping around my father, I raced down the hallway and was brought up short at the entrance to the sitting room, stunned by what I saw.

$$-3-$$

I'd been expecting to find my mother prostrate on the floor, possibly convulsing or bleeding. Instead, what I saw inside the living room was a pair of elderly ladies seated comfortably on the sofa and drinking coffee. One of them was my mother.

Scanning her face, arms, legs, I demanded, "What's the matter? Are you okay?"

"I'm fine, dear, but Ethel is in an absolute state. You remember Mrs. Burns?" my mother said, gesturing to the pale-faced woman beside her.

Tears streamed down Mrs. Burns's heavily powdered cheeks, and her hands twisted a lacy handkerchief like she was wringing the neck of an enemy.

"What's the emergency?" I asked, confused.

My father settled back into his recliner and rubbed his hands as if getting ready to enjoy a spectacle. "There is no emergency."

"How *can* you say that, Bob?" my mother said hotly. Turning to me, she said, "Tommy is missing!"

"Who's Tommy?" I asked.

Ethel Burns was a widow, and as far as I recalled, she had only one child — a daughter.

"My dear, dear boy," Mrs. Burns sobbed.

"Tommy," my father said dryly, "is Ethel's schnauzer."

I spun on my mother. "*Mom*! You called me over here for a *dog*?"

"Not just any dog, dear. Tommy is—"

"Not a person! You scared me stupid. You said it was an emergency."

"It *is*. Tommy is not a young dog, and he's very acceptable to chest infections."

"*Susceptible*," I growled, in no mood for my mother's habit of mangling the English language.

"Your mother's tried to help me." Mrs. Burns indicated the table in front of them, where several tarot cards lay face up. "But so far, we've had no luck."

My mother held up a crystal pendulum. "I even tried this, but sadly, the spirits aren't coming through for me today." Though she wasn't a psychic herself, my mother ran a store in town which sold crystals, candles, dreamcatchers, tarot decks, and every other aid purported to assist in capturing messages from the ether. And she insisted on using them herself. "But as I told Ethel, *you'll* be able to help for sure."

"So, I'm a dog detective now, is that it?"

"Got anything more important going on?" My mother could be sharp when she wanted.

"Yes," I snapped. "As a matter of fact, I do."

"Well, you can tell me all about it as soon as we've found Tommy," she said, undeterred.

Exasperated, I glanced at my father. My look said, *How have you stayed married to this woman for so many years?* The shrug he gave me in return said, *You may as well do what she wants, because there'll be no peace until the hound is found.*

My mother handed me a dog lead blinged to the max with fake sapphires. At least, I *thought* they were fake; given the old dame's traumatic reaction to her dog's defection, it was entirely possible that she loved him enough to lavish real jewels on him.

"I didn't click the clasp on the collar properly," Mrs. Burns confessed, "and he escaped when I opened the front door. I was going to take him for his walk. We always go walkies this time of day."

"Maybe a kidnapper noticed that pattern and nabbed him! And you'll be getting a ransom note soon," my mother said.

She'd been kidnapped back in May, and she'd been understandably paranoid about vans and strange men ever since. The memory of that awful time reminded me of my vow to be kinder and more patient with her, so I bit back the scathing remark about dognapping that hovered on the tip of my tongue.

Mrs. Burns gazed at me, her eyes wide with fear and hope, and I felt a pang of compassion for her. Her daughter, Judy Burns, had gone to high school with me and had always been a cow. I couldn't see *her* rushing to help or comfort her mother.

"He's probably just wandered off to visit a lady friend, Mrs. Burns," I reassured her. "I'm sure he'll be back soon."

"*Please.* Please, will you just try?"

Her beseeching look and trembling bottom lip hit me right in my empathy gland. I sighed and issued my usual disclaimers.

"I can't *make* the clairvoyance happen, and even when it does, it's not always relevant or accurate." Truth be told, it usually was, but my interpretation of what exactly the words and visions actually meant was sometimes way off base. Often, I only understood them with the perfect vision of hindsight, and anyone could do *that*. "You should also know that I've never tried it for an animal."

"Oh, Garnet, if you can do it for humans, why wouldn't you be able to do it for animals?" my mother snapped. "They have souls, too, don't they?"

My father snorted, and I opened my mouth to argue the ludicrous point, but my mother wasn't done talking.

"Not that I mean to say Tommy's crossed the veil into the world of spirit, Ethel, dear, I just mean that he's not an *object*. Though" — she fixed me with a challenging stare — "you've used your gift to find *them* before, too, haven't you? Barns and, and … wells!"

She wasn't wrong.

"So for goodness' sakes, dear, just get on with it already."

I puffed out a breath and shut my eyes, thinking about lost dogs running down roads, getting run over by cars, or being locked in garden sheds.

I opened one eye. "Have you checked the garden shed?" I asked Mrs. Burns, thinking it best to eliminate the obvious before attempting the mystical.

"That was quick!" she said.

"I haven't star—"

"Give me a moment." Mrs. Burns pulled an ancient Nokia out of her handbag and called her neighbor, relaying updates to us every few seconds. "Mr. Yee says he'll go check right now … He's in my yard … He can hear barking!"

My father shook his head and picked up a heavy book — *Killer Code: Cracking the Case of the Zodiac Killer*.

"Oh, heavens, he's there!" Mrs. Burns exclaimed. "Tommy was in the shed all this time, and Mr. Yee says he seems absolutely fine. Oh, thank you, Garnet!"

I accepted her gratitude, even though I hadn't had any kind of a vision. I usually wasn't thanked when I did, so I figured this evened the score a little.

"There, you see? I knew your psychometry wouldn't fail you!" my mother declared. "This is just more proof of your abilities."

"It's proof of her common sense," my father said dryly. "I can't believe the shed wasn't checked in the first place."

Still dabbing her eyes and thanking me profusely, Ethel Burns hurried off to reunite with her schnauzer, and my mother insisted I tell her what important thing was happening in my life. I grabbed a couple of cookies from the plate on the coffee table and told her I was going away for the weekend with Ryan.

"Ah, romance! I should've known. It's right here in the Ace of Cups and the Four of Wands," my mother said, tapping two of the cards on the table.

"You dealt that hand for Mrs. Burns," I pointed out.

My mother looked stumped for a moment but made a quick recovery. "The spirits must have known *you* were coming. That's why these made no sense for Ethel. Unless … perhaps Ethel and Mr. Yee …? She has a real proclensity for falling in love, you know."

"Proclivity," I said automatically.

"Is there something more to this trip, kiddo?" my father said.

"Yes, a new case to investigate." While my mother gathered and shuffled her cards, I told him about it. "Back in July, a family of four was shot dead in their restaurant after it closed for the night."

My mom dealt a line of cards and cocked her head in puzzlement. "Oh."

"Multiple homicides," my father said. "Where was this?"

"New Orleans."

"Aha! That explains this card," my mother said triumphantly. "You're going on a pilgrimage to explore your gift and develop your talents."

"No, I'm going to spend time with Ryan, who's checking out a seemingly solved case."

"New Orleans is a very spiritual and mystical place." My mother's hands danced in the air, perhaps sketching the shape of the ethereal beings she so wished she could see. "It's filled with lingering spirits and supernatural energy."

"Filled with drunks and deadbeats, more like," my father retorted. "What is Ryan's connection to the case?"

"His ex-wife—"

"Ooh, what's her name?" my mother interjected.

"—is friends with the chef at the restaurant where—"

"Is she pretty?"

"—the family was killed."

"She lives in New Orleans, then?"

"—And the shooter was the chef's cousin or something," I

finished, speaking over my mother.

"Oh, an inside job then." My dad's face fell a little in disappointment. He was a true-crime afficionado, but his real passion was reserved for serial killers.

"I don't understand," my mother said. "If they've found the killer, what do they need Chief Jackson for?"

"Apparently, the chef has his doubts about the official version. He wants Ryan to look into it, check that the New Orleans police did a proper job investigating it. And Ryan thinks I might be able to help."

"Of course you will, dear. My goodness, New Orleans! Next thing we know, you'll be in hot demand internationally. However, I do need to warn you about this." My mother tapped one of the cards. "I see an interfering, overbearing female in your future!"

"Just like my present, then," I said, and my father chuckled.

"Would you like me to put together a crystal kit for your quest?" my mother offered.

"No thanks. I already have more than I can carry." On this cool fall day, I'd put on my jacket and found all the crystals she'd previously given me in the pockets. If I were to fall into Plover Pond now, I'd sink swiftly to the bottom.

"Be sure to take the black tourmaline or the obsidian for protection, then," she insisted. "I don't like this woman. I sense danger."

– 4 –

The Thursday-afternoon flight from Burlington to New Orleans was crowded with booze-lubricated football fans loud with team pride.

"The Saints are playing the Patriots at the Superdome this weekend," Ryan explained as we took our seats.

"That right?" I said, with all the interest of a carnivore offered a tofu kabob.

"We can try to catch the game if you like. Find a scalper and score some tickets?" His right cheek dimpled in a teasing smile. Ryan was aware that I knew very little about sports and cared even less.

"If you can score seats to the saints that are going to come marching in on that morning, then I'd be keen," I said, thinking of brass bands tooting out catchy tunes.

"Oh, these guys will be singing that song before long, just wait."

I grimaced and clicked my seatbelt closed. "It's going to be a long flight."

"Did you know that song is about the apocalypse?"

"No way."

"Yup. The verses talk about the sun refusing to shine, the moon turning red with blood, stars falling from the sky, and the horsemen — the Four Horsemen of the Apocalypse, that is — beginning to ride. It's all there in Revelations."

The supporters in blue, red, and silver sitting on the right-hand side of the plane started chanting, "Do your job! Do your job!" And the ones in gold, black, and white, inferior in number but somehow superior in volume, called back, "Who dat? Who dat?"

"Forget the apocalypse. I'm in hell already," I grumbled.

Across the aisle from me sat a teenage girl and her mother, both of whom fired up their phones as soon as we were in the air and given the all-clear. When the flight attendant asked about refreshments, Ryan got us each a soda and some nuts, and I logged onto the airline's Wi-Fi and began researching our case.

"Well, here's a plot twist right off the bat," I told him, scanning a news story on the crime. "All four members of the family were shot, but one, the son, *survived*. Though it seems like it was touch and go there for a while. This article says he was shot in the restaurant's back office, but his family were killed in a refrigerator." I paused for a moment, trying to figure that one out. "I guess it must've been one of those walk-in cold rooms."

"Add refrigerators to the list of places I don't want to die in," Ryan said.

"Yeah." I didn't get a psychic flash, but I could imagine the scene, and that was rough enough.

"Squish the fish! Squish the fish!" The fans to our right yelled, and from our left came the reply: "Bowwwww up!"

"You reckon this is going to go on for the whole flight?" I said.

"You could pick a side. You know, if you can't beat 'em, join 'em?"

"Not going to happen, Chief." I read a few more online articles, trying to construct a timeline of what had occurred. "Okay, so it all happened on the night of July Fourth."

"Clever," Ryan said.

"How's that?"

"The sound of gunshots would've been disguised by fireworks."

"Yeah, you're right! So, it seems this robber was an employee at the restaurant. And he breaks in, waves a gun around, marches the family to the kitchen, then shoots the mother."

"Just like that? Why?"

"Maybe as a message to the others to cooperate?" I toggled between websites. "One source says there was some kind of altercation. The others give no details."

"Hmm." Ryan looked thoughtful.

"Then he, the robber I mean, killed the father and the daughter in the refrigerator." I opened my little bag of peanuts and popped some into my mouth. Better nuts than nails, right? A couple of weeks previously, I'd downloaded a hypnotic induction to stop biting my fingernails, and I'd been listening to it every day since. It seemed to be working for the most part — I now had a thin rim of white on every nail — but I still felt the occasional urge to nibble.

"Why, though? Why not just lock them in the cooler?" I mused aloud. "Would you freeze to death if you were left overnight in one of those?"

"I doubt it. Unless it was a freezer rather than a refrigerator?"

I pulled a newly purchased spiral-bound notebook out of my bag and, just like a real, honest-to-goodness private eye, jotted down a few questions.

Altercation triggered shooting?
Why kill father and daughter?
Freezer or refrigerator?

"I'm keeping a track of lines of enquiry for you, Chief. Right, so where were we?" I consulted my phone again. "Okay, so after he shot the father and the sister, the gunman forced the son to go to the back office and made him hand over the day's earnings. Then, according to *The Inquirer*, the son made a break for it and was shot trying to escape." I checked a bunch of other sources, but each of them seemed to have a different version of what had occurred. "Well, it's not clear exactly what happened next, but the son got shot, and the robber got shot. The robber died on the scene, but even though he was bleeding seriously and going into shock, the son managed to call 911."

"Adrenaline can do that, and he would've been full of it."

Momentarily distracted, I asked, "You ever see a mother lift a car off her kid?"

"No, but back when I was with the Middlebury PD, we were once called out to the scene of a carjacking. The vic didn't even realize he'd been shot" — Ryan tapped his upper arm — "until we pointed it out to him."

"Wow."

In my psychology studies, I'd learned about the role adrenaline played in the body's fight-or-flight response to danger and the pain-numbing effects of the endogenous opiates which were also released in life-and-death situations. But hearing a real-life example from a real-life cop was a whole other thing.

A harassed-looking flight attendant walked past, carrying beers, and the fans behind us sent up a united whoop of pleasure.

"Anyhow, by the time help arrived, the robber was dead, and the son was unconscious. He'd almost bled out." I had to raise my voice to be heard, because some of the football fans were yelling, "Everything we got!" over and over again, which set their opposition to chanting, "Who dat? Who dat? Who dat say dey gonna beat dem Saints?"

"Where did the son get hit?" Ryan asked.

I checked. "Shoulder, according to the *Times-Picayune*, leg according to the *New Orleans Tribune*. Got to say, neither of those sound too serious to me."

"It depends," Ryan replied. "If the bullet hits an artery, it can be life-threatening."

I chased the last of my nuts with a swallow of Diet Coke. "For a while, it looked like the son would follow his family—" I cut myself off. I'd been about to say, "beyond the veil." My mother's woo-woo speak was starting to infect me. "Ryan?"

"Yeah?"

"If I ever start sounding like my mother, just shoot me."

"Nah, I'll keep you around for the laughs."

When, as Ryan had predicted, the liquored-up fans started an off-key rendition of "When the Saints Go Marching In," I plugged in my headphones and hit play on my favorite white-noise track — soft rain on a tin roof. But even at full volume, it wasn't loud enough to block out the words of the song.

"I don't hear anything about bleeding moons and falling stars," I told Ryan.

"That's because they only know the first two verses. The scary stuff comes later."

Returning my attention to my phone, I was surprised to see a friend request on Facebook. I hardly ever used the site; I wasn't interested in what acquaintances ate for lunch or in seeing photos of their precious loin goblins, and I was even less interested in sharing details about *my* private life. So who the heck was reaching out to me now?

Desirae. Desirae Jackson, that's who.

I wasn't sure I wanted to be friends (even virtually) with Ryan's ex. But I *was* wicked curious about her — what she looked like, what she did with her time, whether she currently had a man in her life.

I caught the eye of the teenager sitting across the aisle and said, "Hey, can you be friends with someone on Facebook and see all their posts without them seeing yours?"

"I'm not on *Facebook*," she said, sounding insulted. Judging by the look of disdain she gave me, I may as well have asked her about MySpace or Friendster. "I'll ask my *mother* if you like."

"Yeah, sure, thanks." Not yet thirty, and already, I was feeling old.

After conferring with her mother for a minute, the girl

reported back to me. "No. The friendship thing works both ways or not at all."

Just like high school, then. Cursing silently, I hit the *accept* button and, angling my phone so Ryan couldn't see, pored over Desirae's timeline. I had no doubt that she'd soon be checking out mine. Good luck finding anything juicy in that barren wilderness, lady.

Desirae was a regular poster and seemed to change her profile pic every other week. She was undeniably pretty and photogenic too — another knack I'd never mastered — and she seemed to have quite a following. Her timeline was filled with way too many photos of a tubby cat called Truffle, who seemed to spend the bulk of his life lying around in different spots, and a good many pics of Desirae cooking. In each, her hair and makeup were as perfectly styled as the delicious-looking food. I wondered if she had to pick cat hair off the plates before she snapped the photos. There were a couple of posts of her helping out at a charity where young homeless people were taught the kind of cooking skills that could hopefully help them land a job. She seemed like a good person.

I was probably — definitely — biased, but it seemed to me that she thrived on the attention her posts received and milked the comments for reassurances about her cooking and appearance. I remembered how Ryan had once told me that their marriage had foundered in part because he hadn't been willing or able to provide the steady stream of compliments, encouragement, and reassurances her insecurity required. "Cheerleading," he'd called it if I remembered right. Judging by her posts, she hadn't changed much in the five years since they'd divorced.

I glanced sideways at his profile. How much had he changed since, then?

$$- 5 -$$

By the time we landed at Louis Armstrong Airport, my head was aching, and I was desperate to escape the football fans. The outside air embraced me in a haze of heat and humidity that had me removing my jacket while we waited for an Uber. But I slipped it back on once we were inside the air-conditioned chill of the Prius.

The driver said the trip would take around forty minutes, and while he and Ryan fell into a discussion about the upcoming game, I leaned against Ryan's shoulder and stared out the window. The landscape was flat and dotted with mom-and-pop eateries with rusting signs and boats parked out front. Closer to the city, these gave way to the inevitable big boys — Chick-fil-A, MacDonald's, Taco Bell. The traffic on I-10, already heavy with the influx of tourists, partiers, and sports fans, slowed to a standstill on the Pontchartrain Expressway, trapping us on a section of road with cemeteries on both sides.

"Must be a fender bender ahead," the driver told us. "This is Metairie Cemetery on the right and Greenwood on the left."

"We're in the dead center of town," Ryan said.

I snorted a laugh. Gazing at the marble crosses and statues of angels, at the rows of stone and marble mausoleums laid out in neat rows like city blocks, I asked the driver, "Why are all the tombs above ground?"

"This city is at sea level. Below it in some places. That's why we get flooded every time a hurricane comes through. If they bury the dead in a grave underground, the high water table will just pop 'em right out again."

The traffic crept forward slower than a herd of turtles stampeding through peanut butter. Eventually we picked up speed again and headed toward the jagged line of skyscrapers ahead — the Central Business District, according to our driver, where we could shop 'til we dropped at the South Market District, catch a show at the Orpheum, or visit the Audubon Aquarium of the Americas to touch stingrays and see the famous white alligator.

The driver didn't need to point out the massive beige roof of the Superdome on our right. I could still recall the images from when Hurricane Katrina tore through the city back in 2005. Tens of thousands of people had sheltered there, begging for food, desperate for rescue. I still remembered the horrible stories of what happened inside when the roof leaked, supplies ran out, the power failed, and the chaos increased.

Ryan and I both turned our heads to see it as we passed then exchanged a look with each other. He gave my hand a comforting squeeze, and I nodded sadly. We were getting good at knowing what the other was thinking.

"And this is St. Louis Cemetery," the driver said as we passed yet another graveyard.

"How many cemeteries are there in this city?" I asked.

"Forty-two."

Ryan gave a low whistle.

"This city is full of the dead," the driver said, squeezing the Prius between the lanes of taxis and shuttle buses headed down Basin Street. "And some of them don't want to stay put."

As we neared the French Quarter, the architecture outside slipped back in time, gradually morphing into the type of scenery I'd seen in so many movies and TV shows. Houses and hotels, painted pink, yellow, green, and gray, were built right on the sidewalk and eyed the world from behind wooden shutters. Baskets of ferns and geraniums hung from second-story balconies hemmed in by wrought iron balustrades, and waterfalls of white and cerise bougainvillea spilled over tumbledown walls. Old-timey lampposts — real ones, not the fake touristy rubbish that the mayor of Pitchford had put up on our town's main street — declared the names of roads in black and white signs: Lafitte, Toulouse, Dauphine, Bienville. Side alleys, with overflowing flower boxes and flags between their dumpsters and graffiti-tagged walls, hinted at shady courtyards and secret places.

Canal Street — wide, heavy with traffic, and lined with palm trees, malls, and office blocks — came as a modern shock, but with a couple of sharp turns, we were deep in the French Quarter. The swanky hotels with classical columned porticoes and top-hatted doormen at the top of Bourbon Street gave way to seedier joints the further down its length we travelled. Everywhere, pedestrians crowded the sidewalk and spilled into the road. Signs for oysters, fried chicken, catfish po-boys, and strawberry daiquiris had me realizing how starved and parched I was.

After a noisy altercation with the vendor of a food stand shaped like a giant hotdog on wheels, we got stuck behind a carriage drawn by a pair of mules — "sturdier than horses and better with the heat and the noise," according to our driver — until we eventually reached our destination.

"Here you go." The driver pulled over to let us out, indicating a hotel about thirty yards away. "That's the *La Gargouille* Hotel."

The spot in front of us opened as a limo pulled out, but our driver seemed set on staying where he was, so we grabbed our bags and walked the rest of the way to the entrance of the worn stucco building. Guarded by iron urns trailing ivy and impatiens, the purple front door sported an ornate brass knocker which looked like a gargoyle to me but which Ryan insisted was a lion's head. It took a few hammers, but eventually, the door was opened, and a shaft of the bright sunlight sliced the cool, dark interior.

"Welcome, welcome," said a wizened woman trailing shawls and dust motes that glimmered in the light.

Ryan had made the reservation for our accommodation, and because there were still rooms available at short notice, I'd been expecting the worst. So I was pleasantly surprised by the faded grandeur of the small hotel, even if it was a little heavy on dark wood furniture, faded tapestries, and antique fittings. Our small suite looked clean, and there were no hairs on the toilet seat and no bedbugs in the mattress seams.

"You've got to check — always!" I told Ryan, who was watching my insect inspections with amusement. "Oh, look, we have a balcony."

I opened the shuttered French windows, letting fresh air into the slightly musty room. In the center of the courtyard down below, water burbled from the mouths of stone gargoyles, and pots of flowers promised a scented sanctuary.

"Nice," Ryan said, coming to stand beside me. "What should we do now? Stay and play or get out and see the sights?"

I glanced at the romantic four-poster, with its heavy velvet drapes tied back with tasseled gold cords.

"We definitely need to test that bed," I said.

"That we do."

"Thing is, though, I don't do my best work on an empty stomach."

"Then we should definitely feed you first." He gave me a slow, sexy smile. "You're going to need your strength."

"Promises, promises," I teased, a little breathlessly because he was planting a row of soft kisses just under my jawline.

"I always deliver what I promise," he said, and I wondered how something could sound both threatening *and* enticing.

$$- 6 -$$

I freshened up, changing into black jeans and a flirty top but keeping my Doc Martens on just in case I needed to kick someone out of my way to get to a po-boy stand. I checked my appearance in the enormous mirror standing in one corner, and the gargoyles nestling in its ornamental scrollwork frame grinned back at me.

"These little monsters are all over — did you see the taps in the bathroom?" I said.

Ryan nodded. "This place isn't big on subtlety."

That, I soon discovered, was true of New Orleans as a whole. The Crescent City was many things — loud and proud; chic and shabby; dirty, decrepit, and depraved; but also grand, glorious, and anything but genteel. And crowded! If the French Quarter was this busy in October, what must it be like in the Mardi Gras madness of February and March?

We joined the throng moving down Bourbon street — partiers carrying drinks in neon-green containers shaped like hand grenades, gangs of frat boys being loud and obnoxious, women draped in colored beads hobbling on broken heels, neon signs, sex stores, dives and bars and rainbow flags; thumping music, screams of laughter, drunken shouts, two-for-one offers from doorway touts; takeout windows selling pizza by the slice — all my senses were under attack.

The riot of noise, color, and smells began to blur pleasantly about fifteen minutes after I discovered what Hurricanes were: a slam of light rum, an uppercut of dark rum, a few light slaps of fruit juice and grenadine, all kicked together in an enormous Solo cup for drinking in the street. They went down like a summer breeze and delivered the knockout punch of a heavyweight prize-fighter. My eyes, weird enough already, now seemed to want to focus in different directions. It seemed like half the town was walking around with one of the drinks in hand — New Orleans allowed open drinking in the streets as long as the container was plastic.

"No more Hurricanes!" I said as we entered a jazz club.

The guy at the door didn't bother to card us. Compared to the patrons chugging back booze inside, we must've seemed positively middle-aged. We ordered po-boys — stuffed with shrimp for Ryan and roast beef, pickle, and extra hot sauce for me — and beers. Both went down much better than the music.

"I know jazz is the one true American art form, and I'm supposed to love it."

"But you don't?" Ryan said.

I shook my head. "If epileptic seizures had a soundtrack, it'd be jazz."

Clutching our drinks, we left the club. Outside, the street was heaving with partygoers, tourists, and cops on horseback. People danced on the balconies, tossing down strings of gaudy beads, which I caught and draped around my neck. With every drink I quaffed, it seemed increasingly important that I collect more of the plastic necklaces.

"I want those!" I pointed at the two tantalizing strands of gold and violet beads which were being dangled down above my head by a man wearing an eye mask adorned with silver sequins and peacock feathers.

Ryan agreed that they were indeed amazing and joined me in beckoning for the man to release them into our hands.

"Show us your tits!" the peacock man yelled.

Astounded at this, I looked at Ryan.

"I don't think he means mine," he said.

"Should I?"

"Perhaps I'm just selfish and want them *allll* to myself," Ryan said, then mumbled something of which I only caught the odd word: "soft … lovely … mine."

My hands hesitated at the bottom of my shirt, ready to flip it up and put my puppies on full display. I really did want those beads.

"Hey," Ryan said.

"Hey, what?" I said. Was he leaning slightly to one side, or was I?

"Look at these people." He waved a finger at the crowd around us. "See?"

"See what?"

"Cameras!" he said like he was declaring the answer to the meaning of life.

His warning took a few seconds to meander through the backstreets of my booze-soaked brain, but I got there eventually.

"Right!" I tapped a finger against my temple and gave him a knowing look. "No knockers from me for you tonight, bro!" I shouted up at the peacock man. Instead of beads, he dropped a string of curses on my head then spat a great glob of saliva.

Ryan must've been anticipating something of the sort, because he tugged me aside just in time.

"My hero!" I told him.

He flashed a dazzling smile, steadied himself with a hand on a wall, then led me down a quieter side street. The razzmatazz of Bourbon Street faded to a distant roar as we passed quieter clubs and classier eateries.

"Hurricane shelter." I tugged Ryan toward a restaurant down the way with a striped awning. Maybe we could get some coffee and quiet there. But as we drew closer, I saw that its windows were dark, and a closed sign hung on the door. "Aw," I grumbled.

Ryan sat down on the front step and, with extreme care, placed his cup on the sidewalk beside him. "We could just sit here a lil' while."

"Hold up," I said, backing up on unsteady feet to read the name of the establishment. "This is it."

"Good." Ryan sighed, leaned back against the shut door, and closed his eyes.

"No, this is Broussard's! This is the place where it happened."

Ryan's eyes opened slowly. "What?"

"Where Desirae's cousin's cooks killed all those people." That wasn't right, but Ryan got the idea.

"Oh." He stood up — kicking over the drink — and stared

into the dark interior of the restaurant.

"Shit." I wasn't feeling very merry anymore.

"Are you getting any … you know? Anything?"

I hiccupped and got still for a moment. "Not really."

In that moment, I felt nothing except bad for the folks who'd died inside, the grieving people they'd left behind, and how the nonstop party that was the French Quarter hadn't skipped a beat. I laid a hand on the locked door and closed my eyes to concentrate better.

"Nothing," I said.

Our happy mood from earlier had trickled away like Ryan's drink on the sidewalk.

"Better get you something else to eat," Ryan said, gently brushing my fingers away from my mouth.

Without being aware of it, I'd started nibbling a nail again.

"Sublimation," I said, though it might have come out as *subbination* or *sulbination*.

"What's that?" Ryan said.

"'s a very complicated defense mechanism."

We stopped at a convenience store to buy Cokes and a packet of Gator's Kick chips, which packed a satisfyingly solid wallop in the hot pepper department, and meandered back to the hotel. I'd learned three things that night: that I preferred blues to jazz, that Hurricanes were the literal work of the devil, and that my gift might be inclined to take a hike in the presence of copious quantities of alcohol. I tried explaining all these grand truths to Ryan, but between puffing out hot breaths from the spicy chips and the attack of the yawns which hit me on the way home, the message might've gotten a little garbled.

Back at the hotel, we got as far as half undressing each other before we both passed out on the coverlet of the four-poster. That night, I dreamed of gunshots and grinning gargoyles draped in festive strings of golden beads.

— 7 —

We woke up late the next morning, our hair wild, our throats dry, our heads pounding.

Ryan groaned and pulled the pillow over his head. "I'm getting too old for this."

"Nothing a little Tylenol and greasy food won't cure," I said, speaking from experience. Catching sight of myself in the large mirror, I added, "And eyedrops." The gargoyles in the gold frame, which was now draped in strings of pink, silver, blue, and lime beads, leered down at me, and I found myself pulling my robe closed for no good reason.

"I think we should take it easy this morning," Ryan said.

"No argument from me."

"We're only due to meet up with Desirae for a late lunch, so maybe a gentle stroll along the riverbank or through a park? She says there's a nice market down near the waterfront."

"Wait, what? Back up a second there, Chief. Meeting Desirae? She's in town?"

"Yes, she came to help out her friend and meet with us. Didn't I mention that?"

"Uh, no."

"You sure?"

"I'd have remembered."

I'd have packed nicer clothes, for one thing, and maybe gotten my hair cut.

"Oh," Ryan said. "Sorry. I should've mentioned it. Is it a problem?"

My face must've been showing my feelings again. I turned back to the mirror and practiced a quick succession of enthusiastic expressions while I said, "Of course not! It'll be good to meet her."

It wasn't a complete lie. Though I wasn't exactly looking forward to it, I *did* actually want to see Desirae in the flesh, to watch Ryan and her together, and reassure my jealous-ass insecurities that there was nothing to be worried about. Still, I took more than my usual care with putting on makeup and doing my hair.

A short walk through the Quarter extinguished what little motivation we had for even leisurely strolls. We spent what remained of the morning riding up and down in a streetcar on the St. Charles line, sipping on cups of coffee, and taking in the moss-covered oaks, Greek Revival buildings, and stately white mansions of the Garden District from behind our sunglasses. I found a bag of Roman Candy — which turned out to be long sticks of taffy wrapped in twists of paper — in my handbag.

"Do you remember when I bought this?" I asked Ryan. "Or where?"

His brow crinkled. "I vaguely recall a horse being involved."

My foggy brain gave up no recollections of either horses or

candy acquisition, but I remembered how to eat. The candy tasted like strawberry ice cream.

"It's pretty good," I said, offering Ryan some.

We finished the packet and, judging by how much better we both felt afterward, figured we'd discovered a new cure for hangovers.

Back in town, we moseyed around the tourist district, stopping to watch a basket weaver outside the old French market near the riverside. A sign promising pralines for sale had me dragging Ryan into a store filled to bursting with offerings for tourists — T-shirts, bags, and travel mugs emblazoned with the phrase *Laissez les bons temps rouler!*

"What does this mean?" I asked an assistant.

"Let the good times roll!" he said. "It's the New Orleans motto."

"Seems we're not the only ones," Ryan said, holding up a T-shirt for me to read the glitter printing on the front: *I got Bourbon-faced in Shit Street.*

"It's the New Orleans tradition," I said.

Checking out the shelves stacked with candy and kitschy souvenirs, I finally tracked down pecan pralines for Henry. I was looking around for the assistant so I could ask him whether they stocked Roman candy when I noticed a sign stuck on the wall beside a curtained-off backroom.

Madame Celestine Laveau, Voodoo Priestess
True descendent of Marie Laveau
Tells your Fortune and cures your woes!
Love potions and lucky Charms. Removal of Hexes.
Psychic reader, Spiritual Healer, herbalist, Medium!

"Quite the generalist," Ryan observed wryly. "How about it?"

"How about what?"

A hand pulled aside the curtain, and a woman stepped out of the room. The pure white she wore from her turbaned head to her sandaled toes was broken only by her huge necklace — an elaborate thing of ceramic discs, wooden baubles, and what looked like dried seed pods. Her face was deeply scored with wrinkles, but her hands, with their long, elegant fingers and polished nails, looked like they belonged to a much younger woman. She might've been any age between fifty and a hundred.

"I am Madame Laveau. How can I assist you?" She had a strong New Orleans accent, and her voice was low and gravelly — perfect for maximum spookiness. "A consultation with your ancestors? You want to know what your future brings?" she asked Ryan.

"Um, I don't really—" he began.

But she continued, "Or something more, perhaps? Root work, divination, a conjuring? A *tisane* for your sore head?"

Ryan gave me a look with one eyebrow raised, as if to ask, "How'd she know about the sore head?"

I returned his look with one of my own, which said, "Everybody in the Big Easy has a sore head in the morning."

Madame turned to me. "For you, protection against enemies, perhaps? Or a nice spell for fixing your money matters?"

"No thanks," I said, even though my finances could sure have used some fixing.

"My partner here" — Ryan slung an arm around my waist and urged me forward — "would like a psychic reading."

I gave him another look; this one was less pleasant.

"What?" he said innocently. "You've got to admit it would be nice for *you* to get one for a change."

"Well, *entrez* then, all of you," Madame said, with a quick glance over my left shoulder.

I checked behind me, but no one was nearby except the sales assistant urging a shopper to buy a fabric *juju* doll for his "well-being and protection."

We followed Madame Laveau through the doorway — Ryan without hesitation and me without enthusiasm — and into a dark inner sanctum adorned with the icons and talismans of a dozen religions. A crucifix hung on a wall between a Star of David and a yin-yang symbol. A priestess of voodoo she might be, but she was clearly hedging her bets.

"Y'all from up north?" Madame asked, stepping around a lowered staircase hanging from the attic and leading the way through the cluttered space to the back of the room. I looked up into the open trapdoor above but saw only darkness.

Ryan nodded. "Vermont."

Madame shivered as if the mere thought of snow and ice chilled her bones. "And where you stayin' here?"

"*La Gargouille.*"

Madame glanced back at us, eyebrows raised.

"What?" I said.

She shrugged. "Nothing!"

"*What?*" I insisted.

Madame sat down in a thronelike chair on one side of a small table and waved me over. "Come. Sit down, you."

Ducking under hanging bundles of herbs, roots, and

feathers, I walked over to the deep armchair on the opposite side of her table and sank into it. Now I was at a lower level than her — a slick trick to lend her added gravitas. Realizing I was still wearing my sunglasses — which perhaps explained the gloomy dimness of the room — I pushed them up onto the top of my head. The woman opposite me gasped and crossed herself.

"Oh, here we go *again*," I muttered.

Madame turned to Ryan. "I read *you*, not this one. She give me the *frissons*."

I hadn't even wanted in on this silliness, but now, perversely, I found myself saying, "Oh dear, and you came so highly recommended." By the sign outside the entrance. "But if you're too scared …?"

Madame bristled and thrust her chin forward like a belligerent turtle. "I am not scared. *I* am Madame Laveau, voodoo priestess *célèbre*!"

"Good for you," I said, then blinked as she sprinkled water from a tiny bottle onto her fingers and flicked it at me. "You give all your clients a shower before you start?"

"Only the ones with *fantôme* eyes."

"Are you single, Madame? Seeing anyone?" I asked. "I know this gentleman back in Vermont. The two of you would get along like gangbusters."

She curled a lip and stared over my shoulder. "Well, this is a first."

"What is?"

"Mos' people come to New Orleans to see the ghosts, but you done bring one wit' you."

"What's that?" Ryan said from where he stood behind me.

"You aware you have an attachment, girl?" Madame demanded. "A boy with golden hair and eyes the color of that one." She pointed a thin finger at my left eye.

How did she *know?* The answer came immediately. She was just reading *me.* I'd long believed that some people were much more intuitive than others, that they could read people like I could read objects, picking up on memories and emotions. I found that theory easier to believe than the thought of her actually being able to see some version of Colby lingering in the air beside me.

"Um, well, I mean, yeah, I guess. Kinda," I stammered, feeling Ryan's gaze boring into the back of my head.

He knew I sometimes got visions and heard things, but I'd never shared with him the fact that when I died and came back to life, my first love, Colby, had come back with me.

"No 'kinda' about it. That boy be loving you. Go on wit' you," she said, flapping a shooing hand at the empty air. "Dis girl not in danger now." A moment later, she nodded and added, "There, he done back off a lil'. You want me to get rid of him, girl?"

"No!"

A floorboard creaked behind me.

"I mean, no need, it's not a problem," I clarified, trying to sound more casual. "Don't worry about it."

"You sure? Spirits be like cockroaches — you let one in, you let one stay, next thing, they all stopping by, wanting to abide with you."

I said nothing. Ryan said nothing even louder.

Madame sniffed. "Fine, jes' don' be blaming me if you get an infestation." She pushed a laminated tariff sheet across the table toward me. "So, what do you choose?"

I read through the list of offerings. "Scrying." I'd had enough tarot and crystal readings from my mother to last a lifetime.

"Mirror or water?" she asked.

A flash of the mirror back at the hotel, with its frame of leering gargoyles, flashed into my mind. "Water."

"*Bon.*" She tapped a small platter with a businesslike rap of one of her strangely youthful knuckles.

I stared at it, wondering if it was part of the divining process, but Ryan, quicker on the uptake, placed a fifty-dollar bill on it.

"*Merci.*" Madame Laveau reached behind her for a shallow copper bowl and filled it with water from a matching pitcher while I glanced around the room.

To her left was a raised altar draped in red cloth and surrounded by candles whose flickering glow chased shadows across the Madame's face. On top of the altar, beside an open Bible, an icon of Mary cradling the infant Jesus perched, shedding flakes of gold paint along, I supposed, with blessings for Madame's patrons. Statuettes of lesser saints gazed adoringly at Mary, along with a plastic leprechaun holding a glass of water.

Madame gave me a long stare, then turned to contemplate the collection of bottles lined up on the long shelf behind her. They seemed to be filled with herbs, potions, oils, powders, and more exotic ingredients — shriveled-up mushrooms, tiny alligator heads, and chickens' feet floating in a clear liquid. Nodding as though coming to some sort of decision, she selected a few bottles and set these on the table between us. I eyed them doubtfully. Into a stone mortar, she dropped ingredients — a pinch of herbs, a teaspoon of ashes, a shake of powder, and a couple of substances I couldn't identify. Eye of newt and toe of frog? Then she ground away with the pestle, murmuring some kind of incantation in what sounded like French.

My mother would be in seventh heaven in Madame's backroom. I could imagine her trying on amulets and charms, and asking endless questions about the wooden statue which guarded the corner, with a bunch of ragdolls (none of which had been stuck with pins) resting at its feet. I wasn't wild about the carved wooden mask that watched from one wall nor the dried bat hanging beneath it, so I focused on the less esoteric objects — a cell phone plugged into a charger, a credit card machine, an operating license stuck on the wall — reminders that despite the unsettling décor, this was unmistakably just a commercial enterprise.

Madame bent over, I heard a click, and then the sound of chanting, rhythmic drums, and off-key singing rose from a music system under the table. Unnerving soundtrack? Check. Creepy set-dressing? Check. Actors in place? You bet.

It was time to get this show started.

– 8 –

Madame Laveau scooped the powdered contents out of her mortar and into a dry eggshell, which she handed to me. "Sprinkle it on the water when I tell you to."

I held the eggshell, feeling like my fingers might at any moment convulse and crush it, while she lit a candle and placed it on the table beside the copper bowl. A cloyingly sweet scent rose into the musty air, and the flickering light played over her creased face. The music settled into a low, throbbing rhythm, with high-pitched ululating rising and falling like waves of grief, or perhaps ecstasy.

Madame gestured to the bowl. "*S'il vous plaît.*"

I tipped the eggshell over, and the powder spilled out, forming a blob which floated in the center of the water.

Madame sighed. "I said to *sprinkle* it."

"Sorry."

"Now you must stir. One direction only. No cross currents."

I took the feather she handed me, prodded the floating island of powder, and then gently swirled it around as directed.

I wasn't sure if I looked like five kinds of fool; I sure felt like it. Madame held up a hand for me to stop, then took hold of the bowl, rotated it counterclockwise three times, and started rocking backward and forward as though in a trance. Scoring her a perfect ten for showmanship, I decided I was unlikely to hear anything true, reasoning that if she had any real talent at all, she wouldn't have needed the theatrical flourishes and overdone set dressing. Then again, I thought uncomfortably, maybe I was just a jerk who doubted that anyone *else's* abilities could be real.

While she fiddled and fidgeted, I allowed my gaze to roam around the room, spotting a bottle of luridly pink liquid bearing the label Dragon's Blood Uncrossing Bubble Bath, before drifting back to the wall with the African mask.

"Is that a real bat?" I said.

Madame peered into the water, mumbling incoherently to herself. I saw nothing on its surface or in its depths except little lumps of undissolved powder.

"Who was Obediah?" I pointed to a book of spells.

"You keep interrupting, you mess with my sight," Madame Laveau said, glaring at me. "You scared of what I gonna see, girl?"

"Me, scared? *Pfft!*" I glanced up at Ryan, trying to gauge what he was feeling, but his expression was unreadable.

After more rocking, squinting, chanting, and mumbling, Madame said, "Here it comes … So. Death, but life." She frowned, then repeated, "Death but life. That mean something to you?"

I shrugged, because yeah, it could've meant my near-death experience at the bottom of a pond and subsequent resuscitation, but it was also one of those sufficiently vague statements that could apply to anything or anyone.

"Your mother — *la perplexité*. She is a one, *n'cest pas?*"

Completely accurate. Then again, probably true of everyone's mother.

She looked back into the water and laughed. "Aha, romance!"

Aha, you noticed I came in holding hands with a man, I wanted to say.

"Not easy for one such as you to trust, no?" she said.

Lucky guess, I told myself. Even a broken clock was right twice a day, right? But I was finding it increasingly difficult to write off what she was saying.

"A child with a message. You need to listen … And I see a distant continent … Africa, the motherland!"

Huh. Years ago, after I'd dropped out of pre-med, I'd spent over a year working on conservation programs in South Africa, but I had zero idea how she could've sensed anything relating to that.

"There is something here, something more …" She leaned in closer to the surface of the water, then pulled back with a dramatic gasp.

"What did you see?" I was trying to stay skeptical, but my eyes began to water as they always did when I was creeped out.

Madame Laveau sat back in her chair and stared at me with wide eyes. When she spoke, most of her Creole accent was missing. "You buy sweetgrass in the store, you hear me? And salt. And you fill that place where you're staying with sweet smoke and cross the threshold with salt. And also around your bed, to be sure."

"Why?"

"A bad thing is coming, and that place is a thinning."

"Lovely," I said, as Ryan asked, "What's a thinning?"

"Just what it sounds like," Madame snapped.

"It sounds like the top of a middle-aged man's head," I snapped back.

"What bad thing?" Ryan said.

I added, "Yeah, can you be a bit more specific about that?"

Madame shook her head in a movement that was as much shudder as negation. "*Non.* But for an extra fifty dollars, I can give you a *gris-gris* bag for protection."

"No, thanks. I reckon I'll be just fine."

She muttered a word that sounded like "*cooyon,*" and I raised my eyebrows at her. "Something else?"

"*C'est tout.* That's all." She pushed her chair back from the table and stood up.

I did the same, asking Ryan, "Time to meet Desirae at the restaurant yet?"

"Where y'all having lunch?" Madame asked, seeming more at ease now that we were leaving.

"Jean Claude's," Ryan said. "Over on Toulouse Street."

She clapped her hands in endorsement of our choice. "You get the shellfish gumbo special. They make it nice and spicy, and you" — she pointed at me — "like it hot, *n'est ces pas?*"

"I do indeedy," I said. "And can I just check, you don't see death or serious ill health in my immediate future?"

"*Non.*"

"Great, that helps clarify things, thank you. Very reassuring."

We left, not stopping to buy sweetgrass or salt or any other protections, and chatted while we walked to the restaurant.

"So, what did you think?" Ryan said.

"Generic claptrap and gimmicks for the tourists."

"For someone who gets visions yourself, you're pretty darn cynical, there, Garnet."

"Yeah, but come on. It was all so vague — deliberately so, if you ask me — so that the customer can interpret it to mean anything. There were only two specifics."

"The spicy food?"

"Yup. She must've spotted this." I held up the bag of items I'd bought in the store. Through the transparent plastic, a bottle of hot sauce was clearly visible where it rubbed shoulders with Henry's pralines. "I'll admit I'm a little stumped on how she knew about Africa."

Ryan stopped in front of an antiques store and spun me around to face my reflection in the glass.

"What?" I demanded.

With a forefinger, he flicked one of my earrings. My carved wooden elephant earrings.

I grinned. "You're quite the detective, you know that? Ever consider a career in law enforcement?"

He chuckled, then grew more serious. "What about her scary prediction, though?"

"The one about the big bad coming through the 'thinning?'" I laid heavy emphasis on the word. "I'll bet she does that for all her customers. Gives them something spooky to tell the folks back home. And, of course, it'll always come true."

Ryan cocked his head.

"I mean, something really bad always *does* come along, doesn't it? That's life." I'd long ago decided this was the reason my mother's predictions of doom occasionally seemed to materialize in real life.

"One of the things I admire about you, Garnet," Ryan said, "is your optimistic outlook on life."

I tugged him away from the store window. "That dead bat was a lot scarier than her predictions," I said, trying to convince myself.

"Not as creepy as those stairs to the attic, though. What do you think goes on up there — seances? Channeling of spirits?"

"It's probably where she takes her naps and catches up on *Real Housewives*." Dodging a pool of vomit on the sidewalk, I nearly walked into a chalkboard set outside a café. The message scrawled on it declared, "Come in and try the worst coffee one woman on Tripadvisor had in her entire life."

"It's almost irresistible," Ryan said.

"*Almost*." I took my caffeine seriously.

My hopes that Ryan had forgotten about some of the other things Madame Laveau had said were dashed when he suddenly asked, "That business about your having an attachment, though — what was that about?"

Shit. I'd been hoping that he'd forgotten about that. Knowing that my ex-boyfriend was still hanging around was sure to bother Ryan. He might even feel hurt that I hadn't allowed Madame Laveau to banish Colby, because that had to mean I didn't want him gone. And I truly *didn't* want to hurt Ryan. He was such a good man. Patient, generous, funny, smart. He deserved my full heart. But it wasn't like my heart was divided, not really. It was like I'd kept the old one, the one that Colby owned, and then grown a whole new one for Ryan.

Even to myself, my thoughts sounded uncomfortably like the rationalizations of someone having an affair.

"Who's this boy who loves you?" he asked me.

"Well …" I hesitated, trying to find a good way of explaining the inexplicable. "You know that since my fun times in Plover Pond, I sometimes hear … things?"

"Voices, yeah, you told me. And I know you sometimes get visions."

"Yeah, well, sometimes I get … messages, I guess … from a specific voice. Colby's."

He frowned, clearly trying to figure out who I meant, then said, "Colby Beaumont? Your high school boyfriend?"

It was strange to hear Colby referenced in such an offhand way. "High school boyfriend" was an accurate descriptor, of course, and yet it entirely missed what Colby had once been to me. My be-all and my end-all. The boy I'd loved and trusted with all my being, the person I'd planned on sharing my entire life with. The other half of me who'd been ripped away while we were still at the height and depth of our love for each other. The golden boy with fair hair, tanned skin, and eyes the color of maple syrup who'd wanted to become a cop and help Pitchford hold the line against the opioid epidemic.

"Yeah." I stared down at the sidewalk. "It's like somehow in that pond, when I died where *he'd* died, he kind of … latched onto me."

"Well, hell, Garnet, you never told me *that.*"

"I haven't told anyone. It's pretty crazy, you know?" I forced myself to meet his gaze, trying to read his expression, because worry was settling, cold and spiky as an icicle, in my belly. Would this be a deal breaker for Ryan?

He didn't reply, and we walked on in awkward silence until we reached the restaurant where we were due to meet up with Desirae.

Ryan stopped and turned to face me. "And he still loves you?" He was clearly upset by the thought, and he didn't know the half of it.

"It's like he's frozen in time, how he was and how he felt back then." Ryan frowned his confusion, and I carried on, "I *have* told him to go, to move on." It was a lawyer-worthy fudging of the truth. What I'd actually told him was that he *could* go, he *should* move on. "But I guess he still, you know, lingers."

"Is he here right now?"

"No. Not that I can sense, anyway."

"And you don't want him gone?"

No, I didn't. Colby made me more me. He was the constant thread between the carefree girl I'd once been, the empty wreck I was afterwards, and the woman I was now. And he was my bridge to otherness. *Ryan* was my place to kick back and inhale, and also to lean in and wake up and start living again. Greedy as ever, I wanted them both.

I laid a hand on Ryan's forearm. "Honestly, he's hardly ever with me, and he always keeps his distance when you and I are together. He's growing fainter and fainter. These days, he only comes through when he thinks I need a warning that I'm in danger. In fact, sometimes, I wonder if I'm just imagining it all, and that what I think is his voice just comes from inside of me.”

“And yet that woman back there saw him.”

“Maybe she just really saw *me*. What I think and fear and remember.”

Ryan stared at me for a long moment, then turned and entered the restaurant. Fighting the urge to bite off every single one of my nails, I followed.

$$- 9 -$$

For some reason, perhaps because she'd looked so elegant and put together in her Facebook photos, I'd expected Desirae to choose a fancy restaurant for our meeting. Instead, it was a busy but pretty basic establishment with worn pleather seats and sticky laminate tabletops. A surly server seated Ryan and me in a booth and disappeared before I could ask for a glass of water — my hangover headache was gone, but the thirst remained. While we waited for Desirae, I checked out the menu, pleased to see that it featured plenty of fried food.

"Will you be going with Madame Laveau's recommendation?" Ryan asked.

"Nope. If I follow her advice, I'll die. Literally." At his blank look, I pointed a thumb back at myself. "Shellfish allergy."

"Oh, right!"

"Even more reason to take what she said with a pinch of salt." As I pored over the menu, my mouth began to water at the descriptions of the dishes on offer. "Whatever buttermilk biscuits are, I want some."

"Not tempted by the turtle soup or frog's legs?"

"I have limits."

Ryan raised a skeptical eyebrow.

"I do!" I insisted.

He grinned. "So, what are our plans for this evening?"

"I think you know, sir."

"Yeah?"

"Yeah. You, me, and the four-poster have a date with destiny."

"It's going to be that good?"

"It's going to be *memorable*," I promised, delighted to see the slightest flush color his cheeks. "Worried?"

"Terrified," he said, and the sexy grin made its appearance again.

We were playing footsie under the table when Ryan looked up. "Ah, here's Desirae," he said, getting to his feet.

Ryan's ex-wife's arrival caused a little flutter in the restaurant. Taller than me, thinner, blonder, and way better dressed, she drew almost everyone's gaze as she made her way to our table. Some of the stares were admiring, some were envious. What must it be like to have that kind of impact on people, I wondered, gratifying or ghastly?

"Hi, hi!" Desirae said, all smiles as she reached our table.

She air-kissed the space beside Ryan's jaw and looked set to do the same to me, but I pulled back into my seat, not a fan of PDAs in general, and from my boyfriend's ex in particular. She hesitated, seeming unsure over whether to sit beside me or Ryan. I wanted her where I could see her, so I didn't budge up, and she slid into the seat beside Ryan, opposite me, still wearing her bright smile.

Though her gaze did the usual flick between my odd eyes, she said nothing but, "I'm so glad to meet you in person, Garnet!"

"Yeah, likewise," I said mendaciously.

"But I'm *so* sorry I'm late. I didn't mean to keep you waiting. *Whatever* must you think of me?"

"You're not late," I pointed out.

"Oh! Well, good."

The server reappeared and hovered at our table, his gaze on Desirae. "Good afternoon, Ms. Jackson. Welcome back!"

I flinched at the name and hoped nobody had noticed.

Desirae bestowed a dazzling smile on him. "Now you *know* I can't ever stay away for long, Clète."

He beamed. May even have blushed a little. Amazing.

"What can I get you to drink?" he asked.

"Should we get a bottle of wine for the table? They have a lovely Semillon on their list," Desirae suggested.

Deep inside my torso, my liver trembled. "Just a Coke for me, please."

"Make that two," Ryan said.

"And a tall glass of water, with lots of ice," I added.

Desirae ordered a glass of wine, and when the server left to do her bidding, she turned to Ryan. "Thank you, *thank* you for coming down to help."

"No problem. It gave Garnet and me a good excuse to have a weekend away together."

Together. It was a lovely word, especially coming from him, especially referring to us, and especially when said to her.

"Yes, but in *New Orleans*? It's so ..." She pulled a face and lifted her hands like the bewildered lady in the shrug emoji. Her hands were the only part of her that weren't immaculate; the nails were short and unmanicured, and blue Band-Aids were wrapped around two of the fingers on her left hand. I guessed that in her case, this was due to unfortunate encounters with sharp knives in kitchens rather than to the bad habit of biting nails and picking at cuticles. It was wonderful that, for once, I didn't have to feel any embarrassment at the appearance of my own nails.

"I like this city," I said, though I'd hardly seen much of it yet.

"Of course, sure. It has a rich history and great food. I didn't mean to— I was just … Well, there are prettier towns, but each to his own of course. Or her. *Her* own. I hope this place" — she indicated the restaurant — "is okay, though? I know it's not very *upmarket*, but it does the best Cajun and Creole food this side of the Mississippi."

She had an odd, breathy way of speaking, emphasizing words as though she spoke them in italics and widening her eyes like she was pleading not to be judged for anything she said. It was fascinating to someone like me who opened my mouth mostly to change feet.

Clète, who'd shed his sullen and recalcitrant manner entirely, returned with our drinks. My water had a solitary cube of ice in it.

"Are you ready to order your meal?" he asked her.

"Yes, of *course*. I'll have, um … Why don't you two order first?"

"Can I get more ice?" I asked the server.

He didn't acknowledge by so much as a glance that he'd heard me. But Ryan, bless him, used his fork to fish the ice cubes out of his glass of Coke and transferred them to my water.

"They make a great gumbo here," Desirae said. Then, fixing her bright, blue eyes on the waiter, added, "I don't mean to imply that your other food isn't *terrific*, too, of course. You know I love everything you do here."

I tried to imagine this woman as the boss of a kitchen — shouting orders at chefs, confronting suppliers over imperfect produce, chewing out tardy servers — and failed. She was just so inoffensive, so … *nice*.

The server smiled down at her. "The gumbo *is* pretty great, Ms. Jackson. Can I put in an order for you?"

"No, I, um, can you give me just another minute?"

Whenever I asked for more time, servers tended to disappear and not return, but this guy seemed happy to wait at our table, watching Desirae study her menu. This must be what social justice warriors called "pretty privilege."

Desirae glanced at a nearby table and, lowering her voice, leaned forward to tell me, "I always get a bit anxious ordering in front of other people."

"You do?" I said.

"*Yes*, because you can tell a lot about people by what they *order*."

"You can?"

Ryan's lips twitched. Perhaps he'd heard this theory before.

"*Yes*. Those two, for example?" She slid her eyes to the couple at a nearby table. He wore a comb-over; she wore a perm straight from the eighties and a fanny pack. Both of them were eating blackened fish.

"Grilled salmon," Desirae said. "Safe, predictable, easy. It's probably what they eat at home, and they think they're being daring by having it Cajun-style and served with popcorn rice. Not that I'm *judging* them or anything, it's just a fun *game* I play."

"I'll have the crawfish étouffée with red beans and rice, and a side of collard greens," Ryan told the server. Turning to Desirae, he asked, "What do you make of that?"

"Decisive, wise. You know what you like, and you're smart enough to order a specialty where they're likely to do it best."

The waiter chuckled appreciatively.

"Garnet, what will you have?" Desirae asked.

I'd been thinking about getting the blackened salmon, too, but I couldn't have her thinking of the new woman in Ryan's life as dull and safe. "Um, I'm not sure."

The waiter gave a restrained eye roll and tapped his pen impatiently on his notepad.

"Tell you what, while you wait, why don't you write down *ice?*" I told him.

"How about the Nola jambalaya, Garnet?" Desirae suggested.

I checked the menu and discovered the dish consisted of rice mixed with a bunch of different proteins — chicken, duck, pork, and *andouille* sausage. Was Desirae recommending something with a little bit of everything because she thought I was someone who couldn't make up her mind or commit to anything?

"I'll have the deep-fried alligator," I told the server in as decisive a voice as I could muster. "And make it extra spicy."

Ryan's shoulders shook; Desirae blinked at me. Yeah, lady, consider yourself warned.

"Plus, a side of fried okra and Cajun fries with comeback sauce," I added defiantly. I'd never eaten okra before, fried or otherwise, and had no idea what "comeback sauce" was, but I was on a roll — an admittedly childish roll, like a kid on the playground accepting a double dare to eat a slug.

Ryan gave me a fake-amazed look. "No diablo pickles?"

"*What?*" I ran a finger down the menu, searching. "Here we are — 'Crispy fried dill pickles & fresh jalapeno slices.' How did I miss that?" I turned to the waiter and said, "And a plate of the devil's pickles, definitely. Oh, and some buttermilk biscuits. No, wait — make that a side of hushpuppies."

He wrote down my order without comment, but I could feel the judgment rolling off of him in waves.

Desirae ordered a St. Charles salad, which the menu declared to be an exotic symphony of mixed greens, pecans, cranberries, blood orange, and blue cheese. What in the name of its port wine vinaigrette did this say about *her*?

When the waiter left — my reminder for extra ice following him like a persistent ghost — Ryan turned to Desirae.

"So, tell us all about this case."

$$-\ 10\ -$$

While I drank my Coke, the cold sweetness hitting my veins like some kind of drug, Desirae explained her connection to the case. After her divorce from Ryan, she'd left Vermont, moved to Texas, and gotten a job as a junior chef in a restaurant where Anthony Cooper was the sous chef — which I understood to be a kind of second-in-command in professional kitchens — and they'd become friends. But he'd always wanted to work in New Orleans, where he came from and where his family still lived, so he was thrilled to land the position of head chef in Broussard's restaurant. Even after he'd returned to Louisiana, he and Desirae had remained in contact.

"I'll text you his *number*," Desirae told Ryan. "Anthony's a really great guy. I've set up an appointment for you to chat with him tomorrow and with the co-owner of the restaurant on Sunday."

"Great," Ryan said.

Desirae told us what she knew of what had happened that night in Broussard's restaurant. It wasn't much more than I'd already gleaned online.

"Your friend Anthony and the shooter, Jeron Cooper, were cousins?" I asked.

"No, Anthony was his uncle," Desirae said.

"So, Anthony got his nephew the job at Broussard's?" Ryan asked.

"That's right."

"Then I'm guessing your friend must feel really bad about the murders."

"Oh, *yeah,* he is! I think that's why he's set on finding *something* to mitigate his nephew's involvement," Desirae said. "I mean, the cops aren't wrong. It seems like Jeron really did shoot that family. The facts aren't in dispute. But Anthony is having such a hard time believing and accepting it. *Denial.*" She cast me a quick, bright glance. "As you would know, of course, being a psychologist."

"I'm not a psychologist. I mean, I got the degrees, but I never did the supervised practice hours or wrote the board exam."

"Why not?"

"Reasons." I was beginning to think it would've been easier to have completed the process than to repeatedly go through the process of explaining to people why I'd quit just before the finishing line.

"Oh, I'm sorry, I didn't mean to *offend* you! I just—"

"I'm not in the least offended," I said.

"Truly?"

"Honestly."

"I would hate to think I said anything insensitive." She looked set to apologize more.

Ryan had once said that his ex was thin-skinned and insecure at her core. I was beginning to see what he'd meant.

"If Garnet gets offended, you'll know all about it," Ryan said. "Trust me, she's much more likely to offend you than the other way around."

"Oh," Desirae said, looking from one to the other of us as if expecting drama, but I merely nodded agreement at Ryan's assessment of my levels of sensitivity.

"True story," I said.

The server arrived with our food, setting down Desirae's salad — large as a small garden — first and my deep-fried reptile chunks last.

"*Bon appetit!*" he said.

I lifted my gaze from my humungous spread of fried foods to ask, "My ice?"

He curled his lip. "Coming right up. Ma'am."

Desirae sampled a leaf, declared it to be delicious, and spent a few minutes repeatedly checking that we were both entirely satisfied with our food. The waiter returned and set a giant ice bucket on the table in front of me.

"Will that be sufficient, ma'am?"

"Just about," I said, unembarrassed.

Ryan tucked into his *étouffée*, and I tasted a bite of alligator. It was pretty good and even better when I topped it with one of the hot pickles.

"Anyway," Desirae continued, "Anthony seems to think — or want to *believe* — that there's more to the story, that someone *else* was there that night and did the shooting or *forced* his cousin to do what he did. And I promised him I'd *try* to help. I know, I know, I probably shouldn't have, because what can *I* do, right? But I was thinking of you, Ryan. I know I should've checked with you beforehand, but—"

"It's fine," Ryan said. "I'll ask the locals if I can read the file."

"Oh, *thank* you. I would've hated to have to tell Anthony *no*."

I was happy to let the conversation flow around me while I attended to my food. The hushpuppies — small, deep-fried balls of savory cornmeal goodness — were amazing, and I reckoned the comeback sauce had earned its moniker because it was impossible to have only one dip.

"I'll need to check what district has the case and see if I have any contacts I can hit up for a favor, then I'll—" Ryan broke off and retrieved his buzzing phone from a pocket. Checking the screen, he said, "Excuse me, ladies, but I need to take this."

Desirae stood to let him out and then sat back down behind her mound of leaves. We exchanged a glance and then, by silent agreement, resumed eating. She chewed on a berry and let her gaze roam over my plates of food. Perhaps I only imagined the look of distaste on her face? It was probably awe.

"Want a taste?" I said.

"No! No, thanks. I'm sure it's all *wonderful*, but I try not to eat too much fried food. It's not good for the waistline."

"It's a lot, I know." It was. My mother would've said it was a classic case of my eyes being bigger than my stomach, but she'd always underestimated my digestive abilities. "But I'm doing it to myself, so it's consensual."

Desirae's eyes widened in sudden horror. "I didn't mean to

imply that you— Please, you mustn't think I was *judging* you. I just meant that *I* prefer not to—"

I held up a hand to stem the flow of words. Her constant apologizing and need for reassurance was getting old fast. "No harm, no foul."

"Oh. *Good.*"

I risked one of the fried okra. Beneath its carapace of crispy batter, it was as slimy as a slug. Suppressing a shudder, I swallowed hard.

"Are you sure you like those?" Desirae asked. "Okra's not to everyone's taste."

I nodded resolutely and, forcing myself to spear another with my fork, said, "They're growing on me."

Like a gelatinous mold.

Ryan returned and took his seat, looking unhappy. "Ronnie was cleaning her gutters and fell off the ladder."

"Oh, no! Is she okay?" I said.

He nodded. "She'll be fine, but she broke her ankle and needs to have surgery to put in pins, if I understood right. So she'll be in hospital for the next few days and unable to drive for a while."

"Who's Ronnie?" Desirae asked.

"Officer Veronica Capshaw, the only other full-time police officer in Pitchford." Ryan met my gaze. "Got to go home. I'm sorry."

"Back to Pitchford? Bummer!" I said, seriously disappointed. My last twenty-four hours with Ryan had been terrific — excluding the jazz and the hangover — and I'd been looking forward to the rest of it. "When do we have to go?"

"Tonight, if we can get a flight."

I swore under my breath. So much for our romantic weekend away. Heck, between the previous night's hunger and the morning's headache, we hadn't even test-driven the bed in the hotel yet. When we got back to Pitchford, I planned on having a word with Ronnie. She needed to up her ladder-stability game in the future.

"I'm sorry," he said again, more softly. "It's not how I planned for things to go."

I waved aside his apology. "Sure, sure. It's not your fault."

I wasn't the only one feeling unhappy; Desirae was looking positively woebegone. "Does that mean you won't be able to assist?" she asked Ryan.

"I'll do what I can from Vermont. I can certainly call the detectives down here," he promised her.

"How about if *I* stay on and investigate," I said.

They both turned to look at me, Desirae with confusion and Ryan with dawning comprehension.

"You?" Desirae said blankly.

"On your own?" Ryan said.

"I mean, I'll miss you and all, Chief, but you know, maybe I could find something out that helps."

The idea of staying behind alone while he returned to Vermont wasn't wildly appealing, but the thought of being the one to crack the case? I fancied a shot at that challenge.

"You're an investigator?" Desirae asked me.

I looked at Ryan to answer that one.

– 11 –

He took a deep breath. "Garnet has certain abilities," he told Desirae. "She gets … impressions from objects and sometimes hears or sees things." He frowned, perhaps realizing he was making me sound like someone with a psychotic disorder. "I'm not explaining this very well. She …" He cast me a helpless glance.

"I'm a little bit psychic," I said. "It's fickle and unpredictable—"

"But accurate," Ryan finished, filling me with delight. Then he ruined the effect by adding, "Mostly."

Desirae blinked. "Oh, I see."

She said nothing critical or cynical, and not by so much as a twitch of her lips did she betray that she regarded me with incredulity. But still, I knew.

"So, she could stay and check things out. Try to find out something that the cops missed," Ryan finished.

Now that I had Ryan's vote of confidence, I felt second thoughts sneaking up on me. I *could* stay and investigate, but did I really want to? I'd come here to spend time with Ryan, to

70

see the sights and soak up the atmosphere of the Big Easy. The murder investigation was going to be mostly on him, not me. I'd be in a strange city where I knew no one and where I had no connection to the crime, and no real investment in the deaths of four strangers. I'd have no "in" with the local cops and wouldn't know where to begin. In short, I'd be totally out of my depth.

Then again, wasn't I always?

Desirae looked from Ryan to me and back again. Sounding doubtful, she said, "Okay, then, I guess. Sure. Why not? I mean, it can't do any harm, right?"

At that last question, Ryan's eyebrows knit together, and he sat back in his seat. Reconsidering? I'd been known to do damage in my investigations. As Desirae watched him, an expression of I-*thought*-it-was-a-bad-idea crept over her pretty features.

Ryan opened his mouth to speak, but I got in first. Giving Desirae my biggest, most confident smile, I said sweetly, "No harm at all."

We finished our meal, with me making impressive inroads into the crispy fried everything and dispatching all of the hot pickles. Desirae insisted on paying, and afterward, we arranged for her to collect me the next morning so we could go together to talk to her chef friend, Anthony Cooper. We said our goodbyes outside the restaurant, and after she'd bestowed another couple of French-style air kisses on Ryan and begged him to travel safely, she left.

Ryan and I returned to our hotel. I felt as full as a tick and longed for a nap, but I helped change his flight before parking myself in an armchair by the balcony window, from where I watched him pack. Outside, a breeze played in the leaves, casting moving shadows on the fountain in the courtyard below, creating a mirage in which the gargoyles contorted and writhed under the spray of water. Then again, I may just have been hallucinating, because the inevitable consequences of my overindulgence at lunch were making themselves felt. My belly was distended, a savage flame of heartburn licked at my esophagus, and the food sweats were beginning to kick in. I suppressed a burp, but a whimper escaped me.

Ryan cast me a worried glance. "You okay there?"

"No, Chief, I'm not. I'm suffering from a severe case of deep-fried regret."

"One hushpuppy too many?" he asked sympathetically, digging into his toiletry bag and tossing me a roll of Tums.

I nodded glumly, put two in my mouth, and bit down on the chalky sweetness. Down in the courtyard, the gargoyles' gaping mouths widened in mocking laughter.

"Hey, Ryan? Come over here for a second."

He zipped up his bag and ambled over to stand beside me.

"See anything funny with the fountain?" I said.

He squinted, leaned over the balustrade for a better view, then shook his head. "Water, a fountain. A small table and empty chairs. What am I supposed to be seeing?"

"Nothing. Never mind. I'm imagining things."

He sat down in the chair opposite me, his elbows on his knees. "Can we talk?"

Uh-oh. He wanted to talk about the issue of Colby's continued presence in my life, I just knew it. My heart quickened its beat. What if he was about to demand I send Colby packing? Or worse, what if he, Ryan, wanted out of our relationship?

"I don't think we have time."

"It shouldn't take long."

"You don't want to miss your flight," I said, striving for a cheery tone.

He checked his watch. "I've got five minutes to spare."

Five minutes? That wasn't long enough for a deep discussion, which meant he'd already made up his mind.

"Okay, then. Sure." I wanted to run out into the street with my hands over my ears. Instead, I forced myself to look him in the eye.

"I've been thinking about this thing with Colby Beaumont."

He *had* been very quiet on our walk back to the hotel, but I'd reckoned he was just planning his trip back home. Instead, he'd been pondering the problem of Colby.

"Yeah?" I said.

"At first I felt … really, there's no other word for it — I was feeling *jealous*. Ridiculous, right? To be jealous of someone you loved before you even knew me."

"Yeah, ridiculous," I said, like I'd never experienced it personally, like I wasn't already aware of a growing feeling of jealousy toward Desirae with her beautiful face, successful career, community spirit, and charming manners. She was everything I wasn't.

"I know I need to get over myself. What you had with him was special. I get that. And if he somehow … comes into this world occasionally to help keep you safe, that's a good thing! I should be grateful there's somebody else keeping watch over you."

I nodded several times.

"And besides, it was such a long time ago. It's history, right?"

"Yeah!"

The knot of worry in my chest loosened. I felt like I'd dodged a bullet. Thank goodness Ryan was being so mature about it. But my relief didn't last further than Ryan's next words.

"In fact, this has got me thinking about my relationship with Desirae."

I sat up straighter. "Oh, yeah?"

"It's been a long time since our divorce too. Perhaps it's time for her and me to make our peace."

"I didn't know you were still at war."

"We don't fight, but we *have* kept each other at arm's length. Exchanging texts once or twice a year — it's been awkward."

"Is that so bad, though?" To me, *awkward* seemed like an ideal state of affairs between my boyfriend and his ex.

"I think it would be safe for us to have more relaxed, comfortable contact, because we've moved on. We've healed. We could be friends, you know? I think this case might bring the two of us, what do you call it, closure?"

I thought it might bring on the complete opposite of closure, but I didn't say so, didn't give voice to my unease. Ryan was looking at me with earnest appeal, and I could tell he was feeling proud that both he and Desirae were emotionally evolved human beings, perfectly capable of moving on from a past that had been both wonderful and horrible. I couldn't shatter that for him. Besides, I could hardly object to a friendly relationship between them when I was not yet ready to call it quits with Colby. I might have been many unimpressive things, but being a hypocrite wasn't one of them.

So I merely said, "Yeah, that's great, Chief."

I stood up, groaning at my heavy belly, and ruffled his hair on the way to the bed. Lying on my back like a beached whale was even more uncomfortable than sitting. Trying out various positions, I eventually settled for lying on my side with a pillow shoved under my distended stomach, like I'd seen heavily pregnant women in movies sleep. It was better, even if only marginally.

"I'm really sorry about having to cut short our time together," Ryan said.

"Yeah, me too."

"I'll make it up to you another time for sure."

"I'm going to hold you to that promise."

"And you're sure you're okay with staying on alone to investigate?" Ryan asked me.

I wasn't. But I would rather have eaten another plate of okra than admit that I was feeling insecure, out of my depth, and wanted nothing more than to cling to his side all the way back to Pitchford. Pathetic.

So I said, "Sure I am."

"Good." He planted a gentle kiss on my forehead. "But perhaps you'd better steer clear of fried foods for a while."

"And alcohol, too, I reckon."

"Probably best."

"It's salad and water for me from now on, I promise."

He gave me a doubtful look.

"Well, for the next two days, at least," I said.

– 12 –

As soon as the door shut behind him, the room felt empty and unpleasant. It was like Ryan had kept the dark and the oppressive atmosphere at bay, but now that he'd gone, deep shadows grew in the corners and slid along the floor. The fountain outside was a burbling shout in the silence, and a faint smell of something rotten — mildew, perhaps, or mold? — caught in the back of my throat. I needed to get out of the room, to lose myself in the noise and light of the French Quarter. Only problem was, I felt as sick as the pig I was.

"Ugh! Why do you do this to yourself?" I moaned out loud, even though I knew exactly why. I'd gotten into a childish and one-sided willy-wagging competition, so to speak, with Desirae. She might be beautiful, my actions seemed to declare, but I could *eat*.

It was so stupid. Nothing in Ryan's attitude or behavior had indicated that he had any interest in his ex except as an old friend. I wasn't so sure about *her* — those air kisses, that relentlessly bright smile — but still, I needed to woman up and stop being ridiculous.

I found the TV remote control, hit the power button, and found a local station. A woman in a flowing white dress and wide-brimmed straw hat was presenting some kind of lifestyle segment while standing in front of a typical Louisiana house.

"Few people know the real reason why so many Southerners paint their porch ceilings blue," she said, gesturing to the house behind her.

On the front porch, a pitcher of amber liquid — sweet tea, no two ways about it — sat on a tiny table between two rocking chairs promising rest to the weary. Above them, the ceiling was indeed a light, soothing shade of blue.

"The official name of the color used in this charming tradition is Haint Blue, and while it might give the illusion that you're sitting under a clear blue sky and may even trick wasps into building their nests elsewhere, the origin of the practice has its roots in Gullah culture. The Gullah are descendants of enslaved West and Central Africans shipped out to Charleston during the slave trade to work the coastal plantations of the Carolinas, Georgia, and Florida. The influence of their rich culture of traditions, crafts, food, and spiritual beliefs has spread down as far as Louisiana."

The footage cut to an old man with few remaining teeth. "Now a haint is a wanderin' spirit," he said. "A haint got no rest. He a lost soul and might bring evil on the living. You got to outwit him. Now a spirit won't cross water, see? *Cain't.* So, if your ceiling looks like water, then the haints cain't come down into your house and haunt you."

Looking around at my hotel room, I wished the ceiling of this place had been painted blue. The floor, too, come to that.

"Driving around the South, you may also see bottle trees," the presenter said.

The image of a wire tree on a stand with deep cobalt blue bottles on the ends of its "branches" was followed by footage of a giant crepe myrtle tree with a myriad of blue bottles dangling from strings tied to its limbs.

"Gullah legend says evil spirits wandering around at night are drawn to the prettiness of the glass and then get trapped in the bottles," the female voice said. "When the wind blows, you can hear them moaning. And when the sun rises in the morning, they're burnt away by the light and heat."

"It's pro*tection*!" the old man declared.

It was a protection that would never work in Vermont — not enough heat or sun. Our spirits would have to keep on wandering.

When the segment ended and an advert for hemorrhoid cream came on, I skipped through channels restlessly before muting the TV. I was beginning to feel like I might just survive the aftereffects of my gluttony. I was also feeling a rising sense of excitement. Here was an opportunity to prove myself — to him, to *her*, and to myself. Always to myself.

How cool would it be if I shook things up and turned things over and brought about a whole new understanding of what had happened at Broussard's? I got out my spiral-bound notebook and wrote down a list of questions to ask Anthony Cooper and his sister about Jeron. Then I made a similar list for the man I was due to interview on Sunday — Khurran Bashir, who'd been the co-owner of Broussard's restaurant. I could hardly wait to speak to him; I figured he'd be able to dish the details on the business side of things as well as tell me all about the Broussard family.

Eager to get started, I searched all the social media sites I knew for Jeron Cooper, Khurran Bashir, and Scott Broussard. Cooper's brief flirtation with Twitter in his early teens told me he'd loved rap music and motorbikes, but he'd posted nothing for years. He'd probably moved to other platforms and used a handle other than his name, but I couldn't find him.

I found Scott on Facebook. Judging by the infrequent posts he'd made — averaging one or two a year — he hadn't had either the time or inclination to hang out there. The post announcing the death of his mother, father, and sister had been his last. And as for Khurran Bashir, he had no virtual presence anywhere as far as I could tell. I tossed my phone aside in irritation.

The TV at the foot of the bed was now showing a rerun of an old *Law and Order* episode. I glanced at the empty side of the bed where Ryan should be, wishing he was still there. Outside the French windows, the sun was setting. Inside, the room closed in around me, embracing me in a thick, musty silence. I glanced toward the darkest corner and felt the hairs on my arms lift. Maybe I'd feel better if I closed the curtains around the four-poster? But no, it felt much worse — like a claustrophobic cloth cage.

I switched on the bedside lamp, a move which failed to make much of a dent in the room's darkness, and phoned home, taking comfort in my father's calm and leisurely account of his plans for a fishing trip to Echo Lake. I even enjoyed the familiar irritation that always came with chatting to my mother, who, as usual, enthusiastically predicted misfortune in my immediate future. The cards and crystals had apparently turned up some bad omens.

"An ill wind, that's what it points to," she said. "And seeing as it's hurricane season in Louisiana, I think that one might be headed your way!"

"*Really*, Mom?" I said, wearily.

"Really and truly, Garnet. The cards never lie. Oooh, that reminds me, you'll never guess what happened!"

"Probably not, no."

"Mrs. Burns and Mr. Yee went out on a date! So that's proof right there that the cards know what they're talking about, whatever your father might say." She uttered the last phrase so crossly that I knew the two of them must've had one of their regular arguments about my mother's mystical leanings.

"Why? What did Dad say it was?"

"I believe he called it a momentary surge of hormones from two people old enough to know better."

I laughed. I could just imagine the expression on his face when he'd dropped that gem.

"You wouldn't laugh if you knew how much it exasperated my fears."

"What fears?" I said, resisting the urge to correct her language.

"About you being in the path of hurricanes and tornadoes! I really think you should head for higher ground."

"I'll be sure and do that in the morning, Mom."

"Yes, first thing, mind," she said, then added cryptically, "The wisdom of elephants. Not that I think there are elephants in New Orleans, but if you should see an alligator, say, heading for the hills, then for goodness' sake, run!"

"Mom, what are you talking about? What elephants?"

She gave an impatient *tsk*. "The ones on that island, dear, with the *tsunami.*"

I had no response to that, but she didn't seem to need one.

"How's your case coming on?" she asked eagerly.

"I start my investigation tomorrow." I explained about Ryan having to return home and me going solo.

"So you'll be all alone in the face of the coming storm! I don't like that, Garnet, not at all."

And somehow, even though I was used to being alone, even though I usually enjoyed it, neither did I.

$$- 13 -$$

When Desirae arrived at the hotel the next morning — looking casually elegant in a raw linen dress and knee-high leather boots — I was already waiting out front, happy to be out of a room that I was beginning to dislike.

"Anthony is staying with his sister — Jeron Cooper's mother," Desirae said when I was buckled up inside her car, a giant SUV rental. "They live in the Lower Ninth Ward." Her glance told me this information should mean something to me. It didn't. "It's the part of New Orleans that was worst hit by Katrina back in 2005."

"Oh. Right."

We headed east, out of the French Quarter. Desirae was a good driver, even though her hands were constantly busy with signals to the drivers behind, ahead, and to either side of us: *No, you go first, I insist. You're welcome. May I slip in ahead, please? Thank you!*

"So, how long have you been dating Ryan?" she said when we'd escaped the clogged, narrow streets of the inner city.

I counted off the months on my fingers. "Around six months now." And then, because I couldn't resist, I added, "How long were the two of you together?"

"We were married for five years."

I was thinking of a tactful way to get her take on why they'd divorced when she changed the subject, saying, "And have you always had extrasensory perception?"

"No. Well …" My mother seemed to think I'd had some abilities since I was born, because I'd come out still encased in the caul, and legend said that bestowed the third eye on the individual. But my mother thought a lot of things that had no basis in reality. "No," I told Desirae firmly. "Just since December."

"Do you mind me asking how your abilities developed? I mean, only if you're comfortable telling me. If it's *private* and you'd rather not say, just tell me to poke my nose right out of your business."

I hadn't wanted to tell her more about it — I was generally very circumspect with who and how much I told. But now I felt like I should.

"Oh, you know, I came back to Pitchford for the holidays, drowned in Plover Pond, was dragged out an—"

"*Drowned?* As in, dead?"

"Yup. My ECG line was as flat as New Orleans's topography." That was a word, right?

"Oh my!" That's how she said it. Not *Oh my God* or *Oh my goodness*, just *Oh my*.

"Yeah. Anyway, Ryan rescued me from the pond, and then—"

"*Ryan* saved you?"

"Yeah. He didn't tell you?"

"We don't really talk much anymore."

I glanced at her, holding the silence like a good therapist, hoping she'd spill a few more beans.

"So, if you were dead …" she prompted.

We pulled up behind a bunch of other cars waiting at the St. Claude drawbridge, which was raised to let some water traffic through.

"Ryan gave me CPR until the paramedics arrived, and then they shocked my heart back into a proper rhythm in the ambulance."

"Wow."

"And then from the time I woke up, strange things started to happen."

"Strange things?"

"Occasionally, I hear things or see things that have happened in the past. Especially when I touch something, like an object associated with high emotions or something that was a person's possession."

Her eyes slid over to my left hand, which was resting on the passenger seat of her car, then to my right hand on the armrest.

"Most of the time, I don't get anything," I reassured her. "It's usually only when I'm trying."

"Oh, good. I mean, it's probably better for you that way, isn't it? Otherwise, you'd go through life inundated by other people's memories. You'd have to wear gloves."

I'd never thought of that, but Desirae was right. Of course, sometimes a feeling or vision came from left field, but that didn't happen too often.

The drawbridge descended, and Desirae inched forward onto the bridge spanning the huge industrial canal.

"So you're not a medium, then? I mean, if I understand correctly, they channel spirits and talk to ghosts. But you don't do that?"

"No," I said. No way was I going to tell her about Colby.

"And can you see the future?" she asked.

"I've never tried to."

The past and the present were more than enough, thank you very much.

She nodded slowly, then said, "This is the Lower Ninth."

I looked around and saw an area blighted by poverty and neglect, and haunted by abandoned buildings. Graffiti scrawled on a wall at a deserted filling station read *Ninth Ward Rising!* But frankly, the area didn't look like it had risen very high. Yes, there were a few newer houses here and there that had clearly been built after the devastating floods, but these stood cheek by jowl with the collapsed roofs and crumbling walls of derelict buildings. A community center and a playground spoke of hope, a closed pharmacy of despair. The scars of Katrina's wrath, the knock-on effects of the floods, and a nation's apparent inattention and indifference were etched into the landscape.

We passed vacant lots and even entire blocks of overgrown vegetation. Vines wrapped leafy nooses around tumbled piles of old tires, bushes sprouted through rotting mattresses, grass and weeds reclaimed the places where houses had been destroyed by wind and water, then flattened by bulldozers. Inch by inch, nature was clawing back her territory from the brief centuries of occupation when men, in their hubris, had set themselves up as masters of this wilderness.

Desirae, in her expensive car and clothes, looked about as out of place here as a poppy on a snowfield. I glanced across at her.

"Do you know Anthony Cooper well?"

"Yes! We used to be closer, when we were both working at the Bay Tree in Austin, but you know how it is with special friends — even if you don't see them for months or even years at a time, you can just pick up right where you left off?"

"Sure," I said, though I didn't have any friends of that caliber. "How did you meet him?"

"He gave me my first job after I graduated chef's school. He saved my life!"

"Yeah?"

"I was at such a low ebb. Chef's school was no walk in the park — late nights, hard taskmasters, pressurized kitchens, *constant* criticism. I felt incompetent *all* the time. And this was coming on the back of my divorce from Ryan, and all of that emotional *stuff.* I'd thought moving to Texas would give me a fresh start, a clean slate."

She gave me a quick glance, and I nodded to show I understood.

"But really, it just meant jumping into the deep end on so many fronts. I was living in a strange city with no friends or supports, trying to figure out my new job — and the head chef there was a real PITA, let me tell you!"

"A real what?"

"A PITA." She smiled. "A pain in the you-know-where."

"Oh! Right."

"I was at breaking point, but then Anthony took me under his wing. He mentored me, protected me, showed me the ropes. He even introduced me to his friendship circle so I didn't feel quite so *alone*. We never *dated* or anything, but he was such a good friend. He saved me."

"Right. So you feel you owe him."

A tiny frown appeared between her eyes. "Well, that's a pretty strong way to put it, but yes, I suppose I do, in a way. When I called him for a catch-up, I could just *tell* he wasn't coping. He lost his nephew, he no longer has a job, his sister sounds to be in a very bad way — it would overwhelm *anybody*, wouldn't it? I really want to support him and be here for him like he was for me. Oh, here we are."

We turned down a side road, where a few kids on skateboards glided left and right, stitching up the cracked pavement between water-filled potholes. The Cooper place was a narrow blue-and-white clapboard house. A pair of chickens strutted around a small front yard, and as we pulled up, a crow fluttered up from a litter-strewn gutter, protesting our arrival with loud caws.

"You'll do the talking, right?" Desirae said as we got out of the car. "I mean, after I introduce you."

"Okay," I said and took a deep breath.

Here we go.

$$- 14 -$$

The front door opened before we could knock. I figured the woman who stood in front of us must be Jeron's mother. Her body sagged — shoulders rounded, spine curved, head drooping — like she was struggling to stand upright on a planet where the gravity was too strong for normal humans. Her face wore the blank, immobile expression of someone suffering from major depression.

"Well, y'all come in, then. Anthony's through here," she said, leading us through a short, narrow hall.

My gaze went at once to the man who stood up from a couch when we entered the small living room. Clearly, I was way too influenced by TV cooking shows, because I hadn't expected Anthony Cooper to look more like a tall, broad lineman on a football team than my idea of a chef. He and Desirae shared a long hug, and then she introduced us. I studied his face while we shook hands — his engulfing mine — and noted that while he didn't exactly look full of the joys of life, he didn't have the defeated manner of his sister, Jeron's mother. If anything, he seemed impatient; his brown eyes glittered, and his right foot tapped the floor restlessly.

We sat down, and he turned to face me. "Desirae says you asked to investigate Jeron's case, that you want to interview us?"

My eyebrows shot up at this, and I looked at Desirae for an explanation.

"*I* asked *her*," she said quickly. "I mean, I asked my ex-husband, Ryan Jackson, to assist. He's an experienced cop from up north. But he had an emergency back home and had to return to Vermont. He thought Garnet here might be able to help, because …"

She hesitated, and I filled in the gap, "I have some experience with private investigations."

"That so?" Anthony said, looking unconvinced. "So why you want to investigate this?"

"*I* don't," I said bluntly, annoyed that Desirae hadn't been entirely up front with us. "I was under the impression that *you* wanted someone to take a look at it."

Desirae soothed me with reassurances and Anthony with encouragements. Jeron's mother said nothing, merely stared at me with lifeless eyes ringed by dark shadows. She looked exhausted, punch drunk from all the blows. A bit like the Ninth Ward.

Finally, Anthony gave me a grudging nod, which I took to mean he was on board with my investigation. I took out my notebook, turned to the list of questions I'd prepared, and then looked at Jeron's mother. "Can I just say how sorry I am for your loss? I know talking to a stranger must be the last thing you feel like doing, Mrs. …"

"Cooper," Anthony said.

The same surname as his. So she'd either kept her maiden name or never married. My gaze moved from the picture of a Black Jesus on one wall to a dead plant in the corner beside an electric fan trailing limp ribbons, and came to rest on a collection of photographs displayed on a bureau — a chubby baby in blue, a smiling boy with no front teeth, a teenager with a shadow of peach fuzz on his top lip hugging Mrs. Cooper, and in pride of place in the center, a framed enlargement of a clean-shaven young man wearing a high school graduation cap and gown, grinning widely.

"Is that Jeron?" I asked.

Anthony nodded. Jeron's mother turned her face slowly to the picture.

"Such a handsome young man," Desirae said.

"Can you tell me a little about him?" I asked.

"Dana?" Anthony looked to his sister to answer. When she merely continued to stare at the youth in the picture, he sighed and said, "He was a good kid. I mean, he had his problems, we all do, right? But he was a good kid. No way was he the stone-cold killer the cops made him out to be."

Anthony Cooper sounded like he was trying to convince himself at least as much as me. I wished Ryan was there to ask the difficult cop-type questions, but he wasn't. And Desirae looked like she had no intention of doing anything that might ruffle even a single feather. So it fell to me to wade into uncomfortable territory.

"What kind of problems?" I asked.

"Nothing crazy bad." Anthony sniffed and ran a finger back and forth under his nose — body language typical of either mounting anger or an incoming untruth. "He just—"

Mrs. Cooper stood up and walked out of the room without a word.

"Oh dear," Desirae said, looking contrite. "I hope we didn't ..." Her voice trailed off.

Anthony sighed again and held his hands up in a what-ya-gonna-do gesture. "She don't wanna know. Guess I can't blame her none."

I nodded. It wasn't just the death of her child she was dealing with — and that right there must surely be the worst grief, enough to fell anyone. It was also the death of who she'd thought Jeron was, who he might yet have turned out to be. It was the death of hope. The bright-eyed boy in the photograph had been headed for adulthood, college maybe, and a better life outside the Ninth. Now he would always be remembered for his last day, his final choices, his worst acts. He'd always be a robber and a killer.

"Jeron didn't know what he wanted to do with his life. He was hanging with the wrong crowd. I thought if he got a job, it would keep him out of trouble." Anthony's eyes dropped to his big hands. Did he believe he had blood on them? "Now I wish I never told him about Broussard's, never helped him get that damn job."

"Your sister blames you?"

He looked up, his face tight with regret. "Who else she gonna blame?"

My heart went out to him. It sounded like he blamed himself too.

"You were trying to *help* him, Anthony," Desirae said.

"What kind of problems did Jeron have?" I asked again.

"I think maybe he got into drugs."

Anthony sniffed and rubbed his nose again, and I realized the gesture could also point to a cocaine habit of his own. Had Jeron picked up the problem from his uncle?

"Weed?" I asked him. "Cocaine? Or something worse?"

"I don't know for sure, man. He was just … all over the place, turning up late for work, breaking dishes, that sorta thing. Getting into fights with the boss."

I consulted the notes I'd made about the murders based on news reports. "That would be Mr. Terence Broussard?"

"Terry, yeah. He got into *everyone's* face, though. A real hothead — always interfering, shouting, and cussing out the staff, like he thought he was that guy on TV. That English asshole with the face?" Anthony wrinkled his face and scored deep imaginary lines beside his mouth with his fingers.

"Gordon Ramsey?" Desirae said.

"Yeah, him. Guy's a dickhead, but at least *he* can cook."

"Terry Broussard couldn't?" I said.

"Nah. He was only good at making money." Another sniff. "Until he wasn't."

This was interesting.

"So the restaurant wasn't doing well?" I said.

"Nope."

"Why not?"

"Too much competition, gangs demanding protection, the area going downhill. And Terry wouldn't take nobody's advice, just carried on doing what he wanted."

"So his stress levels went up, and his people skills went down?"

Anthony squinted his too-bright eyes at me. "You trying to say he was harsh, and Jeron killed him because of that? No way, man."

Desirae shifted uncomfortably in her seat. This conversation, with all its hard questions and raw emotions, was clearly difficult for her.

"Why do *you* think Jeron did what he did?" I asked Anthony.

"I don't know! That's what I told her." He gestured to Desirae. "What the fuck would make my nephew shoot a whole family?"

"Any theories?"

Anthony held his hands up in a helpless gesture. "Maybe he owed his dealers, and they put the squeeze on him. Maybe he secretly played the dogs or the ponies, and he needed money. So he robbed the place."

"And shot everyone because …?"

"Things went wrong."

"How, though?" I pressed.

"Things just went wrong!" His fists bunched, and I gave him a moment. When he continued, it was in a calmer voice. "I reckon there were plenty people had it in for Broussard. But the cops only ever looked at Jeron."

Maybe because he was found on the scene of the crime with a bag of cash and the murder weapon. Maybe because there was an eyewitness, I thought but didn't say.

"Young Black man looks like he did it, so he must've, right? Case closed. No more investigating necessary." He rubbed a knuckle into his jaw, kneading at a knot of pain.

"You think there was more to it?"

"I think there's a world of difference between snorting a line and taking a life. Three lives."

– 15 –

I nodded, checked my list of questions. "How did Jeron get on with the rest of the Broussard family?"

"I don't know, man. Fine, I guess. No problems as far as I know. Mrs. Broussard kinda took him under her wing. Maybe she saw he had potential. He was a good kid, you know? Like I said."

I got up and walked over to the graduation photograph, casually laying a hand on the frame, but I felt only a twang of sadness for Jeron and his family. I'd been so focused on the three deaths in the Broussard family that it was only now I fully grasped that a fourth person had died. The youth in the picture was so full of hope and eagerness, and *his* life had been extinguished, *his* family devastated too.

I sat back down. "Will your sister talk to me?"

"I don't think so. She don't talk to no one anymore."

That was a pity but not a train wreck — from what I knew of teenage boys, their mothers were the last to know their secrets anyway.

"That night — July Fourth — were you working at the

restaurant?" I asked Anthony.

"Uh-huh."

"What happened?"

"We had an early rush, but by eleven, the dining room was empty. The Broussards wanted to have a late dinner to celebrate Scott's twenty-fifth birthday, so I made them food, brought out the mud cake I'd baked for them earlier that day, then I left. I haven't been back there since."

"That was the last time you saw them?"

"Yeah."

"How did they seem?"

"Same as usual. Scott was maybe a little excited."

"Because of his birthday? Or something more?"

"When Brittany turned twenty-five, Terry brought her into the management of the business much more."

"Did he plan on doing the same with Scott?"

"Don't reckon he got the chance." He shook his head sadly. "Poor kid. Imagine having to remember the deaths of your family every birthday for the rest of your life. He didn't deserve that. I mean, no one does, right? But he was like the backbone of that place. He did the work. If it wasn't for him, it wouldn't of stayed afloat. And then he gets dealt that hand."

"It's just too *too* awful," Desirae murmured.

"Yeah." I nibbled on the edge of a thumbnail, realized what I was doing, and shoved both hands under my legs so that I was sitting on them. "When did you find out about what had happened?"

"Bashir called me at six the next morning to tell me. Woke me up. He sounded very cut up."

"Yeah?"

"Couldn't hardly breathe, let alone talk. He needed some tranquilizers or something."

"I guess he was in shock, upset."

"Me too, but you don't hear me crying and blubbering."

No, I didn't. In fact, Anthony, while clearly distressed about the loss of his nephew, didn't seem too upset at all about the deaths of the Broussards.

"Did it seem, over the top? Like he was acting?" I asked.

He tilted his head, considering. "It just seemed ... too much, you know? I mean, him and Terry were business partners, not friends. Everyone knew Bashir wanted out of the deal. He didn't have no respect for Terry — any fool could see that."

It was food for thought. I knew that shock could cause people to behave strangely, that everyone reacted in their own way to death and tragedy. But still, Bashir's reaction was interesting.

"So," I said, "what do you think happened?"

"Honest to God, I have no idea. I mean, I thought I *knew* Jeron. I thought he was a good kid. I never imagined ..."

"Drugs can do funny things to a person," I said. "They can change your personality, rob your future, drive you to do desperate things."

He gave me a sharp glance. Wondering whether I was talking about him as well as his nephew?

"I just don't see him as a killer," Anthony said.

Don't or won't? I wondered.

"Can I take a look at Jeron's room?" Maybe I'd get a reading off some of his personal possessions.

Anthony shrugged. "I guess."

He led Desirae and me through to a bedroom with a narrow bed, desk, and a wooden chair with a taped-up leg. A poster of the Joker leered down from one wall, a scuffed skateboard occupied the corner behind the door, and an old-school record player and speakers sat on top of a chest of drawers. A pile of vinyl records were stacked on a shelf, with a pair of Nike high-tops alongside. It looked neater than I'd expected a young man's room to be — certainly neater than my bedroom had ever been. Maybe his mother had tidied up afterward?

Lying on the desk in the corner was a dog-eared copy of one of the *Game of Thrones* books, a Ragin' Cajuns ball cap, and an iPhone with a crack running diagonally across its screen.

"Were you able to get into his phone?" I asked.

Anthony crossed his arms over his broad chest. "Nah. But the cops got records from the service provider — his call lists and texts and such. Said there was 'nothing significant' there."

"May I touch the phone?"

Anthony frowned, clearly puzzled. I gave Desirae a look, and she turned to him with a smile. "Could I trouble you for a glass of water, Anthony? I'm parched."

"Sure, of course. Sorry, I should've offered. Do you—?"

"I'm fine, thanks," I said.

I waited until they'd left before picking up the phone. Holding it between both hands, I closed my eyes and pulled my attention away from the room, the sound of a thumping bass beat outside, and my thoughts of Mrs. Cooper's pain. As I centered all my awareness on the phone, light and color began to shimmer at the edge of the blackness behind my eyelids. No images appeared, but slowly, a feeling blossomed. Grief. Unutterable sadness and despair. The phone was infused with it.

A deep heaviness constricted my chest. Gradually, a picture took shape in my mind's eye: hands holding this phone, tears splashing down onto its screen. Sighing, I opened my eyes and replaced the phone on the desk. The ball cap gave me much the same result. I couldn't get a reading on Jeron, because any significant resonances of him in his belongings had been overlaid with his mother's overpowering emotions. She probably came into this room all the time to pick up his phone, smell his pillow, hug the jacket hanging behind the door.

Feeling like the intruding snoop I was, I checked under his mattress, went through his jacket pockets, and fanned the pages of the book on his desk. A business card for Broussard's restaurant fell out. On the back, a phone number had been written in a loopy scrawl. I pocketed the card, figuring that if the cops had already closed the case, they'd already have conducted any searches they deemed necessary. I pulled open a drawer and was rifling through the tangle of charging cables and cords inside when Anthony and Desirae returned.

Pushing aside a battered PlayStation console, I picked up a Valentine's card with a red teddy bear on the front declaring, *I love you beary much!*

Opening it to read the message inside, I asked, "Who's Camille?"

Anthony took the Valentine's card, ran his fingers over the embossed surface, and then slipped it back into the desk drawer. Close up, I saw that his hands were marked with dozens of burns and scars. Between Anthony and Desirae, I was learning that cheffing wasn't easy on the hands.

"Camille was Jeron's girlfriend," he said.

"Will she talk to me?"

He shrugged. "You can try. You want me to take you to her? They usually hang out on the corner."

– 16 –

We left the house to its oppressive silence — Mrs. Cooper was nowhere to be seen — and Anthony walked us to the end of the block, where a group of teens leaned up against a low wall, hunched over their phones. Desirae took one look at the group — hoodies, saggy pants, tattoos, hand-rolled smokes, chins lifting and eyes narrowing at our approach — and beat a retreat back to the car, murmuring profuse apologies. I didn't blame her. Walking into a bunch of feral teens to ask awkward questions was not for the faint of heart.

Anthony walked up to an itty-bitty bird of a girl of about sixteen or seventeen who sat perched on a low wall, pulling threads out of the frayed knees of her jeans with her long, purple-painted nails.

"Hey, Camille, this is Garnet. She wants to talk to you about Jeron."

Camille lifted her face — delicately boned, huge eyes, stud through one nostril — and checked me over from my boots, up along my jeans (unfashionably intact), over my black sweatshirt, and up to my mismatched eyes.

She scowled. "You police?"

"No. I'm—"

"Then what you wanna talk to me 'bout Jeron for?"

A few of her friends moved in closer.

"Well," I said, "Anthony here thinks there may be more to what happened than the story the cops settled on."

A tall boy built like a brick outhouse cackled at this. "Ain't there always, man? Fucking po-lice."

A chorus of approval for this sentiment rippled through the group.

"You some kind of investigator?" Camille asked me. "Like a PI?"

"Yeah. Can—"

"Like Jessica Jones?"

"Yeah, no. I'm not as kickass as she is. Can I talk to you a little about Jeron?"

She glanced left and right, as if taking counsel from her buddies. Some message must've been communicated in the glances they exchanged, because she met my gaze again, and gave me a grudging jerk of her chin.

"You want me to stay, Camille?" Anthony asked.

She gave him a long, unreadable look. "I look like I want you to stay?"

No love lost there, then.

Anthony gave me a shrug, sniffed hard, and headed back to his sister's house.

Camille watched him go with an impassive look on her face, then asked me, "What's up with your eyes?"

"Same thing that's up with yours."

"Nothing wrong with my eyes."

"Nothing wrong with mine, either."

She gave a soft grunt, which might have meant anything, and returned her attention to her torn jeans. I watched her select another thread and carefully pull it out of the fabric. For someone like me, whose fingers loved to scratch and pick and fiddle, her habit was hypnotic to watch. I needed to get myself a pair of ripped jeans to destroy instead of tearing bits of skin off my fingers and, occasionally, when I was truly crazy upset, my feet.

"What you want to know?" Camille asked.

"Can you tell me a bit about what Jeron was like as a person?"

"He was cool, I guess. A good kisser." The males in the group reacted noisily to this, and Camille snapped, "Didn't knock me around or cheat on me, and lemme tell you, that's unusual with the dickwads around here."

The boys mumbled a few protests, then drifted away, drawing most of the girls with them. One remained — a girl as heavy as Camille was light, with lots of acne, even more makeup, and a mouth full of gum.

"Assholes!" she called after them. To me, she said, "I'm Keisha."

"Hi." I gave them both a smile and, trying to build some rapport, added, "Guys get better as they get older."

But Camille said, "Jeron ain't getting any older."

I cursed myself for not thinking before I spoke. "No. Sorry."

Camille wound the loose thread around and around the first

joint of her pinkie finger. "Not your fault."

"Whose fault was it?"

"His," she said simply. "Jeron was …" Her voice trailed off.

But her friend stopped chewing long enough to chime in, "He was a boy trying to prove he was a man."

"He was a fool." Camille's mouth twisted scornfully. I saw the bravado covering her pain like the thinnest of eggshells.

"You loved him," I said softly.

Immediately, the girl's eyes welled with tears. She wiped them away with a furious dash of her hand, then glared at her finger, pulling the thread tight. The tip bulged and turned wine red.

"Can you tell me about his job?" I said. "Did Jeron like waiting tables?"

"He weren't no waiter."

"No?"

"He was just a dishwasher," Keisha said.

Desirae must've had it wrong. I tried to remember if Anthony had mentioned what type of job he'd helped Jeron get but couldn't recall that he'd been specific.

Camille said, "He *wanted* to be a waiter, for the tips and all. But that bastard Broussard said he couldn't be trusted to wash a dish, let alone carry one to table."

"Jeron and Broussard didn't get on well?"

"You could say that. That's why Broussard fired his ass. He didn't have no good reason otherwise. Just didn't like Jeron."

Fired. Anthony hadn't mentioned that. Either he was hiding it from me or, feeling guilty about getting his nephew the job that ultimately got him killed, he'd subconsciously filtered out any hint of a real motive that Jeron might've had.

"When did Broussard fire Jeron?" I asked Camille.

"About a week before— before the robbery." She examined the tip of her finger, which now resembled a purple Gummi Bear. "He was so mad."

"Jeron? You think he went there to kill Broussard?"

"I didn't say that! I just said I never seen him so mad."

I watched, fascinated, as she unwound the thread and shook her hand, sending blood and surely pain back to the liberated tip.

"His uncle says Jeron was maybe getting into drugs?" I probed.

"Getting into?" Camille repeated with a hard, bitter laugh.

"Just weed? Or …?"

"It started with just weed and coke."

I waited.

"But recently, he was into whatever he could get."

"He was going at it *hard*," Keisha added.

Camille rolled the thread between her fingers and pushed it through the hole in her jeans, tucking it behind an unravelling edge. "Hard, but not all the way, though." The tough, cynical look stole back over her features, and she added, "There was still a lil' blood left in his drug stream."

Keisha snorted a laugh.

"Any idea why he did what he did at Broussard's?" I asked.

Camille looked at me like I was stupid.

Keisha said, "For the money, bitch."

"No, I mean, any idea why he shot them all?"

Camille left off worrying her jeans and began fiddling with

her necklace — a long chain with two halves of the same gold heart dangling on the end.

"Maybe they recognized him," Keisha said. "Cops said he didn't have no gloves on, and he had a tattoo here." She ran a finger over her wrist, just above the spot where a shirt cuff would fall. "Like if they saw it, then he had to make sure they couldn't ID him later. He shoulda worn gloves, man."

"Like I said, a fool." Camille's hand closed into a fist around the broken heart, squeezing the life out of it.

"Your necklace is lovely," I said. "Did Jeron give it to you?"

"He gave her one half, and he wore the other," Keisha explained. "So romantic! Like two halves of the same whole, you know?"

"His mother gave me his half after the funeral," Camille said.

"Can I see?" Without waiting for permission, I reached over to lift the broken heart between my fingers and closed my eyes. Immediately, images bloomed behind my eyelids.

The young man, his hair worn in a shaved fade with twists on top, fastens a gold chain with one half of the heart around his neck.

"I got a plan, babe. I'm not gonna be wrinkling my fingers in dishwater much longer, you'll see. I've got a big job coming up. Easy money."

The girl twists her mouth. "Ain't no such thing as easy money."

"Big money, then. The job's all planned and lined up. And after? Me and you can blow this shithole of a town and start over. Start living."

"What plan, what job? What you talking 'bout?"
A wide grin splits his face. "Aks me no questions and I'll
tell you no lies. Let's just say I'll finally be free of
Broussard when it's done."

"Gimme that!" The real-time Camille tugged the hearts out of my fingers. "What you hanging onto my necklace for? And why your eyes flicking like that — you having a fit or something?"

"No, sorry, I was just concentrating hard, thinking."

Keisha, eyeing me like my crazy might be catching, demanded, "Thinking 'bout what, bitch?"

I said the first thing that came to mind, a line gleaned from a lifetime of watching cop dramas on TV. "Did anyone have a reason for wanting him dead?"

"Jeron?" Camille said.

I nodded.

"His uncle."

"His uncle *Anthony?*"

"Uh-huh. He had life insurance on Jeron. Found that out at the funeral too. He took it out when Jeron graduated high school. Freaking weird."

"Suspicious," Keisha said.

"He *says* he'll give all the money to Jeron's momma, but we'll see," Camille said with the resigned cynicism usually found in women twice her age. "He took one out on her too."

"On his sister?" I said, startled.

Keisha glanced over my shoulder toward the Cooper house. "Guess the old lady better watch her back."

— 17 —

I had Desirae drop me off on Decatur Street, which was easier for her than trying to thread her way back through the one-ways of the French Quarter to my hotel. Plus I needed a walk to clear my head and order my thoughts, *and* I wanted to get something to eat. All I'd had so far that day was a cup of black coffee, and my stomach, which hadn't gotten the memo that it shouldn't be hungry for a month following my orgy of deep-fried excess, was growling.

I spied a line of customers waiting outside a small Italian grocery store and, working on the premise that if people were lining up for it, it had to be good, took up my place at the end of the line behind a man with a battered backpack and a camera bag.

"What are we lining up for?" I asked him.

"Muffulettas," he said. "According to Yelp, Tripadvisor, and FeedMe, these are the best in town."

"What's a muffuletta?"

He grinned smugly. "You'll see."

A muffuletta, as I discovered when I watched it being

prepared fresh in front of me, was basically the biggest, bad-assiest, chef's kiss of a sandwich anywhere, ever. A wheel of bread the size of a dinner plate was sliced in half, spread with olive salad, and stuffed with layers of salami, mortadella, ham, Emmental and provolone cheese, then topped with shredded carrot, pickled cauliflower, marinated mushrooms, and roasted peppers for good measure before being drizzled with a tangy olive oil dressing.

Clutching this wax paper-wrapped promise of heaven against my heart, I hurried to the nearest park — Jackson Square — found myself a sunny spot on a bench, and tucked in. I may have groaned out loud in pleasure. It was several minutes before I could pry my attention away from my food and look around.

The square was large, with tourist-filled paths and pie-shaped wedges of grass studded with ancient live oaks and crepe myrtles. A bronze statue of a soldier on a rearing horse surveyed the scene from a marble plinth at the center of the park. At the north end, a church shone blindingly white in the bright sunshine, its triple steeples piercing the blue sky above. On the other side of the ornate iron fence that hemmed in the square, street performers — jugglers, magicians, "live" statues, mimes, and artists — plied their trade. For a couple of bucks, you could get your caricature sketched in charcoal or your fortune told by a palm reader. Somewhere nearby, a saxophonist played "House of the Rising Sun." I closed my eyes and lifted my face to the warmth and light, blissed out.

As I told Ryan when he called ten minutes into my feast, "I think I just died and went to heaven."

"Again? This is becoming a habit with you, Garnet."

"Yes, but *muffulettas!*"

"Come again?"

I explained all, ending with, "I feel the need to warn you, Chief, that you may have been replaced in my affections."

"You're going to dump me for lunch meat and cheese?"

"Not just any meat and cheese. I've clearly failed to describe the glory of this sandwich. It's so good, so filling, even I won't be able to finish it."

"Defeated by food twice in two days? What's become of the woman I fell for?"

"It's this place; it's corrupting me." I carefully wrapped up the remains of my sandwich in the wax paper. "But — to business! I haven't forgotten why I'm here."

"Desirae says you did great at the Cooper's this morning."

"Oh? She called you?" I said, not wild about the idea that Desirae was giving Ryan status updates on my performance.

"Yes, she said Mrs. Cooper wouldn't talk."

"That poor woman. My heart was breaking for her."

"Three times in my career, I've had to notify parents that their kid died. You watch their faces crumble, their lives collapsing, right in front of you. It's the worst," Ryan said.

"Yeah."

We were silent for a second as the presence of tragedy moved between us.

"So," Ryan said, "did you find out anything from Desirae's friend?"

I gave him a detailed account of my morning, explaining what I'd learned about Jeron, his poor mother, his uncle, Anthony's unflattering portrait of Terry Broussard, and what Desirae had told me on the ride back into town. "She said drug use is rife in the restaurant world. The chefs take uppers to stay awake during long shifts, then they need downers to get to sleep because they're still hyped when they eventually get home. And I have a strong suspicion that dear old Uncle Anthony has a coke habit."

"You like him for a suspect?"

"He knew the lay of the land at the restaurant, he probably needs extra money to feed his nose, and he stood to benefit from Jeron's death because he had taken out life insurance on his nephew."

"Life insurance on a nephew — that's unusual."

"*Right?*"

"But he didn't have anything to gain from the Broussards' deaths."

"Granted, but he never mentioned the insurance to me or the fact that Jeron had been fired by Broussard. Plus, I've got to say, he doesn't seem too thrilled to have me here sticking my nose into his business. Are you aware that he didn't exactly ask Desirae for help?"

"Yeah, she told me she volunteered."

"When?"

"When did she offer to help?"

"No, when did she tell you that?"

"Oh, when we spoke earlier today. I think *she* felt bad that *he* felt guilty on account of having gotten the kid the job instead of backing up his mom about going to college."

So, basically, we were down here because Desirae had felt bad? "Hmmm."

"The thing about Desirae is she's really kind. She loves to help people."

"That's great," I said, insincerely. I didn't want Ryan to praise his ex. Desirae annoyed me. I wanted her to be an annoyance to Ryan too. "Did you get anything from the NOPD?"

"Not much, I'm afraid. It's under the jurisdiction of the Eighth District, and I don't know anyone there. But I spoke to the detective in charge of the case."

"Yeah?"

"She said she 'didn't consider herself obliged' to send me the case file, but she did give me an overview. The deaths actually happened after midnight, so on the fifth of July."

I corrected the date in my notebook.

"And it seems they have solid evidence against Jeron Cooper," Ryan continued. "His fingerprints were on the gun that shot all four Broussards and also on the bag with the cash they found beside him."

"Wasn't it dumb for him not to wear gloves?"

"Not really. He worked there, so it wouldn't be a surprise to find his prints on the scene. And he would've planned on taking the gun and bag with him."

"I guess. Could they trace the gun?"

"No, the serial number had been filed off."

"Damn."

"And he wore a ski mask so they couldn't see his face, but that apparently got yanked off in the scuffle outside the cooler."

"So Jeron shot them because they'd be able to identify him."

"Yup, and the son, Scott, must've known that was coming for him, too, so that's why he tried to take down Jeron and nearly got himself killed in the process."

"Right, that makes sense. So the cops' theory is that it was a robbery gone wrong?" I opened a corner of the wax paper and picked out a marinated mushroom to snack on.

"Yeah. They started with two theories — a botched robbery or a hit on the family made to *look* like a botched robbery. But there was no evidence for the hit hypothesis. Plus there'd been some petty vandalism at the restaurant in the preceding months which pointed toward an inside job, probably a disgruntled employee."

"What sort of vandalism?" I said, licking my fingers.

"Some property damage, and — get this — an awful smell started wafting around the restaurant's dining room. Patrons and staff were complaining, and some bad reviews were posted online. It took them an age to track down, but eventually, they found small pieces of anchovy hidden under the carpet in the corners and tucked into the lighting sconces on the walls. Oh, and pushed into one of the air-conditioning vents too."

"Anchovies!" I laughed. "Yeah, that sort of petty revenge would fit with an unhappy staff member, I guess."

An exhausted-looking woman pushing a baby in a stroller paused near my bench. The baby stared at me and bounced its head as though eager to get going again. Lately, I'd been noticing babies, skirting the periphery of thinking they were cute, wondering if one day, maybe …

The baby dropped its pacifier at my feet, and I bent down to pick it up and then handed it to the mother. She popped it into her own mouth, gave it a good few sucks, and then plugged the now-bawling baby back up. Yeah, I was nowhere near ready to be a mother.

– 18 –

"Did they ever consider the son as a suspect?" I asked Ryan. "I mean, it's mighty convenient that he survived and is now probably the main beneficiary of the parents' estate."

"They interviewed him, but apparently, there was nothing to indicate he had any involvement. All the forensic evidence — fingerprints, blood spatter and trails, footprints, some security footage — lined up with his account of what happened. The DA declined to pursue charges against him."

"They have any other suspects?"

"Not really. They're saying it's open and shut."

"Maybe it is. Maybe Anthony is just in denial about who his nephew truly was."

"But you'll check?"

"Sure, for what it's worth."

My phone beeped with an incoming text from Desirae. On our way back from the Coopers', I'd thanked her profusely for setting up the interview and flattered her shamelessly in an attempt to get her to try to set up a meeting with the sole surviving member of the Broussard family, and she'd promised to give it her best.

"I asked Desirae to set up a meeting for me with Scott Broussard," I said, thumbing open the message.

"Great! When are you interviewing him?"

"I'm not. Desirae just sent a message saying he's 'declined to speak to me.' The people down here sure are polite about their lack of cooperation, aren't they?"

"He doesn't want to talk to a psychic?"

"Maybe, though Desirae didn't say that. Too polite, probably. She just says he doesn't want to dig up all the pain again and can't see the point since the perpetrator is dead. And I guess he has a point. Terry Broussard sounds like an asshole, but so far, I don't see why anyone would want the rest of the family dead. It probably was just a botched robbery."

"Hopefully, you'll find out more when you meet his business partner tomorrow."

"We're going to meet at the actual restaurant. Is it wrong that I'm excited about that?"

"Of course you're excited. I'll bet you get some readings."

One of the things I really liked about Ryan was that he never dismissed my gift.

"Yeah." I brushed crumbs off my jeans. "How's Ronnie doing?"

"Grouchy as a bear with a sore tooth."

"So pretty much the same as always, then?"

"It's only you she's hostile to," he said, laughing. "With me, she's always perfectly pleasant."

"A, I don't buy that for a second. And B, She took an instant dislike to me!" I protested.

"What can I tell you? The universe strives for balance."

"What, now?"

"*I* took an instant — and massive — liking to you."

"You did?" I said, my irritation dissolving. "You never told me it was massive liking at first sight."

"Well, now you know. My liking was so massive, it tilted the planet, and Ronnie had to restore the balance with her dislike."

A warm glow filled my insides.

"Are you smiling, Garnet?"

"Like the *Mona Lisa*, Chief."

He chuckled and, telling me he was missing me, ended the call.

I mulled over my possible next steps for a minute, staring at a tour group headed my way. The park was filling up with visitors and locals on their lunch break, but although the left-hand side of the bench I was sitting on was unoccupied, no one sat down there. Maybe I stank. Maybe I had a resting bitch face. Maybe Colby was there to the left of me, where he'd always sat in life. I thought I caught the faintest trace of cola. Ryan wasn't here; was Colby coming in closer? I let my left hand rest palm upward on the bench, as though inviting him to take my hand. I felt nothing, of course.

Telling myself to stop being as ridiculous as my mother — expecting to hold hands with a ghost, honestly! — I woke up my phone and texted Desirae back.

> Bummer! Can you give me
> Scott's number and address?

Her reply came almost instantly.

Promise you won't mention
you got the info from me!

Pinkie promise

Give me a minute to try and
look up the address.

And send me Anthony's
number? And Mrs. Cooper's
too, just in case.

The tour group drew near, and while I waited, I eavesdropped on the guide — an older man wearing a red bowtie that matched his big golf umbrella. He told his group all about the three-hundred years of Jackson Square's existence — Spanish troops, public executions, slaves, the Battle of New Orleans, and much more besides.

"In short," he concluded, "this square, this town, has seen some *history!*"

My phone buzzed again — Desirae coming through with Scott's phone number and address, and the Coopers' numbers.

Remember, you never got this
from me. And please be gentle
with Mrs. Cooper.

I texted back a thumbs-up emoji and tapped the number for Scott Broussard. After five rings, it went to voicemail.

"Hi, Scott, this is Garnet McGee. I think Desirae Jackson has told you about me. Please, I'd really like to speak to you. Let me know if you change your mind about meeting me." I left my number and ended the call, estimating my chances at getting a call back at fifty to one.

Tossing my phone back into my bag, I headed north through the park, catching up with the tour party again at the steps of the cathedral. The guide was telling the tourists all about how the edifice behind him was said to be haunted by the ghost of a priest and also by a friar, whose voice could be heard chanting something called a *kyrie* on rainy days.

"And speaking of ghosts and ghouls, come this way and have a peep down Pirates' Alley, a street named after the infamous nineteenth century pirates Jean Lafitte and his brother, Pierre," the guide said, ushering us to a spot where we could see down a narrow side street. "Can anyone spot the gargoyle?"

Another one? It was beginning to feel like the grotesque things were everywhere.

This hideously faced creature clung to the corner of a redbrick building. It thrust its tongue out at the world, probably dribbling water onto the passersby below, since, according to the guide, gargoyles were originally designed as a means to allow rainwater to run off the roofs of buildings, kind of like an early gutter. In fact, their name came from the French word *gargouille*, meaning "throat," because the gargoyle statues of gothic architecture had waterspouts projecting from their gaping jaws.

"What do you say when a gargoyle knocks at your door?"

the guide said and delivered the punchline before anyone could hazard a guess. "Is-tat-you?" When only a couple of people in the crowd got the joke, he enunciated, "Is sta-tue?" This garnered a better response and, looking pleased, he continued, "The oldest gargoyles ever found were on a building in Turkey. They're shaped like a crocodile and date back 13,000 years. In medieval times, gargoyle masonry became a common feature on churches, taking the form of hideous mythical humans, fierce lions, or chimeras — those are hybrid creatures formed from different animals. They were made ugly or scary on purpose so as to ward off evil spirits and to devour giants with their open mouths."

So gargoyles were good guys. Who knew?

The guide twirled his red umbrella, gave a theatrical chuckle, and continued in a deeper voice, "But some say gargoyles symbolized the presence of evil in the world, and their purpose was to remind people to live a life true to the Church's teachings or else fall prey to demonic possession. There is also a pagan belief, held by some even today, that the stone carvings can come to life, freeing the evil monsters trapped inside and allowing them to walk among us, reanimated and bent on *eeee-vvvil*." He drew out the last word melodramatically and scratched at the air with clawed fingers.

I tried to join in with the other tourists snickering at the ridiculous superstitions, but my laugh came out sounding forced and too loud. The guide's attention snapped my way. Frowning, he marched up to me, giving me a smile as insincere as my laugh had been humorless.

"Ma'am, if you want to join one of our tours, I'm afraid

you'll have to buy a ticket, just like everyone else. You'll find all the details here," he said, thrusting a pamphlet into my hands. "Next up, the Pontalba Apartments. All *paying* customers, follow the red umbrella!"

– 19 –

When Scott Broussard didn't return my call, I decided to go visit him in person. Maybe his Southern manners would make it hard for him to turn away someone on his doorstep.

The address Desirae had sent was in the Garden District, so I made my way to Canal Street and once again hopped onto a streetcar, headed west on the St. Charles line. This time, without a hangover, I was better able to appreciate the fine crimson-and-green outside of the streetcar, and the polished mahogany seats and brass fittings inside. I entered Scott's address into my map app, got off at the closest stop, and walked the rest of the way, admiring the shady, elegant heart of the Garden District.

The Broussard house was a real antebellum mansion, albeit a small one. Ancient live oaks bearded with Spanish moss held hands over a short drive, forming a green tunnel that led to the main house with Corinthian columns and stone balconies. Somewhere inside, Scarlett O'Hara was lacing her stays.

As I drew closer, though, I noticed signs that the Broussard home was looking a little shabby. The grass out front was overgrown and dotted with weeds, leaves covered the drive, and the windows had that dull, closed look of glass that's gone unwashed for too long. The property was sealed off with fencing and a huge electric gate, so I couldn't march up to the house and knock on the front door, but I pressed the buzzer on the intercom. There was no immediate answer.

I was wondering whether it would be rude to buzz again when a male voice answered.

"Hello? Can I help you?" The tone wasn't rude, but it also wasn't friendly.

"Am I speaking to Scott Broussard?" I said.

"No."

"Well, I'm here to see Scott."

"Who may I say is calling?" the voice said. I pictured a butler in tails and white gloves, determined to keep upstarts and intruders at bay.

"G— Gaby."

"And what is the nature of your business?"

"I want to, um, interview Scott for my magazine, er, *The Bayou's Best.*"

"I believe Mr. Broussard is not at home."

Yeah, right. "Can you check, please? I want to talk to him about a cover piece."

There was a moment's hesitation, and then, "One moment, please." A few minutes later, Jeeves was back. "I regret that Mr. Broussard is not home to visitors."

"Wait! I—" But the intercom went silent, and several long buzzes got no reply, not even one warning me to clear out before the private security company prominently advertised on the gate pillar was summoned.

Crap.

If this was a movie, and I was a private eye, this would be the moment when I took up position in my beater with a cup of coffee and some junk food, and settled in for a long stakeout. But I had no car — and even worse, no snacks — so instead, I leaned up against a nearby tree, keeping an eye on the gates. Maybe Scott would emerge to take his pugnacious bulldog for a stroll. Just like in the movies.

While I waited, I called Jeron's mother.

"Mrs. Cooper? It's Garnet McGee here. We met yesterday."

"What do you want?" Her speech was slow, her voice dead.

"Well, when I spoke to Camille yesterday, she mentioned that Anthony had taken out life insurance on Jeron, and I just wanted to check if that was true."

After a moment's silence, she said, "I have no idea."

"So you haven't received any insurance payout or compensation?"

"Nothing can compensate me for the loss of my boy," she said, a tinge of anger animating her voice.

"Of course not. I didn't mean to—"

"Goodb—"

"Could I just ask one more question?" I got in quickly. "Did Jeron ever talk to you about a new job?"

"A new job? He already *had* a new job."

"Or did he maybe mention some kind of opportunity to make easy money?"

"I think we are done here, Miss McGee."

"Please, call me Garnet."

"No. Me and you are not friends. I don't want to talk to you or anyone else about my son's death, you understand? Jes' thinking about my boy lying in that goddamned place, bleeding to death, makes me want to give up and die."

"I—"

"Don't call me again," she said and hung up.

Great. Far from getting more information, I'd upset the very person I was supposedly here to help. Desirae, I suspected, would've accused me of being not gentle. I didn't get much time to dwell on my failings, though, because at that moment, the gates opened with a soft hiss, and a cliché-red Porsche emerged, giving me a brief glimpse of the young man inside, before it tore up the road with a growl.

I glanced around in frustration — where was a cab when you needed to yell, "Follow that convertible!"?

I pressed the buzzer again. No answer. *Dammit.* I had no clue as to where Scott might be headed, but there was a remote chance someone else might.

Anthony Cooper answered his phone on the third ring.

"Hi, it's Garnet," I told him. "Any idea where Scott Broussard might be headed on a Saturday afternoon with a bag of golf clubs in the back seat?"

"Most Saturdays, he used to leave the restaurant between the lunch and dinner service to get in a quick round at his club and then have drinks at the bar there afterward. He took me a couple of times."

"Right, thanks!"

"Don't get too excited. It's the Live Oaks Country Club. Only members and their guests can get in."

"Oh. Are you a member?"

"I look like I'm rich?"

"Right," I said, disappointed. "Hey, Anthony, while I've got you on the line, can I just check something? This morning, Camille told me that you had a life insurance policy on Jeron." Silence. "Hello?"

"You accusing me of wanting my nephew dead now? Of having a hand in it?" Anthony sounded super pissed.

"No, no, nothing like that," I tried to placate him. "I just wanted to check, you know, whether Camille is honest and trustworthy."

"Huh. Did she tell you my *sister* is the designated beneficiary?"

"No." I silently cursed the fact that I wasn't a cop and couldn't therefore just march into a life insurance company to find out what the truth was. "You see, this is why I always have to check."

After I ended the call, I cudgeled my brains for a ruse to get in at the country club and have a nice, private Q&A with Scott Broussard, and then I ordered an Uber, requesting and extra stop *en route*. When we pulled up to the club's entrance, a female guard with unsettlingly severe micro-bladed eyebrows stepped up to the car's window, asking the driver for his membership card.

He flashed his ID. "I'm just dropping my ride, hun."

The guard peered inside at me. "Ma'am?"

I rolled down my window, tugged on the strings of the helium balloons I'd purchased at a party store on the way, and smiled brightly.

"Hi, there! I'm not a member, but my fiancé is, and it's his birthday. I know he's playing a game of golf right now, and I wanted to get a table ready for him in the restaurant, order his favorite champagne, and so on."

She consulted her list. "Has he put you down as a visitor today?"

"No, like I said, it's a surprise!"

She began shaking her head.

"Oh, please, I've flown in all the way from Vermont. Help a girl out, will ya?"

Her scary brows drew together, but she didn't dismiss me. "Who's your fiancé?"

"Scott Broussard. Little red Porsche?"

"I know who Mr. Broussard is. He came in about an hour ago."

"*Please.* Scotty's been having such a rough time of it lately, you know, with his family and all. I just wanted to give him a happy day."

Fortunately, a car waiting behind us honked just then.

"I'm so sorry, are we blocking the way?" I said sweetly, trying to mimic the apologetic expression Desirae so often wore.

"Fine," she said. "You go on in and try cheering up that poor boy. And you," she told the driver, "had better be out within two minutes."

– 20 –

The boom barrier rose, and we drove inside, crunching up a gravel drive that was bordered on either side by the emerald green of a perfectly tended golf course. The Uber dropped me off at the main clubhouse, and I ran up the stairs to the entrance like I belonged there. Inside, I wandered around until I found the bar. Choosing a seat at the polished wood counter from where I could keep an eye on the doorway, I tied my balloons to the bar rail beside me.

"Meeting someone?" the barman said.

"You bet."

"A drink while you wait?"

I hesitated. I needed to stay clear-headed. "I'll have a G&T, hold the G."

He frowned. "You want a tonic water with ice and lemon?"

"I want to stay on the wagon without anyone knowing." I gave him a wink, and he nodded his understanding. All's fair in love and war and supposed recovery. When he brought me my drink, I added a sweet tip to my payment, telling him, "If I order another round, or if my date does, bring this again, will you?"

The bar was mostly empty. Seemingly, the lunch crowd had disappeared onto courts and courses and into saunas, and the predinner folk had yet to arrive. Good, that suited me fine; I didn't need any gym-bunny competition. I was reaching the end of my first drink when Scott came through the doors, walking with a slight limp. He was freshly showered and wearing designer jeans and a navy-and-white-striped polo shirt — the brand with the little crocodile on the pocket. His face was thin, with light eyes beneath dark-blond hair, and he looked like he was in good physical shape. Not bad looking, overall, even though his expression seemed a little sulky.

His gaze slid over me without stopping and scanned the rest of the interior before he grabbed a stool at the bar counter a good way away, greeted the barkeeper, and ordered a vodka and orange. I was close enough to hear his voice, and I recognized it at once. *Jeeves.* It was the voice I'd heard on the intercom at the Broussard house. Why would Scott pretend to be his own butler? Maybe his inheritance hadn't come through yet, and what with the restaurant being closed, he'd had to get rid of the home help. I could empathize with the condition of empty pockets — the reward I'd been promised for tracking down the serial killer in my last case still hadn't made its way into my bank account.

It occurred to me that if I recognized his voice, *he* might well recognize *mine* from our intercom exchange and the message I'd left on his voicemail. I'd need to change it up when I spoke to him. *If* I got to speak to him, because he wasn't making any moves to chat with me, and the golden rule of fishing is to let them approach you. When he glanced my way,

I gave him a smile then glanced down at my phone as though checking messages and sighed loudly. He didn't take the bait. Maybe the real reason he pretended to be his own butler was to keep people like me at bay.

I waited a minute, then checked my phone again, and said, "What the hell!" in a stage whisper.

At that, he met my glance. "Everything okay?"

"Yeah, but I need another drink," I said, using a voice deeper than my usual register and adding a rasp of vocal fry on the last word for good measure. I caught the barman's attention and tapped my glass in a *same-again* gesture. "Can I buy you a round?" I asked Scott.

"Sure." He downed the remains of his drink and moved closer. "Thanks."

"No problem. I hate drinking alone." I gave him my friendliest smile. "My name's Kimberley."

"Scott."

"Well, hi, Scott. It's not, by any chance, your birthday today, is it?" When he shook his head, I slapped the balloons and said, "I bought these for my boyfriend, but it looks like I've been stood up. And I came all the way down from Vermont for the occasion. It was supposed to be a nice romantic surprise, but it seems he has other plans. Man, I sure can pick 'em!"

"His loss, I'm sure," Scott said with that smooth Southern politeness I was learning to expect.

"How come you're alone? A guy like you …"

"I just came in for a quick drink after my round. I wasn't planning on staying long."

"You played golf?" I said, like that was interesting.

"I tried. But I have an injury, which is making it hard for me to get in more than a couple of holes."

"An injury?" I asked, knowing that people *loved* to talk about their aches and pains. But Scott merely nodded. "And who won?"

"The other guy generally wins when you forfeit," Scott said, his expression riding the line between irritation and amusement.

Giggling, I said, "Sorry, I don't know much about golf." I finished my drink and set the glass back on the counter just a little too hard. "I'll bet you usually win, though."

He merely shrugged. Damn, I was having to work for it. This guy was ignoring all my openings.

"Another?" he said with a head tilt at my empty glass. "Or would you prefer something else? A glass of wine, maybe?"

"Same again would be good."

"Same again it is," he told the barman.

"My mother taught me never to mix my drinks. Or my men, either." I allowed myself the slightest of slurs on my *S's* and giggled again. But he didn't join my laughter or my playful mood. And that gave me an opening. "If you don't mind me saying, Scotty, you look kinda sad. Are *you* okay?"

He breathed out a long sigh, took a swallow of his vodka orange, and said, "I'm fine."

"You don't sound fine. Something bringing you down?"

He shook his head, clearly unwilling to talk about it. Time for me to try another tack, one that might work better with someone who was competitive.

"You don't want to talk about it, huh? I get that. I felt the same when I was at my lowest. Grief," I told him. "It's a bastard, you know?"

Scott glanced at me with interest.

"My high school boyfriend, Colby. We were so young and so in love. We were going to spend our whole lives together and wind up sitting on a bench, holding hands, watching our grandchildren play. I could see my future — our future — just rolling out ahead of us." I stretched out an arm into that life that had once lain ahead of me. It had felt as solid as the one I was living. "Then he died. Murdered." Scott's chin tucked back in surprise, and I nodded glumly. "Took my heart and my hope with him." I stared morosely down into my drink and added softly, "It doesn't get worse than that, you know?"

"But it does, though," Scott said. "It really does."

I gave him a questioning look but said nothing, allowing the silence to stretch out to breaking point.

"I lost my family," he finally said.

"What? They died? All of them?"

"They were also murdered. In an armed robbery."

"*Shit!*"

Scott stared down into his glass, then tipped the remains down his throat. A fresh drink arrived a moment after he set the glass down; clearly, the barman knew his customer.

"I'm so sorry," I said, reaching over to give Scott's forearm a consoling squeeze.

And it wasn't an act. I did feel genuinely sorry for him. I even felt bad that I was manipulating him into talking to me, but sometimes, you had to bite the bullet and do what you had to do. And what I had to do right then was to get the sole survivor telling me exactly what went down that night in July. Besides, it wasn't doing him any harm. In fact, it might make him feel better to share it with someone — that, after all, was the basis of psychotherapy.

"How did it happen?" I said. "If you don't mind me asking."

He looked at me for a long moment, perhaps trying to judge whether my interest was rooted in true compassion or voyeuristic nosiness, then said, "Did you hear about the family murder at Broussard's?"

"No. Should I have?"

"Maybe it wasn't a big enough story to make the news up north," he said, a definite bitter edge to his tone. "It was all anyone reported on down here for a while."

"So, tell me." I sucked on my straw, keeping my eyes wide and fixed on him. Everyone loves an audience.

"My mother, father, and sister were killed by a robber at our family restaurant. I was shot, too, but survived."

I allowed my jaw to drop open. "But, like, what *happened?*" He seemed reluctant to open up, so I used another therapist's trick — guessing wrong. "So a guy ran in and robbed all the customers, and then … started shooting?"

"No, we'd closed up for the night and were sitting at a table in the restaurant, having a late celebration dinner."

"What were you celebrating?"

"My birthday."

"This happened on your *birthday?* That's brutal."

"In case you hadn't noticed, the world is not a kind and gentle place." The attempt at humor didn't mask the bleakness in his voice.

"Who did it?"

"A guy called Jeron Cooper. He'd been a dishwasher at the restaurant."

"Wow. Did he just march in?"

"He was there already. Must've been hiding in the restrooms or kitchen or something, and he came out threatening us with a firearm. Told us to cooperate or he'd kill us."

"You must've been so scared!"

"Not at first. I just figured it was a robbery, that he'd take the money and go. He forced us to walk to the kitchen. I think he planned to lock us in the cooler. Well, to lock most of us there and take one of us to the office to open the safe."

"But that's not what happened?"

"No."

When he didn't continue, I said, "So, what did happen?"

"Look, you don't want to hear this. It's awful."

"I *do*." My mind scrambled for a reason — other than the real one — why I would want to hear all the details of his experience. I decided to take a leaf out of Desirae's book. "The thing is, when I was in a really bad way, someone got me talking, got me to tell them every last thing. And I felt better afterward. It helped to get it all out. So I'm just paying it forward."

Scott traced a finger down the condensation on his glass, and a droplet slid like a tear down the side. "Well, when he, Cooper, told the others to get in there, my father charged at him, trying to take him down, I guess, and the gun went off. My mother got shot." Scott's voice was faint on the last few words, like he still struggled to believe it, like the words were impossible to say loudly or clearly. "I just … the world just dropped out from under me. I went over to her to try to save her. But she was already gone."

"Oh, *man!* I can't even imagine how awful that must've been for you."

But Scott didn't seem to be listening. His eyes were fixed on something in the distance, perhaps imagining his mother's face in the moment before she was shot. And the moment after.

"And right then, I realized it was all over. Everything was gone. My life had turned to shit. I mean, she and I were so close." Scott scrubbed a hand over his face. "I was still holding her when I heard him order them — my father and sister — into the cooler. He shouted at me a bit, and then he shot them."

"Fuck," I said because really, what else was there to say? *Sorry?* Sorry is something you say when you step on a stranger's toe or when your friend gets dumped by her boyfriend. There are no adequate words for having your family annihilated in your presence. On your birthday.

Scott gave himself a little shake. "He was panicking. His mask had come off in the scuffle, and he knew we'd recognized him. He just freaked out and started shooting."

"So you don't think he originally planned to kill everyone?" That, at least, would be some small piece of comfort I could give to Jeron's mother and uncle.

"No. No, I don't believe so. He just lost control of the situation. And my father—" Scott placed his palms on the bar counter and pushed back, blowing out an exasperated breath. "He was always such a hothead. Looking back on it now, he would *never* have listened to orders, just cooperated and allowed his money to be taken. He always bailed in without thinking about the consequences. Act first, think later. He was just that kind of guy."

Terry Broussard sounded like a fool to me.

"What happened then?"

Scott gave me a small smile. "Well, I was next, wasn't I?"

– 21 –

"You were next?" I repeated. "What does that mean?"

Scott edged his drink a half-inch forward and backward then left and right, widening the pool of condensation on the counter. Saying nothing.

"Did— Did Cooper shoot you too?" I said like I didn't already know.

Still looking down at his vodka orange, he said, "Cooper put a gun to my head and marched me to the back office. I gave him the day's cash takings, but he wanted me to open the safe. When I refused, he hit me. I don't know why I held back, why I didn't just open it for him immediately. I mean, what did it matter then? What did anything matter?"

I met his glance and nodded.

"But I was so shocked, you know? I could hardly breathe, let alone think."

I could understand that. "If you can't fight or flee, you freeze. Er, that's what they say."

"Yeah, I was kind of frozen. Numb. But the pain of the beating sort of woke me up, and I realized he was going to kill me as well. I'd seen and recognized him too, right? He was going to eliminate me as soon as he had access to the contents of the safe. So as soon as I opened it, I turned around and tackled him."

"Brave!" I said.

"I got a bullet in my leg in the process." He rubbed his thigh as though feeling again the punch of a bullet, the spreading burn, the lingering ache. "But I got the gun away from him and shot him as he was coming at me again." There was no hint of gloating or satisfaction in Scott's voice, just a numb recounting of the facts.

"Wow."

He looked at me as though pleading for absolution. "I didn't mean to kill him, I just meant to stop him from killing me, you know? But it all happened so fast."

"Dude, it sounds like legit self-defense to me."

"Yeah, but still … Taking a life — it's a big thing. It changes you." Again, he stared off into the distance, maybe seeing the self he was before the Fourth of July.

"And then?" I prompted.

"I was bleeding badly, but I had to get back to the kitchen to check on my father and sister."

"You thought maybe they were still alive?"

"I didn't know, not for sure. Cooper had closed the cooler door after he fired his gun."

Rationally speaking, he should have called for help first. But psychologically, the need to check up on his family made complete sense to me.

"I mean, I think I *knew*, in my gut, but I had to make sure they were ..." He swallowed hard. "If there was any chance they could still be saved ..."

"But they couldn't?"

He shook his head.

"I'm so sorry," I said, wishing there were bigger, better words for the magnitude of losses such as these. "And what was happening with you?"

"I knew I was dying. I'd lost a lot of blood by then, I was feeling cold, shaky, like I was going to faint. I couldn't stand. But I had to get to the dining room."

"Why?"

"Before he took us to the kitchen, he'd taken all our phones and piled them on one of the dining tables," Scott said. "So I half crawled, half dragged myself there."

"*Shit*," I said, seeing the scene play out in my mind's eye. "You made it, though?"

"Yeah, I got to my phone, called 911. Then I passed out."

"You're lucky you didn't die."

I'd no sooner said the words than I wanted to take them back, because I realized it was like saying, *You're lucky your family died and you didn't*, and having your whole family murdered isn't lucky. Not at all. Fortunately, Scott seemed to understand what I'd meant.

"The doctors said a quarter inch to the side, and the bullet would've punctured my femoral artery, and I would've bled out within three minutes. Or if the paramedics had arrived fifteen minutes later, I would've bled out anyway, because it did hit a vein."

"Man, I am so freaking sorry. It must be the pits to be the

sole survivor. On the one hand, you must feel relieved, happy to be alive, and all that. But on the other, I mean, not that you did anything to feel bad about, but I can imagine that you still felt guilty."

I'd felt guilty after Colby died. Guilty for the fight we'd had, guilty I hadn't foreseen the unforeseeable and prevented it. Guilty simply because I was still alive and he wasn't.

Scott's gaze snapped to mine. "You *get* it." He gave my hand a hard squeeze and released it. "Like, why me? Why was I the one lucky enough to survive? And unlucky enough to lose everyone I loved?"

He didn't seem to expect an answer, which was a good thing, because I didn't have one. Why did anything happen to anyone? Why had Colby died so young, while others survived wars and car wrecks and cancer, and lived to a hundred and two?

"Sorry," Scott said with a small, sad smile, "I'm killing your buzz."

I waved his concern away, and asked, "What were they like?"

"Who?"

"Your family?"

"Oh. Well, they were ..." He paused as though unsure where or how to begin describing them, and for a long minute, he didn't speak. Then he gave the bar counter a double tap with the tips of his fingers and said, "It hurts to talk about it all. And I really need to go."

He stood, pulling his wallet out of his jeans pocket. As he got out cash to pay, a piece of paper fell, and I automatically caught it.

It was a strip of five small photographs, the kind you get at a photobooth, of a young man and a—

Scott Broussard jams the cowboy hat on his head and polishes the tin sheriff's badge on his chest with his red bandanna. The woman sitting beside him — older, with a pixie cut of gray hair and soft pink lipstick — giggles and flings a white feather boa around her shoulders. Then she perches a wide-brimmed straw hat on her head, turns it around to show the fake flowers and ribbons around its brim, and adjusts the angle to give it a flirty tilt.

Scott leans forward to press a button. "On three, Mom! One … Two …" The flash pops a fluorescent burst of light, and the woman throws back her head, laughing.

"I wasn't ready! I wasn't even smiling!" She presses the sides of her forefingers under her lower lashes to catch the mascara running from her leaking eyes.

Scott is handing her his bandanna when the next flash explodes. They both scream with laughter, and, gasping, Scott yells, "Swap!"

He snatches her boa and straw hat, and thrusts the Stetson at her, but the burst of light comes too soon, illuminating them mid-swap.

"Quick, quick!" she yells.

They both face the camera, smiling. She holds up a finger gun, and he peeps coyly out from under the curved brim of the floppy hat. The light flashes.

"Phew!" The woman swipes the hat off Scott's head and

ruffles his hair. "You're a crazy boy, you know that?"

"I get it from my momma."

She flicks his ear. "You're lucky I love you."

"To the moon and back," he says.

"To infinity and be—"

"Hey, hey!" Scott was shaking my shoulder. "Kimberley!"

I opened my eyes and blinked hard, trying to bring my jet-lagged awareness back to the here and now. "Who's Kimberley?"

His eyes bulged a little in alarm. "Are you okay?"

"Oh! Sorry, yeah, I'm fine."

"What happened there? Your eyes were closed and, like, flickering."

"Sorry, sorry," I said. "I must've forgotten to take my seizure meds this morning with all the excitement."

"Seizures? Should we call a doctor? 911?"

"No! No, I'm really fine."

"You forgot your name!"

"I remember it now — Linda, right?" I said with a huge fake grin and a wink.

He didn't smile, and I noticed that his face was thinner than it had been in the vision with his mother. Pain will do that to you.

"I was worried," he said.

"Thank you, and sorry I gave you a fright, but honestly, I'm fine now. Sometimes I just, you know, go AWOL for a second or two. It's nothing major."

"Wow, okay. If you say so."

He seemed really concerned that I might have a medical

emergency in his presence. Poor guy, he'd witnessed more than his fair share of those and didn't need me scaring him, too.

"Um, can I have my pics back?" he said.

Following his gaze, I saw that I still had the strip of photos grasped in my hands. "Oh! Of course." I tried to smooth out the crinkles I'd crushed into them. "Here. Sorry about that."

"It's just that these are my favorite pictures of her. Of my mother."

"Right, yeah. Of course. It looks like it was a fun moment."

"Last year. At the amusement park over in Baton Rouge."

Tears welled in his eyes, and I felt shame heat my cheeks. I'd tricked my way in here, used false pretenses to get him to spill his traumatic beans, because I'd been following the money trail, and he'd been the easy suspect. But I'd had him all wrong. In my vision, I'd seen the truth of his relationship with his mother, and his emotion had been genuine. Scott Broussard was just a traumatized young man who'd loved his family and was devastated by the loss of them. Orphaned and set adrift, he was trying to hold his life together by clinging to the old places and routines, the old memories.

Jeron and Scott, I mused, were two young men from two entirely different worlds. They'd been born into radically different circumstances and lived on opposite ends of this crazy city, and yet one tragic night had ruined both their lives and destroyed both their families. I felt tears pricking my eyes too. Until now, my quest had been a half-hearted attempt, reluctantly undertaken when my plans for a romantic weekend with Ryan had gone to hell in a handbasket. Heck, I'd been way more interested in New Orleans's food than the intersecting story of these two clans.

In that moment, I resolved to get serious, to double down my investigative efforts and get to the bottom of what exactly had happened at Broussard's on the Fourth of July. I still believed I'd probably only wind up confirming what everyone already knew or guessed, but so be it. I didn't believe in the concept of "closure" — I'd never been able to close out Colby, never even wanted to — but surely, certainty would bring some degree of satisfaction.

"Can I give you a ride somewhere?" Scott asked.

"To the front gate would be great. That's one long-ass drive," I said and followed him outside.

As we exited, I waved at the security guard from the passenger seat of the fanciest car I'd ever caught a ride in. She gave me a big smile, clearly happy to have played Cupid. As soon as we were out of the gates, Scott pulled over. I clambered out of the low bucket seat and just had a moment to thank him before he closed my door and zoomed off. Feeling eyes on me, I looked back toward the country club entrance. The guard was there, hands on her hips, disappointment and puzzlement written large upon her face.

I threw my hands up and called out, "Men! Am I right?"

Poking the air with an indignant finger, she yelled back, "You said it, sister!"

– 22 –

I felt a little down and a lot tired after the afternoon's encounter with Scott — seeing visions always left me tapped out, as did feeling someone else's emotions — so I decided to have a quiet night in at the hotel. Besides, I suspected that exploring the French Quarter's nightlife on my own wouldn't be nearly as much fun as it had been with Ryan.

I bought a bottle of beer on the way home and went directly to the hotel's shady courtyard, where a small bistro table and two chairs sat invitingly beside the fountain. Unwrapping the remains of my muffuletta, I took a bite, pleased to discover it tasted as good as I remembered, and chased it down with a swig of beer. The floral-scented courtyard was peaceful in the fading light of dusk, and the soothing trickle of the fountain's water masked the noise of the wakening streets beyond. A pigeon fluttered down and strutted about, chest puffed out like a self-important mayor as it pecked at the breadcrumbs on the paved ground near my feet. How did birds always know when there was food around? Could they smell it? Were they always watching us?

Rolling my shoulders to ease the tension I always stored there, I reviewed the day's events. Though I'd learned some interesting and surprising things, I'd found nothing to disprove the police's conviction that they had their man and their motive. So far, I had no evidence for a feasible alternate theory. Yes, two men linked to the case stood to benefit financially from the deaths, and neither was keen on the investigation being reopened, but could I honestly see Anthony having a hand in his nephew's death? Or that sad, lonely momma's boy somehow organizing a hit on his family? No. Neither of them were truly likely suspects.

I crumbled the last crust of my bread and scattered it for the pigeon, but soon, he had competition. A crow clattered into the courtyard with raucous caws and graceless wings, scaring off the pigeon and claiming its crumbs. Another of the ragged black birds lighted on the back of the chair opposite. It regarded me with a quizzical eye, tilting its head from side to side as though evaluating my potential as edible material. An image dropped into my mind as though from a memory vending machine: a scene in an old Hitchcock movie where hundreds of silent birds gathered on a playground jungle gym behind a woman seated on a bench, biding their time until they attacked.

I glanced over my shoulder, but no line of crows waited on the courtyard wall. The bird watching me hopped onto the table, pecked at a scrap of lunchmeat on the crumpled wax wrapper in front of me, and swallowed it in two jerky gulps.

"Shoo!" I waved my hands at it and its crony, and they retreated to a spot on the ground a few feet away, putting their heads together. Discussing strategy?

I needed an improved strategy too; I didn't have a handle on this case yet, and I had only one more meeting scheduled. Desirae had set up an appointment with Broussard's business partner at the restaurant on the following day, and I seriously hoped I'd get valuable input from him. But was there anyone else I should speak to or any place else I could visit before then?

The sun sank lower in the sky, stretching the shadow of the fountain's gargoyles across the courtyard so that their jaws seemed to open wide for the conspiring crows. The carved stone faces leered, their clawed limbs contorted in the fading light, and the trickling water now sounded more like sinister whispers than a soothing burble. Damn gargoyles. Who in their right mind had thought *that* would be a fun theme for a hotel? Even the Uber driver, I now realized, hadn't wanted to come too close to the entrance of this place.

When the creepy crows hopped closer to me, I abruptly stood up. Time to head inside.

But my room didn't provide much of a refuge from the heebs and the jeebs. Madame Laveau may have described this place as a "thinning," but to me, it felt more like a thickening. The oppressive atmosphere seemed heavier, and the shadows in the dimmest corner seemed even deeper, like the darkness was gathering itself into something more substantial, more tangible.

It was all pure imagination — I knew that. The creep factor of the Crescent City was getting to me, with its talk of cathedral ghosts and evil gargoyles coming to life. Still, for the first time in my life, I wished I was staying in a nice, generically bland room in a soulless hotel chain instead of in the sort of place which advertised itself as "steeped in local flavor."

In the bathroom, I thought I detected a hint of a different kind of flavor — cola Chapstick. Immediately, my unsettled mind put two and two together and came up with 666. If Colby's spirit was present, then danger must be imminent, since that was the only time I really sensed him these days.

"Colby?" I said out loud.

There was no answer. No *Run, hide, watch out!* Maybe I'd just imagined the scent, because I didn't detect a whiff of it on my way to check that the room's door was locked and the windows closed.

Keeping my eyes averted from the murky corner, I returned to the bathroom, locking the door behind me. Part of the "historical charm" of this place was the ancient plumbing — pipes which juddered and groaned when you turned on the faucet, and a shower with piss-poor water pressure set over the bathtub at just the right height for a hobbit. I let the water run until it was hot, clambered inside, and drew the curtain, immediately imagining that a knife-wielding madman was creeping up on the other side.

"Girl, you've watched too many slasher movies," I told myself and then started singing the first song that came into my head — Taylor Swift's "Shake It Off." If someone *was* about to go psycho on my ass, at least I'd go down jaunty.

I was rinsing conditioner out of my hair when I heard something. A knock at the door, maybe? Stopping my song mid-shake, I listened. Nothing. Forgoing a leg shave — it's not like Ryan was there to prickle anyway — I shut off the water and wrapped myself in the too-small towel. Apart from the slowing drip of water from the shower nozzle, all was silent. I brushed my teeth, mentally directing myself to ignore the feeling that I was being watched, but still, as I wiped the misty mirror with a swipe of my forearm, I half expected to see someone standing behind me.

It was then that I heard the knock again. A confident triple rap — the sort that room service gives when it delivers the goods. Perhaps Ryan, knowing me all too well and loving me anyway, had ordered up a snack for me.

"Coming!" I slipped on the courtesy bathrobe hanging behind the door and went to answer.

First, I peered out of the peephole; I'd listened to enough true-crime podcasts that not even the lure of food could make me open a door to a possible stranger without checking first. But the hallway — what I could see of it anyway — was empty. No food cart with a silver dome, no ice bucket with a bottle of bubbly, no person holding a tray bearing a grilled cheese sandwich speared with a cocktail onion on a toothpick.

"Colby?" I asked the air again.

Getting no reply, I slipped the security chain on, opened the door a crack, and peered out. No one was there.

Knock-knock-knock.

This time, the sound came from behind me, from *inside* the room.

– 23 –

I spun around, scanning the space. Empty. My eyes began to water, and my scalp tightened. But then my gaze rested on the French windows, and I sighed in relief. Of course! One of those damn crows was no doubt perched on the railing outside, its black feathers hidden by the night. It must've pecked at the glass, demanding more food. I marched across the room, intending to fling open the windows and scare it off, but as my hand touched the handle, a strident noise startled a yelp out of me.

My phone was ringing. Snatching it up from the bed, I checked the display. "Hi, Mom."

"Garnet! Thank goodness! Are you all right, dear?"

"Of course I am." Physically, at least, anyway. Mentally? Well, I wasn't so sure about that. "Why wouldn't I be?"

"I'm sorry to say that there are bad omens."

"Been reading the tarot again?" I headed for the bathroom and began brushing my hair. That night, in that gloomy place, I found my mother's dire warnings comforting rather than disconcerting. They were familiar and routine. If there was one thing I could count on, it was that when she read the cards for me, they *always* forecast some kind of disaster. "Do the cards never predict a nice, calm, safe period ahead for me?"

"Well … You do lead rather an eventful life, dear."

Fair enough. "So, what do they say this time? Murder and mayhem? Fire and flood?"

"No, no, none of that. Though I suppose we can't rule out *flood* entirely. But a storm, definitely. A hurricane, no doubt, or possibly a tornado."

Back in the bedroom, I marched back over to the windows and peered outside. Any birds that might have been there were gone now. "There isn't as much as a soft breeze here, Mom."

"But what else could 'a disturbance of air' mean?"

"A fart?"

I tapped a knuckle against the glass of the window; it sounded nothing like the knocks I'd heard earlier, but a beak and a knuckle were two different things.

"Garnet, you never take these warnings seriously enough! The Knight of Swords, too. Cold weather and biting winds."

"Maybe in Vermont. Down here, the weather's still great. Honestly, between the food and the weather, I'm beginning to wonder why anyone lives up north. No wonder Desirae turned snowbird."

As I spoke, I grabbed the hotel ballpoint pen from the bedside table and tapped the metal nib against the window glass. The resulting clicky tick also didn't resemble what I'd heard earlier.

"Who's Desirae?" my mother asked.

I yanked the drapes closed, shutting out the darkness

outside, shutting *in* the darkness inside. "Ryan's ex-wife."

"So *that's* her name! Now, there isn't any trouble between you and Ryan, is there?"

"No!"

"Because perhaps *she's* the interfering female I warned you about. And here's the Tower, too," my mother intoned in a deep, ominous voice. "Breakups, the end of weak relationships …"

"Our relationship is not weak," I said, irked.

"What's she like?"

"Desirae? Depressingly perfect."

"Oh dear." My mother seemed stumped for a moment, then rallied with a reassuring, "I'll bet *she* doesn't have any psychic gifts, though."

"Not a one." She was well endowed in seemingly every other respect, though. Beautiful, elegant, monied, talented. I'd bet she slept between thousand-thread-count Egyptian cotton sheets and wore silk pajamas. Pulling on my own sleepwear — an oversized T-shirt I'd pilfered from Ryan — I clambered under the coverlet.

"There you go, then," my mother said. "What's her star sign?"

"Don't know. Don't care."

"Probably a Virgo. Insufferable," my mother mumbled. Tutting, she added, "But then we're back to the Tower."

"What tower?" I said, still thinking about Desirae, about how I had yet to discover anything that might lead her to believe that Ryan's girlfriend was capable of more than bad food choices.

"*The* Tower. The Tower card."

"Wait, haven't you drawn that for me before?" I had a faint recollection of a lightning-struck turret, with bodies tumbling from its blazing windows.

"Yes. And *it* could mean severe weather too."

"*Could?*" I knew my mother's habit of picking and choosing her interpretations to fit her superstitious beliefs. Cognitive bias, that's what it was called in psychology. "What else *could* it mean?"

"Danger, crisis, destruction, being blindsided by a sudden unforeseen change. Nothing good, I'm afraid, dear."

"Lovely."

"Though some do say the lightning bolt can symbolize a sudden inspiration, a life-altering revelation, a flash of truth, something like that."

"I could use one of those. Let's go with that interpretation."

"I *would*." She stretched the word out into two uncertain syllables.

"But?"

"But I drew the Devil, and that's just the tip of the icing on the cake, because he was in the upright position, too—"

"Better and better," I grumbled.

"*—and* the Seven of Swords."

"More swords?"

"Exactly! And you know what that means."

"I'm happy to say that no, no, I don't."

"What's that?" my mother called to someone on her side. "Your father sends his love and says the potatoes are starting to burn. I'd better go."

"Tell him I say, 'Hi,' and don't worry, Mom. I promise to keep a watchful eye on the weather."

"Yes, please do. And I'll set a crystal grid for you and send a light blessing."

I plumped my pillows, switched off the bedside lamp, closed my eyes, and failed to fall asleep. My tired flesh was willing, but my spirit was restless, and my imagination was still in overdrive. I put the light back on, cursing its piddly wattage — the small pool of light it provided made no impression on the thick darkness in the corner nearest my head. Turning on the TV, I switched to a local channel and was pleased to see a weather report predicting another day of uninterrupted sunshine.

While I was checking the weather app on my phone, Ryan called, and we caught up on each other's day. I told him the room was playing tricks on my imagination; he told me he'd cut his thumb slicing green beans.

"If I was there," I said, "I'd kiss it better."

"Then come home! You can kiss me better all over."

"I've got a job to do."

"Are you sure — like, *totally* sure — that you're okay with this, Garnet? I mean, being alone in a not-so-safe city, staying in a spooky room? The whole helping-out-my-ex-wife thing? It doesn't seem right."

"I'm good. I've got this."

"You don't have to prove anything to me, you know."

"I know." But I wanted to prove something to others, to one other in particular. "Goodnight, Ryan."

"Sleep tight."

Without consciously intending to, I found myself googling the Seven of Swords in tarot. *Feeling powerless* — check. *Sudden loss, a threat to health, natural disaster* — no doubt, this was the interpretation that was fueling my mother's fear of a tropical storm. *Money woes* — heck, I always had *those*. The last group of meanings seemed more relevant to my current situation: *betrayal, stealth, deception, someone getting away with evil deeds.* Possibly right on the money, I conceded, but not specific enough to be of any use.

Much like the whole of tarot, really.

One final note of warning was listed: if the Seven of Swords had been dealt in the "future" position of the spread, whatever that meant, it indicated that I should prepare for upheaval and calamity, because I'd yet to reach rock bottom. Great. Just absolutely wonderful. I ran a search on the Devil card, suspecting that it would bode even worse tidings. I wasn't wrong.

"Well, hell," I muttered when I saw the goatlike satyr whose manic eyes glared back at me from beneath its curved horns.

One of its hands was raised in what might have been a wave, but between the pentagram nestled between its curved horns, its reptilian wings, and the wild profusion of pubic hair, the overall impression was deeply unsettling rather than friendly. Things weren't looking good for the naked male and female humans held captive at its clawed feet, either. Their chains might be loose, but they both had tails, and the man's appeared to be on fire. On the off chance that this particular artistic rendition of the card was especially malevolent, I checked out other versions. In some, the devil had cloven hooves instead of talons, or breasts instead of a man-chest and potbelly, but none of them was any less disturbing.

A quote from a play or a poem bounced around my head.

Something about having stepped so far through blood that turning back would be more tedious than forging on — *Macbeth*, maybe? *Hamlet?* Whoever had said it, that's how I felt now. Like I'd waded so far into a river of stupid superstition that I pretty much had to know the worst. I read up on the meaning of the devil card, then wished there was a backspace button in my brain.

According to Miss Golinda Lightly's Tarot Truths blog, The Devil pointed to some kind of toxic relationship in my life.

"My relationship with Ryan is *not* toxic, lady," I muttered.

But, I read on, that relationship could be with either a person or a substance. Ah, okay. So maybe I had issues with food, and occasionally, I drank too much. Big demonic deal. The card was a warning not to succumb to my bad habits. Realizing that I was nibbling at the rough edge of a fingernail as I read, I made myself fold my arms.

The chained Adam and Eve figures, the blog explained, signified lust, shamelessness, and the reckless pursuit of earthly pleasures. Apparently, sex positivity wasn't a thing in the Middle Ages or whenever these dumb cards were created. While the feckless humans were chained to an ideal, a belief, or a person, the horned fiend himself symbolized temptation with a capital T that rhymed with D for Devil. In short, it seemed like I was due to be tempted into hedonism, addiction, self-gratification, materialism, and prideful wants. Pretty much par for the twenty-first-century course, I reckoned.

Golinda suggested that my time of impending temptation would lead my soul to an "important crossroads on the soul's journey," and I got the sense that she wasn't thinking of a daiquiri joint *en route* to my meeting the next day. Golinda warned that taking the easy path might lead to short-term gratification but long-term disaster, and urged me to resist my temptations so that I could overcome the darkness and move toward the light.

She added that as I walked the thin line between good and evil, I should also either embrace my shadow self or fight it, "depending." Giving Miss Lightly a C-minus for clarity, I switched off my phone and placed it on the bedside table. The too-soft mattress sucked me in and hugged me close, and as I slipped from consciousness, I thought I heard the distant sound of a soft triple knock.

– 24 –

I woke up at the ass-crack of dawn, feeling unrested after a night of uneasy dreams about storms, swirling clouds, and blistered fingers. I drank about a gallon of water, checked the gloomy corner — utterly empty and not even particularly dark in the gray light — and then slipped back into a deliciously deep sleep from which I finally surfaced just after ten. Clearly, I'd already failed at resisting the temptations of sloth and idleness.

During my morning shower, I heard no knocks, smelled no scent of cola, and felt no eyes watching me. The gargoyles in the mirror frame were just ornamental shapes, and those in the fountain, when I peered down into the courtyard below, were as still as stone should always be.

Feeling more like myself, I set out into the streets of New Orleans. They were already teeming with football fans headed to the stadium, which lay southwest of the Quarter. Ducking away from the open arms of a man in navy, his silver-painted face topped with what looked like an overturned ice bucket, I stumbled into a trio in white robes embroidered with gold *fleur de lis*, wearing stiff gold hats of the sort the pope normally wore. They each had a single word written in bold black script on the headdress; from left to right, it read: *Bless You Boys*. Everywhere were scarves, flags, banners, giant whistles, and people screaming threats, cheers, and war cries. Whoever had said sport was a religion had underestimated the situation.

I needed to get away from the hubbub, but my meeting at the restaurant was scheduled for one o'clock, so I still had a couple of hours to kill. Watching a cop separate two men determined to head-butt each other made me recall that, according to Ryan, the Eighth District had the Broussard case. On a whim, I googled the address of the police station, and when I found it was located only a short walk away on Royal Street, I headed in that direction.

Thumbing my way to my list of favorites on my phone, I tapped one of the three numbers stored there.

"Good morning." The deep, sexy timbre of Ryan's voice was reason enough to call.

"Hey," I said by way of greeting. "I need information."

"And how're you doing this morning, Garnet? How was your evening?"

Ryan had a thing for manners and was trying to get me to learn some. If he got any worse, he'd have to relocate to the South.

"Better. I think I was just weirded out by my mother's mumbo-jumbo last night." Even as I spoke, I recalled that some of the odd stuff had happened *before* she called, but I wasn't going to let facts stand in the way of my clear head and good mood. "How are *you* doing?"

"Great. I just had the pancake special at Dillon's."

"Now can I ask my question?" Without waiting for a reply, I said, "What was the name of the cop in charge of the Broussard case?"

He gave me the name, spelling out the surname for me. "Why, are you planning on talking to her?"

"I thought I'd give it a shot."

"She wasn't that helpful, to be honest, and I doubt she'll be in the station on a Sunday, but it won't hurt to try. What else is on your agenda today?"

"I'm meeting with Khurran Bashir, Broussard's business partner."

"Right. Taking Desirae with you?"

"*Desirae*? What for?"

"I thought you might like the company."

"Hmm. I think you *mean* to say, 'I thought Desirae might like to be included.'"

He chuckled. "Yeah, you're right. I think she just feels a bit out of the loop."

So they'd been having more backchannel chats? I *knew* this "we can be friends" business was going to lead to more contact between them.

"I'm sorry she feels that way, but I think it might be better if I went alone."

"Hmm. I think you *mean* to say, 'I wish I could do everything alone.'"

"Smartass," I said. "You just tell Desirae if I discover anything, she'll be the second to know. Better yet, don't you tell her. *I* will."

"Ah, like that?" Ryan said.

"A little," I admitted.

"Noted."

"Anyway, back to the case. I don't know who else I could speak to. I'm beginning to think this might all be what my mother would call a wild goose chase."

Actually, knowing my mother, she'd probably call it a wild duck run.

"Still planning on coming home on Tuesday?" Ryan asked.

"Yup. I'm … I'm missing you." I was better at snark than schmaltz, so I had to squeeze the words out. But although my delivery might've been forced, the sentiment was genuine.

Ryan's heart was more open. "I'm *definitely* missing you, beautiful."

A little glow of pleasure lit up somewhere in the region of my heart at that. It was good to be the person that someone missed, and it felt *really* good to be called beautiful. A bitchy voice inside wanted to know if Ryan used to call Desirae beautiful, if he still thought of her that way, but I told it to shut up.

"Yeah?" I said.

"Yeah. So bad it's even affecting my appetite. I couldn't finish my pancakes *or* my bacon this morning."

"Oh, Chief, don't worry about it," I said in a sweetly sympathetic tone. "It happens to every man sooner or later. The important thing is not to feel ashamed. And not to put pressure on yourself to *finish*. This doesn't make you any less of a man."

He barked a laugh, insulted me fondly, and ended the call.

The Eighth District had to be the prettiest police station in the nation. A black wrought-iron fence with decorative spikes surrounded the massive two-story structure. The entrance — a raised portico supported by eight classical columns — sat just behind a pair of open gates inset with wagon wheel motifs, and more soaring white columns stood sentry all the way around the sandy colored building. I craned my neck to take in the ornamental stone balustrade, running like a tiara around the roof, and was relieved to see that its pedestals were topped with urns rather than medieval monsters.

The inside of the station was no less impressive. Sumptuous chandeliers dangled from high ceilings, gold-painted scrollwork crowned yet more columns, and elaborate cornice moldings garlanded the walls. If I were a cop, I'd want to be stationed there. The local officers were apparently proud of their division, because two vending machines stood along one wall, offering NOPD T-shirts for $25 a pop. I toyed with the idea of getting one that said, "Police line — do not cross," but I'd already spent too much on this trip, so instead, I approached the officer on duty behind a long, polished-wood counter and asked to speak to Detective Carolyn Dupre.

"What's it in connection with?"

"The Broussard multiple murder case. I have something that could help her," I said.

His eyebrows lifted slightly. Reaching for the desk phone, he said, "You're in luck. I think she's in today. What's your name?"

The police officer who emerged a few minutes later from the back of the station was short and slight and looked to be in her forties. Her hair was twisted into braids as severe as her expression, and she wore a long-sleeved blue button-down shirt with a silver police badge above one pocket, her brass name tag above the other, a circular badge on her black tie, metal insignias on each collar point, and embroidered badges on either sleeve. Did all cops wear this much uniform bling, or was it an NOPD thing?

"Ms. McGee?" Detective Dupre said.

"That's me." I stuck out my hand.

She didn't take it immediately. "Are you in any way, shape, or form a reporter?"

"No."

"Are you associated in any way with any media outlet?"

"No."

She nodded and shook my hand with a firm grasp. "You have information for me on the Broussard case?"

"Yeah. Quite possibly."

"Follow me."

She led me past three tall brass poles flying the nation, state, and NOPD banners and into a busy open-plan area and gestured to a visitor's chair on the other side of her own neatly ordered desk.

"Well," she said. "What do you have for me?"

Since I was really here to find out what *she* had for *me,* I needed to swing the conversation around. I was tempted to use Ryan's name but decided not to just in case things didn't go well. As my mother had pointed out the previous night, things often didn't go too well for me.

I gave Detective Dupre a bright smile. "Um, am I right in thinking that you believe Jeron Cooper shot the Broussard family in the course of a robbery gone wrong?"

"That is what happened, yes."

"And you think that he was acting alone?"

"You have evidence that indicates otherwise, ma'am?"

"'Evidence' is such a strong word," I hedged, but she didn't return my smile. I noticed she was wearing a bracelet with a silver charm in the shape of a letter M ending in a swirling curl. I'd spent enough Saturdays working in my mother's esoteric store to know what *that* symbol meant. "You're a Virgo?"

Following my gaze, she shook her wrist so that the bracelet disappeared beneath her cuff then met my gaze again. "What of it?"

I regarded Virgos in the same light as every other star sign, which was to say that people born in that month shared nothing particular in common with each other. Wishing that I'd paid more attention to my mother's horoscopic ramblings, I glanced at her workstation with its tidy stacks of files, minimalist pen holder, almost-empty in-tray, and immaculate desktop planner. Nothing was out of place. The Broussard file was probably shipshape and neatly slotted into its final resting place in the police archives.

"Well, Virgos are fabulous people, aren't they?" I said. "So organized and efficient!"

A smile twitched at the corner of her mouth, and in a marginally less abrupt tone, she said, "You wanted to talk about the murders at Broussard's?"

"Right, yeah, let's get to business. I, um, well, I wondered if you'd collected any physical evidence from the scene of the crime?"

"We always do that."

"And would you permit me to see it?"

First prize would be to see and touch the firearm used that night. Surely, that would trigger a flood of images in my brain. But Detective Dupre was looking more perplexed than enthusiastic.

"Ma'am, I'm failing to see your angle in this. You told me you had information for me."

"I *did* say 'maybe.'"

She frowned at this hairsplitting, but her landline rang just then, and she took the call. I seized the opportunity to look at the files, trying to read upside down. At a glare from her, I cut it out and checked my phone instead. Henry had texted, reminding me to bring him pralines and Roman candy and inquiring how the good people of New Orleans were reacting to my witchy eyes. I was just composing a message that the city had decided to crown me its queen when Dupre began wrapping up her phone call, telling the person on the other side — someone at the coroner's office from the sounds of things — to call her as soon as the results were in. As she gave her cell number, I captured it in my message app. You never know when you might need a direct line to a cop.

Ending the call, Dupre turned her attention back to me. "Why do you want access to physical evidence?"

Here it was, the moment at which conversations so often unraveled. And I still hadn't figured out a way to explain myself so that logically-minded people would hear me out, let alone lend any credence to what I said.

I sighed. "Okay, so the deal is: I'm a psychometrist." I hated that word and objected to its appropriation from the field of psychology by mystics and mediums. But it didn't stop me using it when I hoped it might bamboozle the listener into thinking my skills were more scientific than intuitive.

"That something like a psychologist?" From the way Dupre tucked in her chin, I already knew how the conversation was going to unfold. If she was skeptical of psychologists, then she'd have zero time for anything more mystical.

"No, it's a kind of psychic." She opened her mouth to speak, and I rushed on, "Sometimes, when I touch objects, I get—"

I didn't get a word further. Thirty seconds later, I was being escorted, in an orderly and efficient manner, back past the flags, and Detective Dupre was berating the desk sergeant for not keeping out "kooks and quacks."

To me, Dupre said, "Goodbye, Miss McGee. I wish I could say it was a pleasure meeting you, but the police force doesn't do business with 'psychics.'"

"Not even in New Orleans?"

"Especially not in New Orleans." She spun on her heel and marched off.

The desk sergeant gave me a filthy look, but a man in a natty black-and-yellow three-piece suit approached me with a smile that showed two gold front teeth.

"You a fortune-teller? You got a tip for me for the American Pharoah Stakes?"

"Steer clear of Virgos and devils," I told him and headed for the door.

"Virgos and devils?" he repeated, and as I stepped out into the sunshine, I heard him call after me, "Bitch, that horse ain't even in the race!"

– 25 –

I'd known when I entered the PD that my chances of getting any official cooperation were lower than the necklines on the witch and nurse Halloween costumes displayed in seemingly every other store window, but it had been worth a try. Racking my brains for someone else I could speak to, I headed in the direction of Broussard's and got there over an hour early for my meeting. The restaurant was still dark and locked up, but a SOLD sign was now prominently displayed in the window.

I found a fun-looking bar two doors down where I could wait. It wasn't yet noon, but the city wasn't called the Big Easy for nothing, and already, the cool interior was filling up with tourists in a hurry to hand over their cash for overpriced drinks. I took a seat at the bar counter and scanned the blackboard behind the bar, where a list of cocktails was written. Sazeracs, mint juleps, absinthe frappes — they all sounded exotic.

"What's a cafe brulot diabolique?" I asked the barman, a tall man with wavy black hair and a tanned face.

"Brandy and Curaçao on fire, served over a twist of orange

peel." His accent was thick — French sounding, but with an unidentifiable slant. His words were softly rounded, with hard consonants dropped from the ends. "You wan' one?"

"No." It sounded like a flaming headache on wheels.

"How 'bout a Hurricane?"

I shuddered, and he grinned. "Looking for sometin' lighter, you?"

"Yup."

"How 'bout a Ramos gin fizz — tastes like lemon meringue pie."

"What's in it?" I asked, not sold on the idea of a sweet pie beverage but also wanting to hear more of his sexy accent. New Orleans, man. Come for the mayhem and murder, stay for the food and the accents.

"Lime, lemon, orange blossom, and gin, frothed with heavy cream and egg white."

I winced. "You lost me at the egg. Got anything with a kick?"

"Got an *envie* for hot peppers today, you?"

"If an *ahn-vee* is a craving, then yeah, I got one every day."

"One Creole bloody Mary coming up," he told me. "Double horseradish?"

I gave him a hand signal which said *Bring it on, you don't scare me.*

"Good call," I said when he brought over a tall glass of innocent-looking tomato juice adorned with a stick of celery, and skewers bearing pickled okra, a split green chili, a ruffled rasher of crispy bacon, and a pimento-stuffed green olive. "Wow."

"Just a bit of this and that." The way he said it, it came out *dis* and *dat.*

"And this?" I said when he slid a small plate with an oyster and lemon wedge, and an enormous bottle of Tabasco sauce my way.

"A *lagniappe.*" At my uncomprehending look, he explained, "A lil' something extra."

"Some-ting," I repeated the way he'd said the word. "What's that accent. French? Creole?"

"Cajun," he said proudly. "I'm from Lafayette."

I lifted my glass. "Cheers."

"*Santé.*"

My first sip confirmed the drink was going to be worth every cent of the eye-watering thirteen dollars the blackboard promised it would cost me. I gave a soft mew of pleasure.

"*C'est bon.*" The barman lifted his chin in delighted acknowledgment. "It's the pepper-infused vodka does the trick."

Ignoring the celery, I dipped the bacon in the cocktail and ate it in one bite. The devil, it seemed, was already winning the tug-of-war for my gluttonous, sybaritic soul.

"Cool place you've got here," I said, taking in the copper beer taps, exposed pipes, analog dials, and brass pressure gauges of the bar's steampunk interior. The counter was burnished steel studded with rivets; it looked like the wing of an old plane. "You own it?"

"Own it, work it, love it. Damn near sold my soul at the crossroads to pay for it."

"I believe you. Nothing in this town comes cheap." I nibbled on the sliver of okra, and my eyes widened. "This is so much better pickled than deep fried."

"Most things are." He picked up a dishtowel and began polishing beer mugs.

"Hey, that restaurant a couple of doors down — is that the same Broussard's where those shootings happened back in July?"

"Uh-huh."

"Can you tell me anything about it?"

He hung the beer mug on a hook above the counter. "You a reporter or investigator?"

"Something like that."

He gave me a slow smile. "Like you say, nothing comes cheap in this town, *cher.*" He pronounced it *sha.*

I slipped a twenty onto the counter and then, at the look he gave it, placed another on top. If only there was an actual paying client in the case to cover expenses. As he pocketed the bills, a young girl in denim dungarees ran out from the backroom, handed him a piece of paper with a sketch on it, and demanded his verdict. She was at that awkward age around eleven or twelve when your arms and legs and teeth are all too long, and you want to be both a cool teenager *and* a little kid getting praise from your dad.

Telling her that it was indeed a marvelous artistic effort, he said to me, "This is my daughter, Lisette. It's my weekend."

"Hi, Lisette."

"*Bonjour!*" she sang.

"So, were you working that night when it happened?" I asked the girl's father.

"*Mais* yeah. Fourth of July is one of the busiest nights of the year. Everyone was helping out. Even Lisette was here to save the dishes." At the mention of her name, the girl lifted her eyes from the oyster, where they'd been fixed. "Remember the fireworks, *Boo*?"

"Uh-huh. I saw them and I heard them." Her accent was softer than her father's. "I heard the shooting, too."

"Did you?" I asked.

Before she could answer me, her father said, "You can't know that's what you heard, *Boo*, not with all the fireworks going off that night. We done spoke about this before."

"I *heard* it," she said emphatically. "Bang … Bang. Bang … Bang-bang, bang-bang."

"What made you think they were gunshots?" I asked.

"You going to eat that oyster?" she demanded.

"Lisette!" her father chided.

But I pushed the plate toward her, saying, "It's okay. I can't eat shellfish."

Both of them gaped at me, horrified, then the man patted my hand and whispered, "*C'est une tragédie*."

"What's that?" I said.

"He thinks it's sad," Lisette said. "But I think it's lucky for me."

She dressed the oyster with lemon, black pepper, and a drop of hot sauce, lifted it to her lips, and sucked it up with a loud slurp.

"Well?" I said, when she replaced the empty shell on the plate.

"Fireworks sound like explosions." She opened her hands in twin bursts, splaying her fingers, making percussive *boom* noises. "But gunshots sound" — she frowned, pinching her thumbs and fingers together — "*narrow*. Like *pew-pew-pew!*" She pecked at the air with her pinched fingers.

"But *you* didn't hear shots?" I asked the barman.

"No. I was too busy *pouring* shots to pay attention to anything but declined credit cards and drunken *couyons*."

"A *couyon* is a fool, an idiot," Lisette translated for me.

"First thing I knew about the murders was all the police coming down," her father said.

Lisette imitated the sound of police sirens loudly and accurately enough that a shady-looking character in the corner sat up suddenly and peered worriedly out of the window.

I sipped on my drink for a minute, then asked, "The Broussard family — what were they like?"

"Brittany was pretty," Lisette said. "She dressed real nice. Always wore high *high* heels." She made a clicking sound of heels as she wiggled in her seat. The kid was like a walking, talking sound effects machine.

"We weren't friends or anything'," her father said. "I didn't know them well."

"But …?"

"I hear things, me."

"Such as?"

"Well, that old man Broussard was a real *tête dur!*"

I looked to Lisette for a translation.

"A hard head." With a mischievous grin, she added, "A stubborn asshole."

"Lisette!" Her father flicked the dishcloth at her, but she just giggled.

"What did he do to make people dislike him so much?" I asked.

"He paid minimum wage, was always firing his cooks and servers, cursing them out in front of customers, that kind of thing. We share one or two of the same suppliers, and they say Broussard screwed them on prices, paying late, finding fault with perfectly good produce." He hung up another polished glass. "The other restaurant owners in the Quarter didn't like him much, no. They say he set up fake accounts online to leave bad reviews for them and five-star ones for his place." He gave an exaggerated shrug, palms upturned. "Then again, maybe he just pissed off the gangs, and that's what got him *défunt*. Making an example, like they say."

That would fit with the cop's secondary theory of an organized crime hit.

"Who's *they?*" I said.

Another shrug. "I heard it on the grapevine. Don't know specific names, me."

"And what gangs?"

"Drugs, the mob, the 39ers." *Take your pick,* his tone implied.

"And the wife, Melissa Broussard? What was she like?"

"She wasn't at the restaurant much, but people liked her better than him. Good-looking woman for her age." Screening his mouth from his daughter's gaze, he mouthed, "Great body!"

"And the son and daughter? Brittany and Scott?"

"From what I know, they seemed like good enough kids. Didn't hear nothing bad about them anyways. I don't think Broussard saw eye to eye with his *podna* in the business either."

"That's interesting."

Lisette rolled her eyes like she thought the opposite. She grabbed her drawing and her hand drifted over to my plate, looking set to purloin my olive. I quickly popped it in my mouth and chewed it with relish but offered her the celery. Narrowing her eyes at me, she repeated her *pew-pew* pattern under her breath, fingers pointed at me.

"What sorts of things didn't they agree on, Broussard and his partner?" I asked.

"According to my supplier friend, they didn't agree on so much as the color of the tablecloths."

"Hmm." I downed the rest of my cocktail and sighed in satisfaction.

"You want another drink, you?"

I shook my head, already beginning to feel the kick of the vodka. "So, what do you think went down that night?"

"Everybody knows what went down. The dishwasher came in to rob the place, shot the Broussards so there would be no comebacks, then got put to rest himself."

"Yeah, that makes the most sense, I guess."

"But the Broussards got too much bad fortune for one family. Maybe ..." His eyes slanted sideways as though to check the coast was clear, then he leaned in close and whispered, "Maybe someone put de *gris-gris* on them."

"A curse, black magic," Lisette said.

"Right." I checked my watch. Finally, it was time to visit the scene of the crimes. "I've got to go, but you've both been very helpful. Thank you."

"Anytime ..." the barman paused expectantly then said, "I didn't catch your name, *cher*?"

"Garnet."

He smiled. "*Joli!*"

"Pretty!" Lisette translated.

"I'm CJ," he said.

I slid off my stool. "See you later, CJ."

"*Au revoir,*" Lisette said. "Bye-bye."

"You come by again, yes?" her father added, and I thought I saw a gleam of interest in his eyes.

Then again, it might just have been a glint of appreciation for the fifty-three bucks I'd dropped in his establishment.

– 26 –

The man waiting on the sidewalk outside Broussard's was both shorter and slimmer than me and looked every inch the gentleman. He wore a finely made gray suit, and the edge of a pink silk handkerchief peeped out from his breast pocket.

"Khurran Bashir? I'm Garnet McGee."

The bright black eyes in his unsmiling face assessed me while we shook hands. "Pleased to meet you. Would you like to go inside?"

"Yes, please." I tried to say it casually, but I was excited, no two ways about it.

This was it, the moment I'd been waiting for. Behind the door that Terry's partner was unlocking was the actual place where four people had lost their lives; that *had* to have left an imprint on the place. The answers I wanted might be mere minutes away. It would feel so good to figure this out one way or another and to be able to tell Desirae — and Anthony, of course, primarily him and his sister — what exactly had happened. Perhaps I might even come up with something that poked a hole in Detective Dupre's armor of contempt.

Khurran Bashir held the door open for me, and I stepped into an interior so dim that I could make out only shadows.

"Are there lights?" I said.

"Yes, of course."

He hit a switch, and by the discreet golden glow of wall sconces, I took in the largely empty space. Chairs and tables stacked with teetering towers of white tablecloths and huddles of brass-bottomed lanterns had been shoved against one side of the dining room. The floor was still covered with a fitted carpet of oxblood red, but bare patches on the walls marked the spots where paintings had once hung. The stale air caught in my throat.

I ran my fingers over the surface of one table and tried to imagine what this place would have looked like on a busy night before July Fourth: servers threading their way between tables covered with starched tablecloths and set with gleaming silverware and fresh flowers; crystal chandeliers bathing the diners in an intimate glow of light; and all underscored by a mellow soundtrack of low conversation, soft music, and the clink of glasses. It must've been an elegant haven from the rough and raucous energy of the French Quarter.

I glanced back at Bashir. He still stood just inside the doorway, a frown contracting his features.

"You okay?" I asked him.

His shoulders lifted fractionally in a tight shrug. "Yes, I guess. I just … I haven't been inside since the day after the murders. It's bringing stuff up."

It was bringing stuff up for me too. My breaths were coming

faster, my stomach felt cold and unsettled, and my head was starting to fizz. This was more than nervous excitement about possibly settling a mystery. Four people's lives had been taken here, and every cell in my body seemed attuned to that fact, to their absence.

Or was it to their presence?

I made myself blow out a steadying breath. A hostess would once have stood behind the counter to my left, greeting guests, checking her reservations list, charging credit cards. Now, uneven rows of bud vases gathered dust on its surface, and a dead fly lay slowly desiccating. Two framed photographs hung on the wall behind the counter. The larger picture was of a group of five people holding drinks up in a toast and looking straight at the camera.

"That's Terry on the left," Khurran Bashir said, noticing my interest. "Then Brittany, Scott, Melissa, and me on the right."

Moving closer to study the picture, I was immediately struck by the contrast between the two business partners. Terry Broussard was tall and wide-shouldered, with a hale and hearty physical presence compared to Khurran Bashir's slight build and retiring stance. Broussard's arm was slung around his daughter, and he grinned confidently at the camera, while Bashir wore a somber expression, and his attitude came across as reserved, almost diffident. Broussard's face, his cheeks rosy as medium-rare beef, looked like it belonged on a jolly innkeeper in Provence; Bashir's fine-boned features would have suited an ascetic monk in a monastery on a mountain.

They looked about as alike as oil and water. And according to both Anthony and CJ, they'd blended just about as well.

Terry's wife, Melissa, stood beside Bashir. She was indeed attractive and had a classy, elegant style that reminded me of Desirae. It may have been my imagination, but her smile looked a little strained. Was it relevant that she stood on the other side of her children rather than next to her husband? Psychologists gave children a projective test called the draw-a-family-picture test and drew all kinds of inferences by interpreting the appearance and arrangement of family members. If this was a drawing for me to analyze, I'd wonder if the children had served as a buffer between their parents. Scott, his arms folded confidently and his head tilted slightly toward his mother, stared straight out from the picture, while Brittany wore a cheeky expression and had a hand raised in bunny ears behind her father's head.

In the smaller photograph, which hung just the slightest bit askew, Terry and Brittany stood inside an auto showroom, beside a red Porsche with a giant ribbon draped across its hood. An ecstatic smile split her face, while Terry's mouth was pulled into a smug smirk.

Seeing the direction of my gaze, Bashir said, "That was his birthday gift to Brittany when she turned twenty-five a couple of years ago."

"Was he planning to get Scott one for his twenty-fifth?"

"Possibly. Terry and I did not discuss family matters with each other."

I tapped the picture. "He looks mighty pleased with himself."

Bashir expelled a little sound of disgust but said nothing.

"What were they like, the Broussard family?" I said.

Bashir cleared his throat. "Forgive me, Miss McGee—"

"Please, call me Garnet."

"I am not sure of your role here. I agreed to meet with you, but I am still not clear on the reason why."

"They've asked me to investigate what happened here. I guess Anthony is struggling to come to terms with what his nephew did. He asked me to see if I can find out more, something that will help him understand and reach some kind of acceptance."

"And what makes you believe you can find out more than the NOPD did?"

"I, uh" — I took a moment to adjust the angle of the photograph on the wall — "I use a different set of skills."

"I see. And what might those be?"

Here we go again. I had never yet come up with a succinct and sane-sounding explanation.

"I have psychic abilities," I said baldly.

"I see," he said, though I doubted he did, and his serious expression turned anxious.

Immediately, the needle on my suspectometer flicked to the red zone. What was he nervous about? What didn't he want me to find out?

"So, what *were* the Broussards like?" I asked again.

He blew a breath of air out along the counter, sending dust motes dancing in the air. Buying time.

"They were good people who did not deserve to be murdered in cold blood," he said eventually.

"Uh-huh." I glanced at the photo again. "Something tells me Scott was closer to his mother, but Brittany was a daddy's girl?"

Bashir's stance relaxed slightly. "Oh yes, she was his precious princess. In his eyes, she could do no wrong."

"And in other people's view?"

"She could be a piece of work." Registering my expression, he added, "Oh, not in any *bad* way. Not really. She was just … ridiculously spoiled and knew how to wind her father around her little finger. She was the elder of the two children. She knew she was in line to take over this place one day, and she was already beginning to throw her weight around."

"How did that go down with Scott?"

"He didn't say anything to me about it, but I think it must have hurt him. He worked hard, but Brittany had her father's number — flattery and fawning, those were the keys to Terry's heart."

"You sound bitter."

Bashir ran a hand over his face, ironing out his frown. "Let me not speak ill of the dead."

"How about Melissa Broussard? What kind of a person was she?"

And in that moment — whether I'd read it in the faintest softening of his expression or intuited it with my gift — I *knew*.

– 27 –

"You and Melissa!" I said to Khurran Bashir

His face tightened. "Me and Melissa what?"

"You had a relationship."

"What? No! What are you accusing me of?"

"You did, though, didn't you?"

He flushed and dropped his gaze.

"How long?" I asked.

Several seconds passed before he sighed and said, "Years."

In that single word, I heard the weight of devotion and longing. This, then, explained Anthony Cooper's description of his highly emotional reaction to the news of the Broussard deaths.

"You really loved her." I said the words gently, inviting him to open up to me.

He stared at the ceiling for several seconds before meeting my gaze. Fighting tears? "With all my heart. And she loved me, I know she did."

"But she didn't leave him. Are you married? No? Well then, what was stopping her from divorcing him?"

He looked away, out the window, longing, no doubt, to be away from here. Away from the memories and my probing questions.

"At first, she stayed for the sake of the children, then for the sake of the business. She once said that on principle, she would not leave him while he was struggling financially."

"Stand by your man and all that?"

He smiled wryly. "Not at all, Miss McGee."

For whatever reason, it seemed he preferred not to use my first name, and he hadn't, I noted, asked me to use his. Maybe Khurran Bashir was just an old-fashioned kind of guy. Lucky for me, because his good manners were probably the sole reason he was talking to me.

"She'd supported him when they were just starting out," he continued. "Worked to pay for him to go to business school and struggled alongside him through the hard days of building up the restaurant. She told me she would divorce him only when the business picked up again or he sold it. Or if he had a heart attack and left her with the insurance payout."

My eyebrows rose at that.

"She was only joking," Bashir said quickly. "You mustn't think her cold or mercenary. No, no. She was a lovely person, lovely! It was just her little joke. I mean, if we don't laugh …" He lifted his hands as though to signify the only other response to life's vagaries was despair. "But I think she was coming close to leaving him. She wanted out; she'd had enough."

"Enough of what?"

"Her marriage. Her life with Terry was hell, you see."

"In what way?"

"He did what and when and who he wanted."

"He had affairs?"

"Nothing so serious. Just a carousel of one-night stands and short-lived liaisons. If it wore a skirt, he chased it. Wanted to possess it. He was greedy that way. It got so as Melissa would no longer hire female staff."

"It must've broken her heart."

"Initially. But we can get used to anything, I think."

I wondered what he'd gotten used to — playing second fiddle to the bigger, bolder Broussard whom he neither liked nor respected; being a partner in a business that, according to Anthony Cooper, was just limping along; spending years waiting to be with the woman he loved. In my book, that amounted to a whole lot of motive to be rid of Terry Broussard. With his partner dead, Bashir would've been free to love and live how *he* wanted for a change. Only problem was that Melissa was now also dead. All that wasted love.

Then again, I had only Bashir's word for it that he'd loved her.

"Did you have life insurance on Terry Broussard?"

"Of course," he said and added, "And he had insurance on me, too, in case you are getting any ideas. It was a mandatory clause in our business contract."

"So how much do you get now?"

"Not enough!" His face contorted with anger. "Not enough to compensate me for my loss. All the money in the world couldn't make up for that." He fixed his gaze on Melissa in the photograph, and tears welled in his eyes. "Excuse me, please."

He strode off, presumably in the direction of the restrooms, to regain his composure. I had the sense that emotional control was important to Khurran Bashir. Taking advantage of his temporary absence, I hurried to the back of the restaurant, pushed open the double swing doors, and stepped into the kitchen. The beat of my heart kicked up a notch. My breathing shallowed. Ahead of me lay a long plating-up area, with stainless steel counters and a series of gas grills behind. In the back left-hand corner were several sinks and a door, which presumably opened onto a back alley.

As I closed my eyes, a fluttering like panicked crows' wings churned up a succession of random impressions — a chef laying lobsters on the grill; a wad of cash changing hands; the smell of garlic and onions, a phone falling into a bucket of soaking dishtowels; the clatter of plates and saucepans; a gun, yelled orders, frightened screams.

I needed to do this quickly, before Bashir returned. When I had visions, my eyes rolled and my eyelids fluttered. I sometimes moaned or fell. It tended to freak people out, and I didn't want to freak Bashir out; there were still lots of questions I needed him to answer.

I tuned in to the frequency of the screams in my mind and followed it. It was like that old game where you hide something and then give the searcher clues — "colder, warmer, hotter, red hot!" The sounds echoing inside of me amplified as I walked to the far right of the kitchen and drew near to a stainless-steel door with a handle. It resembled a giant safe with heavy-duty hinges and a bolt on the outside. I rubbed my hands together. Then, hesitantly, I reached out and laid my right palm against the dented, scratched surface of the cooler.

The vision came in like a freight train.

Overlapping voices shout.

How dare you?

Don't touch me, you filthy pig!

Shut up!

No, no, no!

I mean it, I'll kill you!

Stay calm!

Four people stand in a tight group, each face etched with an emotion. Fear, shock, disgust, anger.

A fifth person, wearing jeans, a dark jacket, and a black ski mask, points a gun at them, herds them toward the cooler. "You three, get inside. And you," he says to the younger man in the blue button-down shirt, "open it, then shut it after them. You and me are going to the office."

"You'll never get away with this," the older man yells, his face mottled red with rage.

"Terry, just stay calm," the older woman begs him. "Just do as he says, for the love of God. And we'll all get out of this safely."

The young man opens the cooler door, stepping aside with the swinging door.

"You three, get in there," the gunman says. "Don't try anything stupid."

The beefy man takes a step toward the cooler, then spins, hurling himself at the gunman, tackling him around the waist. The arm with the gun moves up. A deafening report reverberates in the tight space. The older woman crumples to the ground. Scarlet blooms from the hole in her forehead.

The young man collapses beside the lifeless body. "Mom! My God, Mom!" His screams are raw with shock and pain.

The young woman stares down in frozen, open-mouthed shock.

The older man grunts under a barrage of blows and falls back, lip bleeding, releasing the gunman.

"Get in there, you dumb fuck!" The man in the mask trains the gun on the older man. His hand is unsteady, and the weapon wavers.

"You've killed her!" the young man cries. "Why did you kill her? Mom!"

The gunman waves the weapon between the older man and the younger woman. "Get inside!" he screams, spit flying. "Now, or I'll kill your son too!"

The young woman lifts her gaze from the crumpled form on the floor and stumbles into the cooler. The older man shuffles backward, his gaze fixed on the weapon.

"Get up!" the gunman yells, but the man kneeling on the ground just rocks to and fro, cradling his mother's limp body against himself.

"It's all over now," he keens, kissing her face. He's trembling. Waves of shivers ripple through his body.

The man with the gun turns toward the cooler.

"Miss McGee?" Bashir's voice, calling from back in the

restaurant's dining room, jolted me out of the vision.

I rubbed a hand over my chest, where Scott's gut-wrenching agony still flooded through me. I was running out of time to see more here unobserved by Bashir. Opening the cooler door, I stepped inside. Empty shelves ran the length of the space, but my eyes were riveted on the far end. That was where Broussard and Brittany had died, I could *feel* it. The skin on my scalp tightened, and I sucked quick breaths around the tight constriction in my chest. This was going to be bad. Wanting — and not wanting — to see more, I crouched down onto my haunches and braced myself for an onslaught of images and emotions. I closed my eyes and reached with the fingers of my mind into the present past.

Father and daughter are huddled against mesh sacks of potatoes and onions stacked against the back wall. She sobs loudly in his arms. He mutters reassurances through gritted teeth. They both look up as the man steps through the open cooler door.
Her eyes widen. He opens his mouth to speak.
A double shot punches red holes into his chest. Two more quick shots hit Brittany in the face, one through an eye, the other smashing into the cheek below.

The force of the impacts knocked me sprawling backward. My elbow hit the shelf behind me, zinging pain up my arm and driving any lingering visions from my mind.

"Miss McGee?" an astonished voice said.

– 28 –

Bashir stood silhouetted against the open cooler door, staring down at me. "What on earth are you doing?"

"I, uh …" I rolled onto my knees and, spying something on the floor under the shelf, reached for it. "Look what I found."

"What is it?"

I stood up and opened my hand for him to see. A small, clear button lay in my palm. At once, images of the Button Man — his house, his face, his needlework, his agonized sobs — flashed into my mind. But these weren't visions, merely flashbacks. Memories of another place and a different killer.

"Is it a clue?" Bashir asked.

"Could well be."

Probably wasn't, though. Surely, the cops would've searched every inch of this cooler. What were the odds I'd find something they hadn't? Hearing that thought, I had to suppress a laugh. Discovering something they hadn't — that was precisely the reason I was there. I tried to read the button, got no impressions, and shoved it into my pocket.

"Sometimes a cigar is just a cigar," I murmured.

"I beg your pardon?"

"Freud," I said. "Sometimes things are just what they appear to be, nothing more."

"Well, you'd better come out. We don't want you getting trapped in there."

I craned my head to examine the back of the cooler door. "No way to open it from the inside? That seems like a serious design flaw."

"It's a very old model," Bashir said, shutting the door once I was back in the kitchen. "We begged Terry to update it, but he didn't listen. He was never one to invest in practical upgrades; he preferred to spend money on the flashier stuff that diners would see."

"Who's we?" At his blank look, I added, "You said, 'We begged Terry to update it.'"

"Oh. Melissa and me. Scott too. We were always trying to upgrade equipment and limit Terry's excesses."

"Such as?"

"New carpets, fresh flowers every second day, those chandeliers out front, which cost thousands of dollars each."

"What was the share split in the business?"

"He had fifty-one percent, and I had the rest."

"So what *he* wanted was ultimately what happened?"

Bashir nodded. "I was more of a silent partner."

I trailed my fingers over the plating counter, receiving only a distant impression of bustle and business.

"The two of you didn't have the same vision for this place?"

"Terry wanted to continue the family tradition of a fine

dining establishment. I thought the market had changed and that the heart of the French Quarter wasn't the best location for the type of eatery he wanted," he said, speaking slowly as though choosing his words carefully.

"The restaurant wasn't doing well?"

That sparked something like a smile from him. "You could say that." I waited, and he added, "I thought it would be a good idea to sell. So did Melissa and Scott. We'd had good offers from big franchises who wanted to open in this spot."

"But Terry wasn't interested?"

"His philosophy appeared to be that when you're in the bottom of a hole, you should keep digging. He doubled down on what he'd always done. Spending more money, incurring more debt, buying the best food and linens, hiring an inferior and interfering interior decorator to spend even more on unnecessary embellishments, and turn his head from what he should've been focused on. What Melissa and Scott and I knew needed doing."

"And Brittany?"

"She went along with whatever he wanted."

A family split into factions. Terry had wanted to give his customers the best dining experience, but he'd screwed his suppliers, bullied his staff, and divided his family. He could have authored a book: *How to Win Enemies and Alienate People*.

Ultimately, though, it was Bashir who'd gotten his way.

"You've sold now, though? I saw the sign in the window."

"It was auctioned off last week."

"For how much?"

He gave me a hard look. "I may have wanted to sell the

restaurant, I may have wanted out of the partnership, but I never wanted it this way. Do you understand?"

The look he gave me was so fierce, I nodded like a chastened schoolgirl.

"Now, was there anything else you wanted to see, Miss McGee?"

"I'd like to see the place where Jeron died."

Not looking enthusiastic about it, Bashir led the way to the back office. I stepped into the small space with trepidation, but it was just an empty room with bare shelves and no furniture, not even a carpet beneath my feet. The walls were bare except for a door to a safe.

"This is where Scott did most of his work," Bashir said from where he stood outside the room. "Terry liked being front of house and talking to the customers, managing the staff. Scott was in the back room, you know, doing the bookwork, planning the orders, counting the night's takings."

A line from the old "Sing a Song of Sixpence" nursery rhyme came to mind: "The king was in his counting house, counting all the money." Only here, it hadn't been the king, it had been the prince, who — if I remembered right — wasn't even mentioned in the ditty.

"Was this where Scott was on the night when Jeron Cooper appeared?" I asked, wanting to hear Bashir's version.

"No, he was out front, eating a late supper with his family. They were all together."

"Where were you?"

"At home. Watching television. Alone."

I turned on the spot, taking in the room. "Can you tell me exactly what happened here that night?"

"I can do better than that. I can show you." He pointed to a small security camera mounted in one corner of the room.

"There's video? Wow! Okay. Can I see that?"

"Yes, I have a copy on my phone. But let's do it outside. This room gives me …" His voice trailed off. "This way."

I followed him back through the dining room and out into an adjacent courtyard, where iron tables and chairs were stacked against a wall frosted with white bougainvillea. Weeds pushed through the paving stones, and a water feature in one corner sat dry and silent.

"This was our outside seating area," Bashir said.

I forced myself to comment on its beauty before I asked him again about the video and whether there'd been any other cameras in the restaurant.

"The camera in the office was the only one."

Another of Terry's false economies? Or merely a savvy businessman knowing it made sense to trust nobody when it came to money?

Bashir pulled out his phone and tapped the screen. "Here."

I took it from him and hit play. The camera angle was stationary and focused on a desk, a small segment of carpet, which I realized must since have been ripped up, and the wall with the safe. In the grainy footage, the safe was covered with a framed certificate of some sort. A date and running time stamp in the corner of the picture confirmed the footage was from July fifth, at twenty-three minutes past midnight.

In the courtyard, bamboo windchimes tinkled, though I felt no breeze on my face. On the small phone screen, Scott entered the camera frame. Jeron came in right behind him, gun trained on the back of Scott's head, and gestured for him to sit in the chair behind the desk. Jeron's face was twisted with anger and something else. Panic? And although the video had no sound, I could tell he was shouting.

Bashir glanced over at the screen. "According to Scott, Cooper was demanding the day's takings at that point."

I watched Scott open a desk drawer and pull out a slim banking bag. Jeron was clearly dissatisfied with the amount of cash it contained — most diners would've paid by credit card, I guessed — and yelled some more at Scott. According to Bashir's ongoing commentary, he was demanding that Scott show him where the safe was and open it for him.

Scott shook his head adamantly and was rewarded with a punch to his jaw, which sent him spinning in the swivel chair. Jeron threatened him again. And again, Scott shook his head. Jeron slammed the pistol against Scott's temple, then he pointed the gun at his knees, his chest, his head. I didn't need Bashir's explanation to know what he must've been threatening at that moment.

Scott lifted his hands in surrender and nodded. Jeron waved the gun, and Scott obeyed — standing up, lifting the certificate off the wall, and setting it on the floor. Then he turned the dial left and right, and as the door of the safe opened, he stepped back, spun around, and drove his shoulder into Jeron's midsection. Both men disappeared from the camera's limited field of vision.

"There's nothing more to see on the tape," Bashir said. "Scott got shot, then he got control of the gun and shot Cooper, who died in the hallway. There was blood" — he indicated the floor at the threshold of the room — "all over."

I checked the video. According to the time stamp, less than ten minutes had passed since Scott and Jeron had entered the picture. Crazy to think how lives could change — could *end* — in mere moments.

"What happened then?" I asked Bashir.

"Scott called 911. He nearly died before help arrived."

"When did *you* find out?"

"At five o'clock the next morning, when the police called me. Look, Miss McGee, I have another appointment. Can we conclude this meeting now?"

"Sure, I guess. Unless— Is there anyone else I could speak to, to get a fuller picture of the family?"

Bashir huffed an irritated breath. "You could try Melissa's sister. Though I doubt she'll talk to you."

I got the number from him, and we walked back through the restaurant. My gaze drifted back to the family photo on the wall behind the counter. How strange that it had been left there.

"Don't you or maybe Scott want to take that pic?" I asked.

"It doesn't come off the wall."

I stepped behind the counter and took hold of the framed photograph. It came off without a problem. "Here you go."

Almost reluctantly, Bashir took it from me.

We said our goodbyes outside the restaurant, and I watched him walk away, feeling dissatisfied, turning the button over and over in my pocket. I'd wanted to find out more. *Expected to.* Yet now I wasn't sure if I'd learned anything relevant.

On a whim, I followed him. If I *was* Jessica Jones and on

his tail, he'd immediately go make contact with his co-conspirator. It wasn't easy to stay unnoticed, though. The Superdome had inhaled all the football fans, and many of the usual vendors had trailed after, leaving the usually crowded streets emptier than I had yet seen them.

At the first corner, Bashir glanced over his shoulder and spotted me. I shoved my hands in my pockets and pretended an interest in the nearest store window. It was a sex store, and the display — some of it Halloween themed — completely distracted me. You could do that with a pumpkin? I was still staring, half fascinated, half grossed out, when a finger tapped imperiously on my shoulder.

"Are you following me?" Bashir demanded.

"No! I, er …" I pulled the button out of my pocket and held it out to him. "I just wondered if you would take another look at this button?"

He gave it a dismissive glance. "This is harassment. Kindly leave me alone."

Clearly, even *his* politeness had its limits. He stalked off down the sidewalk, and a man with a sweaty, eager face emerged from the store, his arms full of paper bags. As he passed by, he jostled me, and the button flew out of my fingers. I fumbled and made a grab for it as it hit the sidewalk and snagged it just before it could disappear between the rusted grates of a street drain.

– 29 –

Stepping into a quiet side street, I dialed the number Bashir had given me.

"Good afternoon," an older male voice said.

"Hi, can I speak to Sarah Lannister, please?"

"Whom shall I say is calling?"

"My name's Garnet McGee. I'm a private investigator looking into the Broussard murders, and I wondered if I could speak to Sarah to get a better perspective of her sister, and the whole Broussard family, really."

"I'll ask," he said, sounding doubtful. "Sarah, Sarah! There's a woman on the phone who wants to speak with you about Melissa and the murders."

"No comment, Dad," a woman's voice called impatiently in the background.

"She sounds very nice."

"No. I've told you a hundred times, I won't speak to reporters. Please try to remember."

"She says she's a private investigator."

"*No. Comment!*"

The man came back on the line. "I'm very sorry — Miss McGee, was it? But my daughter won't speak to reporters or private investigators."

"I'm also a psychic," I said, because what the heck.

"Is that right?" The old guy sounded interested. "I'm sorry to say that I don't believe that will make a chat with you any more appealing to her."

"Right. Okay, well, thanks anyway."

"One moment, young lady. You *are* young?"

"Yes," I said.

"Are you pretty?"

"Are you flirting with me, sir?"

"I'm an ancient, decrepit man with a very boring life. My wife died twenty years ago, and it's been dull as dishwater since then. Don't deny me my tiny pleasures," he said with a chuckle.

I gave him a pass on what might, from a younger man, have sounded creepy. Because this gent sounded like he came from a way earlier generation, when it was considered acceptable — charming even — to flatter young women.

"All righty," I said. "Just yesterday, I was reliably informed by an officer of the law that I am beautiful."

"Then you come on over, and *I'll* speak to you. I'm Walter Reed. Like the hospital."

I took an Uber to the address he gave me and, as directed, walked around the side of the house. I found him sitting in a wheelchair under the spreading boughs of an enormous tree.

"Walter Reed," he said. "Forgive me if I don't stand."

"Garnet McGee." I shook his hand. "Thank you for meeting me, and in such a lovely spot."

"Magnificent, isn't it," he said, gesturing to the canopy of glossy green leaves above us. "Southern magnolia. Fifty-five years old. You should see it in May or June when it's in full bloom." He indicated the lawn chair nearby. "Do sit down."

Walter Reed had reached that advanced age where it's difficult to estimate exact years, but if he wasn't yet in his nineties, he was getting there. His face was a map of deep lines and blue veins beneath thin, liver-spotted skin. He wore a gray suit, with a patterned silk scarf knotted around his neck, and his leather shoes were polished to a fine shine. A Panama hat was perched at a jaunty angle on his head, and a pencil mustache graced his upper lip. He looked like an old silent-movie star. Thankfully, however, he turned out to be anything but silent.

"I wish I could say I chose this spot deliberately for its beauty, but the truth is, my daughter won't allow you in the house. She was pestered by reporters after the tragedy, and it's given her a deep antipathy of talking to outsiders."

"I totally understand, but I'm not a reporter."

"Yes, but you are a nosey Nellie." He held up a hand to forestall my defense. "Don't deny it. No need to anyway; I *like* nosey people. It would be fair to say that I'm one myself. I was curious to see *you*, for example."

"You were?"

"Indeed. My life is very boring. I wasn't going to turn down the opportunity to while away the afternoon with a lady who talks to ghosts."

"I don't really talk to ghosts," I said. Well, only one of them. "Mediums do that. It's more that I just get messages."

"Is the correct term 'psychic,' then? Or do you prefer

clairvoyant? From the French *clair*, meaning clear, and *voyant*, seeing, I suppose. I think the distinctions between these categories have not been precisely defined, yes?"

"In that, sir, you are one hundred percent correct."

"Whatever you call yourself, I welcome the opportunity to chat with you!" He barked a phlegmy cough then offered me a glass of sweet tea from the pitcher on the little table beside him.

"Thanks. I'll get it." I poured myself a glass and took a sip. It was good — very cold, not too sweet, definitely homemade. I sat back down and began, "First of all, my condolences on the loss of your daughter and granddaughter and son-in-law."

Walter's eyes grew moist. "Thank you. I miss the girls. I try not to dwell on it, but I miss them terribly."

His words hung in the air for a minute until a light breeze carried them away. I glanced up as the leaves above us rustled.

"It's a Southern magnolia," Reed said. "Fifty-five years old. You should come back in summer to see the blooms. Magnificent!"

"So I've been told," I said, smiling gently. "I wondered what you could tell me about Melissa and Terry and their children."

"Well, now. Melissa was a good girl, the sensible, responsible older sister. And she was always a very loving child." He paused, swallowed hard, then continued, "Smart, too. She had a good head on her shoulders, all right. Took after her mother in that way. The only truly bad decision she ever made was marrying that scoundrel."

Another person who wasn't a fan of Terry Broussard? This was getting to be a recurring theme.

"Her husband?" I said.

"Yes, *him*. Oh, he was handsome when he was young and

charming enough when he wanted to be. Swept her off her feet. These whirlwind romances, they seldom last. I warned her that I didn't think he was a steady character, but young ladies are rendered insensible by infatuation. Ah," he added with a twinkle at me, "present company excluded, I'm sure."

I smiled to show I'd taken no offense. I had once been rendered insensible by infatuation, and it *hadn't* lasted, though that had been due to murder and not any deficits in Colby's character. Not for the first time, I wondered if we would have lasted, if we would have been one of those rare childhood sweetheart stories that defies the odds. I liked to believe so.

"You turned out to be right about Terry?" I prompted.

"Indeed I did! He had a succession of failed businesses, you know, before the restaurant. And *that* only succeeded because Melissa took a real hand in it. And the boy. He's another sensible one."

"Scott?"

"Uh-huh. A no-nonsense sort of fellow. Does what needs to be done and doesn't have his head turned by fantasies and passions."

"And Brittany? What was she like?"

"She took after her father," he said in a tone laced with regret. "She got too emotional and did things she regretted later. Always chasing after the latest fashion and fad, spending on fripperies. Like her father, she liked the finer things in life."

"Even when they couldn't really afford them?" I asked, but Reed seemed not to be listening. He was staring up into the depths of the tree above us, possibly getting ready to tell me its species and age again.

"I'll tell you a little story about them."

"About Brittany and Terry?"

"About the family."

"Okay." I sipped on my tea while he spoke.

"We once went on a vacation to some resort on the Outer Banks of North Carolina. Supposed to be some of the best fishing in the world there. Terry hired this fancy yacht that came with its own skipper and all the best tackle, and the whole family went out at first light to go fishing on the ocean. Now, I've fished a time or three in my day, and one thing I know is this: y'all have got to have the right *temperament* to fish."

"A patient one?" I guessed.

My own father loved to go fishing and regularly tried to get me to join him. But sitting around all day, watching a line in water and being alone with my thoughts, wasn't my idea of fun. I got restless within twenty minutes, irritable within forty, and by the one-hour mark, I was bored out of my mind.

Reed nodded. "And see, Terry wasn't the patient type." He gave another bark of laughter. "Come to think of it, no one on the boat that day was the patient sort except maybe the skipper."

"What happened?"

"Terry fished on this side of the boat then that. With bait and flies and all manner of cursing. Scott did his best to land one, too, mostly to try to win his father's approval, I think."

"How old was he then?"

Reed rubbed his chin and narrowed his eyes, clearly scanning the inner banks of his memory. "I reckon he must've been about twelve or thirteen years old. Brittany would've been around fifteen or sixteen."

"Did she also fish?"

"Not her," he said with a chuckle. "She wasn't one to get her hands dirty or smelly. No, as I remember, she spent the day suntanning and swimming off the boat and occasionally making her father something to drink. For hours, we caught nothing! And then, *finally*, in the heat of that endless afternoon, there was a big tug at the end of Terry's line."

– 30 –

"We gathered around Terry, watching him try to land that fish," Walter Reed said. "And he put up a good fight, I'll give him that."

"Terry? Or the fish?"

"Both of them," he conceded after a moment's consideration. "And at long last, Terry hauled his catch onto that deck. Fat Albert!" he added with disgust.

"Excuse me?"

"A Fat Albert, that's the name of the fish. Well, I suppose the common name is a false albacore, and the taxonomical name is a *Euthynnus alletteratus*. A good species for game fishing but not something you'd ever want to eat."

"No?"

"No! Mushy as cat food, oily as a mechanic's rag, and a potent fishy smell. They say the best way to cook them is to grill them on a plank with fine herbs and a touch of salt, then throw away the fish and eat the wood!" Reed slapped his thigh with a pale, thin hand and laughed, clearly enjoying his story of that long-ago day. "Terry was celebrating, thinking he'd caught himself a good-sized tuna, but I told him it was a Fat Albert. And, my dear, that was the *polite* way of saying FA, because if you've landed one of those, what you have is worth—" Reed cut himself off, clearly not wanting to use bad language in front of me.

Was ever polite restraint more misplaced?

"Fanny Adams?" I suggested.

He gave me a big wink. "I knew you'd be fun! More tea?"

"Thank you." I refilled my glass.

"Where was I, my dear? These days, I seem to lose the thread ..."

"You were telling me how Terry thought he'd caught a tuna?"

"He insisted it was so! Argued with me, kept saying it was a true tuna, a bonito no less." Reed shook his head at this foolishness. "I said, 'Now, Terry, a Fat Albert is not a tuna, it's more like a big old mackerel. A stinky one.' But he wouldn't hear sense. He wanted a picture of himself holding it. Said he'd frame it and hang it on the wall of his eatery. And I could understand that — it was a decent-sized fish, must've been about ten or twelve pounds — but the problem was, we didn't have a camera on board. Everyone had left their bags and cell phones behind at the rental place's office for safekeeping. So Terry wanted to go back to the marina with that damned fish, which was flip-flopping around on the deck all the time we were having our little dispute. I pointed out that we'd have to kill it to take it back — couldn't let the poor thing suffer — and that'd be an utter waste, because we'd just have to toss it after the damn photo. Because it was a *Fat Albert!*"

I nodded vigorously to show I, at least, didn't contest his classification.

"We all knew it. Even the skipper said it wasn't a tuna. But

Terry simply wouldn't listen to reason. Now, I don't hold with killing animals for sport." Reed gave me a hard stare.

"I agree. You kill it, you'd better be prepared to eat it."

"And I told Terry as much. But he just wanted that dashed photograph to brag with. *Vanity!*"

"How did the others react?"

"Brittany would usually go along with whatever her father wanted, but she was distressed by that fish thrashing around, still on the hook. She got half hysterical, said we should just cut the line and toss the fish back in the ocean."

"With the hook still in its mouth?"

"I see that you and I, young lady" — Reed pointed a finger between the two of us — "are of one mind when it comes to the humane treatment of animals. But my granddaughter prized her own comfort above another creature's pain or even life. She just wanted it gone, out of sight and mind, as quickly as possible. Brittany," he said with a sigh, "wasn't cruel so much as *selfish.*"

"What was Scott?"

Walter considered for a moment. "Pragmatic. Good in an emergency. Brittany was still screeching, and Terry and I were arguing with each other. And that useless excuse for a skipper was just looking on and umming-and-ahing while Terry demanded why *he* didn't have a camera on board as a matter of course. And then Scott just did what needed to be done. He got down, grabbed that fish, slapped it against the deck to stun it for a moment, and removed the hook as quick as you please. Then he tossed it back into the ocean. Did it all so fast that his father didn't have a chance to stop him."

"How did Terry react?"

"Furiously! Thankfully, Brittany stopped her ruckus and set about consoling him. Scott tried to explain that he'd done the only sensible thing, but Terry stomped into the cabin and sulked like a toddler for the next two days straight."

"And Melissa? Where was she during all this?"

"She was still sitting at the back of the boat, reading a book and sipping her wine. She missed the entire hullaballoo."

"Deliberately?"

Reed cackled and pointed a finger at me as if to say I was a sharp one.

"Was that how Melissa was generally?" I asked. "Tuning out? Wanting out?"

His face crinkled in confusion. "What do you mean?"

"Did she want out of the restaurant business? Perhaps even out of her marriage?"

"She'd been trying for years to persuade Terry to sell up, but she had no plans to leave her marriage, my dear."

I raised my eyebrows; this wasn't what Bashir had told me. "She was happy with Terry?"

He smoothed his mustache, considering. "Happy enough, I would say. She may have hit the occasional speed bump in her marriage, but last I heard, they were planning on renewing their marriage vows. They'd been doing a bunch of that whatchamacallit — couples counseling."

"So she definitely wasn't thinking of leaving Terry, maybe starting a life with someone else?"

"Oh, no, she'd never have done that. Terry was … a *charismatic* man. Magnetic. For all his foibles — and he had a great many, let me tell you — he was charming and irresistible. Generous, too, when he wanted to be. Compelling, you understand? It's not easy to leave a forcefield of that strength. Other men tend to look a little insipid in comparison."

I thought of Bashir. He *did* seem bland compared to the Terry that Reed had described. Nicer, sure, but duller. And some women, I knew, preferred *exciting* to *nice*.

"She loved him, even if she didn't always like him," Melissa's father concluded.

Could it be true? Had Melissa hidden her real intentions from her lover, or had she told her father a pack of reassuring lies?

"This is a touchy subject …" I began.

He waved a hand for me to continue.

"Was Terry faithful to Melissa?"

"I doubt it." He puckered his lips and glanced upward as though looking to the leaves for solace. "I planted this tree when she was born, you know?"

"This tree?" I pointed to the green canopy above.

"Uh-huh." He nodded solemnly, looking suddenly very tired. "It's a Southern magnolia. Such a beautiful memorial. My wife, Leonora, and I love to sit here in the evenings, remembering the old days when the girls were little."

Wait, what? I thought Reed had said that his wife died twenty years previously.

"So, if you're a psychic, can you tell me when I'll be shuffling off this mortal coil?" he said. "The thing is, I particularly want to make my ninetieth birthday."

I could've told him the truth: that I'd never yet been able to see into the future and that by the frail look of him, I was surprised he'd held out against the Grim Reaper this long. But I knew the power of placebo — how remarkable feats could be achieved when a person truly believed they could. So instead, I said, "You want me to tell you your future?"

"Yes." His tone was emphatic, but the look in his eyes was uncertain, almost frightened. I leaned over and took both his cold, bony hands in mine, closed my eyes, and pretended to go into a trance, throwing in a slight sway for added effect.

"I see you making your peace with all those around you," I said in a low, trancelike voice. "And I see cake and candles. Balloons."

I fluttered my eyes open and shook my head as though to clear the mists of my future visions. "You, Walter Reed, are going to make it to ninety and beyond!"

"Thank you, my dear." His tired smile turned into a yawn.

I figured he needed a nap, so I got to my feet, saying, "It's time for me to go. Thank you for speaking to me. It's been very enlightening."

"The pleasure has been all mine, all mine. And I'll tell her you stopped by."

"Tell who?"

"Melissa."

"Right, thank you," I said and left.

At the garden gate, I turned back to give him a goodbye wave, but his eyes were already closed, and his head rested against the back of his chair.

– 31 –

That evening, my exhaustion reached down to my very bones. I was utterly tapped out by all the visions at the restaurant and weighed down by the emotions that had swamped me. Strangely — extraordinarily so for me — I wasn't even hungry. All I wanted was a hot bath, an early night, and refuge from the ruckus outside. The Superdome had exhaled all the fans, and celebrations outside were in full and raucous swing. I certainly wasn't in the mood to talk to my mother, so when my phone lit up with an incoming call from her, I sent it straight to voicemail.

Three minutes later, it beeped an incoming message.

> Dear Garnet, are you okay? Is
> there any sign of a tornado or
> hurricane or other disturbance
> of air? All the portents! I am so
> worried! LOL, Mom.

Like many people of a certain age, my mother texted in full sentences, was clueless about emojis, and thought LOL meant "lots of love." By way of reply, I sent her a screen grab of my Weather App's forecast — clear skies, no wind predicted. She responded almost immediately.

> Dear Garnet, And is there any
> sign of the overbearing,
> interfering woman? LOL,
> Mom.

It took all of my limited resources of maturity and restraint not to point out that she was the woman she'd warned me against. I merely replied:

> Everything is fine, Mom.
> Really. Stop worrying.

A minute later:

> Dear Garnet, I am so confused.

No argument from me on that count.

> Beware, beware, beware. That
> is what the cards are telling
> me over and over again. LOL,
> Mom.

> Goodnight. Tell Dad I say hi.

My call with Ryan was a lot more pleasant, even though I really didn't have much substantial to report in terms of the case. I told him about my visit to the restaurant and what I'd gleaned there between my visions and my chats with Terry Broussard's partner.

"So, both Terry and Melissa were having affairs? Interesting," Ryan said.

"Very," I agreed. "Bashir comes across as very reserved and gentle — a complete contrast to the impression I've gotten of Terry. And he had lots of good reasons to want Broussard out of the way: he'd get a life insurance payout, be able to sell the business as he wanted, and he'd get the girl," I said, then added, "Except, of course, he didn't."

"But according to both you and Scott, Melissa's death happened accidentally."

"Yeah."

"So he's not out of the picture. Did he seem cut up about it?"

"Oh, he's heartbroken, all right, but at the death of *Melissa*. He doesn't much seem to care about the loss of Terry Broussard or their partnership. Or even Brittany."

I recounted what I'd seen on the video footage, how that matched what Scott had told me, and gave him a quick update on what Melissa's father had told me about the state of the Broussard marriage.

"Any way of discovering which was the real state of things?"

"Phenomenologically speaking, there are as many truths as there are participants and witnesses. Truth is subjective."

"Maybe to shrinks," Ryan said dryly. "Not to cops. Find out anything else?"

"Not really," I admitted. "Thing is, I don't know if there even *is* anything to be found. Maybe it was just what it looked like — a robbery gone horribly wrong. Broussard took Jeron by surprise, the gun went off, Melissa was shot accidentally, and then Jeron killed the other two to cover his identity. And maybe also because he was pissed at being fired. Then he got killed by Scott. End of story, nothing more to see here."

Who was it that said evil was banal? I was tempted to look it up there and then. It was a question that would have an easy answer, unlike seemingly everything else in my life.

"I honestly don't know what else to do or who else I could talk to," I continued and filled him in on my lack of success with the NOPD.

"Time to call it quits, you reckon?"

"I'll sleep on it tonight. But if I don't get any bright ideas, I'll move my flight up to tomorrow afternoon."

"Good idea! I can't wait to see you," he said and treated me to a few delicious details of what our reunion was likely to include.

The call was the high point of the evening, but Ryan's phrase — "Call it quits" — looped around in my head afterward. I didn't want to be a quitter. I wanted to be the gal who saved the day. I wanted to find out something that would make Jeron's mother feel better and lessen the guilt Anthony Cooper was carrying. I desperately wanted to deliver some useful goods on the psychic front so as to impress Desirae. But it was probably time to admit I'd done what I could.

Besides, I was eager to get out of this place. I glared at the dim corner of the bedroom. It was looking — no, *feeling* — even darker, like the shadows there were coalescing into something substantial, into a form which had an active presence rather than merely the absence of light. I turned on my bedside lamp, which must've done something to the old electrics, because it caused the main overhead light to flare, flicker, and die.

Screw this. I grabbed the bedside lamp and set it down close to the creepy corner, as far as the cord would allow. An icy draft swirled around my ankles, but though I felt around the wall and baseboard, resisting the sense that something hid there, ready to bite my fingers, I couldn't locate the source of the cold air. The lamp gave off a feeble glow, which didn't penetrate the thick gloom, like it was pushing against the darkness and losing the fight. Surely, it had been brighter when on the bedside table. I was probably only imagining that; bedside lamps were always dim, and this one had an old tungsten light bulb. Still, I removed the lampshade and stepped back to check the effect. Now at least it gave off enough light for me to see into the corner and to reassure my fevered imagination that nothing lurked there.

After a long bath, I went to bed and, despite all the thoughts swirling around in my head, fell asleep instantly. I woke up just a couple of hours later. Someone was knocking at the door. Or was it the window? I was lying on my left side, facing the dark corner. The light of the lamp I'd placed there was almost completely dimmed; I could just make out the glowing orange filaments of the old light bulb and, behind that, deeper shadows.

The room was silent. Had I dreamed the knocking?

I closed my eyes but snapped them open at a rustling, skittering sound coming from the corner. Part of the gloom there was darker than the rest. And was it … moving? With a prickle of horror, I sensed that someone or *something* was there, squatting on its haunches beyond the reach of the meagre light. Watching me. I sucked in a breath. The air felt heavy and thick, averse to filling my lungs. I needed to jump up and escape the room, but I was too terrified to move a muscle in case I drew attention to myself, so I lay perfectly still.

With a creaking like the sound of old bones, the dark form in the corner shifted position. I made out the silhouette of a shape — a head with short, curved horns; a ridge of sharp bones along the spine, folded batlike wings. The head slowly turned to face me. Two shining spots reflected the faint light.

Eyes.

– 32 –

Pareidolia! I thought-yelled to myself.

My brain was just seeing patterns in random shadows and attempting to make sense of normal background noises. But the meaning it had assigned to the sensory input was horrible, far-fetched, and utterly absurd. *Ridiculous!* There was no monster in the corner. I was trying to talk myself into standing up and doing something mundane — checking my phone for messages, drinking some water, going to the toilet — when I heard knocking again. A triple rap.

"Hello. Can I come in?" It sounded like a little girl's voice. "Let me in, please."

I glanced at the window, where the voice and knocking had come from. No one was there. Of course no one was there — my room was on the second floor.

A change in the light drew my gaze back to the corner, where the bulb now glowed brighter, sending light all the way into the corner, showing me it was empty. Sweet relief flooded my limbs and slowed my heart a fraction. I *had* just been dreaming, imagining the knocks and moving shapes. But now

216

I was fully awake and back behind the wheel of my rational mind. No one was knocking at the window. Nothing was lurking in the corner, ready to pounce. I—

The mattress moved beneath me.

It was behind me. Crouched on the bed, shifting its weight. Inching closer.

My body began to roll into the depression caused by its weight, and I screamed. But the sound stayed locked inside my tight throat, trapped behind my clenched teeth and frozen lips. It was all I could do to draw a ragged breath of the reluctant air.

Behind me, the creature muttered unintelligible sounds in a low, hoarse voice. Then it licked its lips. Hunger radiated off of it. No, it was more than hunger. It was *greed*. The thing wanted … me.

"Aaaahhh," it sighed, and a putrid odor swirled through the air.

Horror tightened my skin with goose bumps. A cold sweat broke out on my top lip, and my eyes watered. The beast behind me — now, I knew it to be a gargoyle — grinned, showing needle-sharp teeth and black saliva. It stroked a hand over my hair, lightly raking my scalp, then my back with sharp claws. A shudder rippled through me. Inside, beneath the paralysis of my flesh, I was a tumult of chaos, fear, and revulsion.

"I know," the gargoyle rasped beside my ear, bathing my face in the hot stench of death and decay. "I help."

Just a dream! A nightmare. *This isn't happening. It's not real.*

Then the coverlet slid back over the bare skin of my arm. The beast behind me was pulling the covers off of me, exposing my body to its covetous gaze.

"*Nooo!*" I screamed with all my might. The protest came out as a soft croak, hardly audible above the creature's whispered, "Soon ..." But it was enough to break the spell binding me. "Go away!" I yelled, my voice louder, stronger. "Get out!"

I leapt off the bed and spun around in a rapid circle. Nothing was in the spot behind where I'd lain. Only the lamp and its circle of light occupied the corner. No child was at the window.

Of course there was nothing. What an *idiot* I was. Now that I was fully awake, I knew that I'd just had an episode of sleep paralysis. I'd never personally experienced it before, but my racing brain searched for what I remembered learning about the condition in my psychology studies. It was a sleep disorder in which you somehow got stuck in a hypnogogic state somewhere between sleep and waking. Because you became mentally aware before the chemically induced muscle atonia of dream sleep wore off, you were awake (sort of) but paralyzed. Sufferers felt extreme fear and often reported hallucinations of shadowy evil beasts or hags, though no one knew why.

That's what had happened to me. That's all it was. None of what I'd seen or heard or smelled had been real. Not the foul smell or the creaking bones or the knocking at the window. Not the creature's horns or its whispers or its blackened needle teeth. The teeth! How could I possibly have seen those when I was facing the opposite direction? How could I even have known it *was* a gargoyle? I couldn't have. That right there proved it had been just a hallucination. A remnant of a horrible nightmare that had intruded into my state of wakefulness.

I'd only dreamed about a gargoyle because I'd been

inundated by the horrible things ever since I'd arrived in New Orleans — taps and mirror frames and fountains, the statue in the alley, and even that damned devil card I'd looked at online. I glanced at the coverlet. It was bundled in a bunch directly behind where I'd been lying, precisely where it would've landed when I'd thrown off the covers. Precisely where it would've been if it had been tugged off of me.

Stop it! I ordered myself. *Stop being so stupid.*

I sniffed the air and smelled nothing. Not even, I realized belatedly, the faintest whiff of cola Chapstick. And that also proved the episode hadn't been real. If I'd been in any danger — and surely, from such a hideous creature, I would've been — Colby would've drawn close to warn me.

I took a deep breath and forced myself to blow it out slowly. I was safe. I was fine, just a little spooked. I checked the time on my phone: 2.13 a.m. It was way too early to wake up, but the thought of getting back into that bed repelled every fiber of my being. And despite what I knew to be logically, rationally, and objectively true, I still couldn't face staying in the room for a minute longer.

With trembling hands, I threw my belongings into my suitcase, grabbed my handbag and phone, and left the room, slamming the door shut behind me, silently apologizing to any other guests I may have startled awake with the sound and my screams earlier. Then it occurred to me that in the days I'd been staying in the hotel, I hadn't seen a single other guest. *Shit.*

I marched down the carpeted stairs, feeling lighter and safer with every step I took farther away from my room, but when I discovered that the front door of the hotel was locked, with no key in sight, I came perilously close to panicking. I rattled the door, searched the little table beside it for a key, and slammed my hand down on the valet bell at reception over and over again.

"Hello?" I yelled. "Help!"

A distant door opened and closed. The light over one of the dark hallways that led off the foyer came on, and the old woman walked toward me, moving way too slowly.

"What is it?" she asked, not complaining at being disturbed at that hour of the night, not even seeming annoyed. If anything, her expression looked … unsurprised.

"Open the door, please," I said. "I'm leaving."

I expected her to ask why, but she merely sighed. The horrible thing upstairs had sighed too.

"There's a key for the front door on your room key ring," she said.

"What? Oh. Well, I left my keys in the room."

"Then I'll open it for you," she said, moving way too slowly toward the door. "Did you consume anything from the minibar?"

"What? No. Maybe, I don't know. Just charge my card, okay? But open that door now. *Please.*"

Without another word, she opened a hidden drawer in the little table, removed a key, and unlocked the front door. I bolted outside and half walked, half ran down the sidewalk as if the hounds of hell were at my heels. Perhaps they were.

– 33 –

I found a big, brightly lit hotel with "Bourbon" in its title. It seemed like an omen — the good sort. I checked in, crossing my fingers that the hold on my credit card would go through, then crashed in an inoffensively bland and modern room and slept like the dreamless dead until dawn, when sunlight streaming through the undrawn drapes woke me.

My mind immediately returned to the night before.

Not before coffee, I told myself, and since the horrible pod stuff in the room didn't count, I dragged on my jeans, boots, and a long-sleeved tee and headed out.

At seven-thirty on a Monday morning, the streets of the French Quarter were deserted. It looked like an apocalyptic storm had rolled through, blasted away the humans, and left a barren world in its wake. Bars and storefronts were shuttered, and the streets were empty except for the detritus of the bacchanalian revels of the night before, which littered the gutters and sidewalks. Squashed plastic cups lay like splotches of neon blood on the pavement; gold, purple, and green beads from snapped necklaces crunched underfoot; crushed cans, broken bottles, and food wrappers piled in drifts against walls like dirty human snow. And used condoms and needles lay where they'd been dropped at the entrance to narrow alleys.

The rank smell brought back a flash of the foul odor of the creature that had visited me in my bed. *Visited me in my dream,* I corrected myself, running my hands hard over my face, scrubbing away the night before.

The unforgiving sunshine showed more of the Quarter than was visible at night, revealing the split personality of the city. Boarded-up stores and graffitied walls rubbed shoulders with the old-time splendor of grand architecture and ornamental ironwork. New Orleans, in its mashup of historical grandeur and contemporary squalor, was a funny old place. At first, I'd noticed only the façade of fun, but now, I felt like I'd seen the dark beneath the neon, the lack beneath the excess, the fear beneath the frenetic party.

A woman wearing thigh-high boots and a mangy feather boa the same vivid purple as her hair slowly minced across the road ahead of me, placing her unsteady feet in carefully selected spots as she walked her pet on its lead.

"Step on a crack, break your momma's back," she yelled to no one in particular.

Drawing closer, I saw her pet was a baby alligator. I blinked. Was I hallucinating again? Was it a dog wearing a costume? But nope — the reptile was real.

The woman caught me gaping and let me have it. "What you looking at? Huh? What you looking at? You never seen a lady with her baby before? Close your mouth! Open your eyes! There's a world all around you. See it! Love it! I will love*love*love it! And use your eyes, see what's there —alligators and flowers and reptile people all over the place, scurrying, scurrying."

Honestly, there was wisdom in her words. She had me right up until the part about the reptile people.

With a final glare, she stalked away from me, back down the way I'd come, her voice echoing in the empty street and alleys as she berated the air and promised to *love, love, love* like it was a threat to kill.

I needed caffeine and sugar, and Google offered up the name of one place that was sure to be open at an hour which the Big Easy clearly considered to be ungodly. Turning at a corner occupied by an old absinthe house, I headed east, down toward the river. A truck was offloading seafood deliveries outside a restaurant. A man in a bloodied apron opened the lids of the Styrofoam containers to inspect glistening octopus, frozen shrimp, and oysters on ice. A fishy smell rose into the air. Again, the fetid odor of the gargoyle knocked at my awareness. Again, I pushed it away.

A street-washing truck crept up the road, spraying jets of water out front and to the side, driving the litter into the gutters. Two cleaners with rakes, snow shovels, and wheeled trashcans walked behind, gathering up what remained of the *bon temp.* I wished I could squash the horror of my nightmare as easily as a Solo cup then dump it into a trash can and be done with it. It had just been a dream, I reminded myself for the umpteenth time. Just a dream.

It hadn't felt like a dream, though. It had felt more like some kind of spiritual attack. I swore and kicked a soda can in frustration. I was beginning to sound just like my mother. At the thought of her, I remembered the chilly draft, the little eddy of cold air in the dark corner before I'd seen the entity. Had that been the ill wind she'd warned me about?

No. I needed to stop thinking like a superstitious kook and remember that I was a logical, scientifically trained, almost-psychologist. What I'd experienced the night before had just been a really intense and horrible nightmare, with the added awfulness of sleep paralysis thrown in. Images of what I'd seen online and what my mother had told me had threaded their way through the subconscious dream images, and my insecurities about my seeming inability to add any value to this investigation had manifested as the gargoyle offering assistance at a time when I could've used some help.

Café du Monde was located near the river and adjacent to the old French market. It stayed open twenty-four hours a day, three-hundred-and-sixty-five days a year, and even at this hour, it was already busy. I snagged a seat at one of the outside tables, where I could soak up the thin morning sun and watch the city wake up. While I waited for my order to arrive, I answered Ryan's good-morning text, adding:

> I had the freakiest nightmare last night! There was a gargoyle in the corner of the room. Then somehow it was squatting on the bed behind me, whispering. Ugh!

My shoulder rose to wipe away the hot, moist breath I could still feel on my ear.

It's all the gargoyles in that place, Ryan replied.

Absolutely!

How's the investigation going?

It's not. I've got nothing new. Honestly, I'm feeling pretty useless.

Ryan sent me a GIF of two pandas hugging and the message: *Time to come home?*

Yeah, I think so.

I'd wanted to go home feeling victorious, proud of using my gift and my brains to uncover some missing information and help a family. Instead, I was going to retreat with my tail between my legs, feeling humiliated and looking like a fool. And I so did not want to look like a fool, especially in front of Desirae. I'd wanted nothing more than to impress her, to get the old popular, pretty-girl clique stamp of approval that had eluded me when I was a kid.

From the outside looking in, those girls with their clear skin and sleek hair had seemed to possess everything, to *be* everything, that I wanted. I'd been an odd child — too smart for some, too different for others, and with my offbeat sense of humor and strange parents, the business of making friends and having playdates and sleepovers had come hard. Jessica Armstrong had been my one true friend. We'd bonded by mocking the giggling gangs of popular girls who ruled the hallways of Pitchford High, searing us with scathing comments and contemptuous looks — or, worse, with their blithe indifference, like we were pieces of furniture beneath their notice.

Jessica had laughed at my snide commentaries, wasn't put off by my father's passion for killers, and had even enjoyed my mother's regular dire predictions, declaring my parents way more interesting than her own. She'd even cheered me on when Colby and I started dating, and suddenly, I was one of the cool crowd, elevated from obscurity to acceptance by the attentions of the hottest boy in school.

For that shining, glorious time, I'd not only been wildly in love, I'd been on the inside of Girl World looking out. I'd laughed and flicked my hair and painted eyeliner wings on my eyelids with the best of the senior bitches. Then Colby had died, taking most of me with him. And even Jessica couldn't connect with the inert lump of grief left behind. I could hardly bother to wash my hair, let alone play nice with others, and I was flung back into the outer orbits of the social system, stranger and lonelier than before.

And now here I was, twenty-nine years old and mature enough — psychologically sophisticated enough — to know that I was bringing transference from my childhood into this situation but also seemingly still immature enough to crave

Desirae's admiration and respect.

As though my musings had somehow summoned her, my phone rang with a call from Desirae. After a good few minutes of polite pleasantries from her side — asking whether I'd slept well, wanting to know if I was enjoying the city, apologizing way too profusely for calling so early — she got to the point.

"I'm at the airport, about to board my flight back home. I was just *wondering* if you'd managed to, you know, discover anything?"

"Not really," I admitted through gritted teeth. "Nothing significant, at any rate."

"Oh. Well, it's just that Anthony contacted me last night. And he thinks we should call it a day."

"Does he now? Why's that?"

"He says his sister is really upset by your opening the wound again."

"*Me?* By *me* opening the wound? You're the one who asked us to come!" I said, outraged.

"Yes, yes, *sorry!* I didn't mean to imply— I should have cleared it better with him before asking and warned him what to expect. It's all my fault. I'm not blaming you at *all*. It's just he says she hasn't stopped crying since you— since *we* visited. And he wants us to stop."

"I wonder if that's the real reason."

"What do you mean?"

"Nothing," I muttered.

"I think, if you haven't turned up anything new, I mean if your … *gift* hasn't, you know, revealed anything, then perhaps we shouldn't waste any more of your time."

"I'm sorry I wasn't more helpful," I said, begrudgingly conceding defeat.

"Never mind," Desirae said, and I was sure I wasn't imagining the note of condescension in her voice. "It was worth a *try*."

– 34 –

My order arrived, and I dove into the heaping plate of *beignets* — hot, deep-fried squares of donut heaven. Crispy on the outside and pillowy soft inside, they were smothered in a thick dusting of powdered sugar that melted into the sheen of oil on their surface. The bitter chicory kick of the café au lait was the perfect accompaniment to their melting sweetness.

Desirae's tone had been as sugary as the *beignets*, but the note of condescension beneath all her polite apologies and disclaimers had rankled as deeply as Detective Dupre's open scorn. I'd been ready to call it a day and head home to Ryan and to Henry's untidy office, where I was confident I *did* add value, but now — goaded by Desirae's judgement and even by Ryan's too-ready acceptance of my failure — I felt a mulish need to keep on investigating.

I stabbed my fork into another sugared square, realized I was pouting, and brought myself up short. Maybe the caffeine and the sugar were kicking in, or maybe I was getting a little more mature with age, but I realized that if I continued, I'd be doing the right thing (perhaps) for entirely the wrong reasons. I'd be acting from a misplaced sense of *I'll show them.*

A weight of depression settled itself on my chest. Not getting to do what you wanted — was this simply what adulting felt like? Doing the right thing, taking others into consideration, putting the whiney needs of ego aside — it sucked. I'd learned in my studies that alcohol and drug addictions press the pause button on personal development and that when the addict kicks their habit, they take up where they left off — at the level of maturity they were at when they lost themselves to numbness, dissociation, and a refusal to deal with life. Now I wondered if that hypothesis held true for deep grief as well. In many ways, I'd been fixated in my growth path, stuck with odd spots of immaturity. It was time, beyond time, really, to do some growing up. And it was absolutely time to go home. I'd head out to the airport and grab an earlier flight. Hopefully, I'd be home with Ryan by bedtime.

I paid my check, couldn't resist buying a reminder of my trip — a T-shirt saying *Beignet, done that* — and hurried back to the hotel, keen to get going now that I'd made a decision. I had just started packing when my phone rang with a number I didn't recognize. I hit the answer button anyway and had my ear assaulted by someone yelling incoherently. Assuming it was a wrong number, I ended the call, but almost immediately, it rang again, and this time, the shouting and swearing were even louder. It took me a few moments to figure out the identity of the caller.

"Anthony?" I said when the voice paused to draw breath. "Is that you?"

"Yeah, it's me, and don't you dare hang up on me again!"

"Sorry, I didn't know it was you. What's wrong?"

"I'll tell you what's wrong. My sister is lying in hospital — and it's your fault!"

"*What?* What happened?"

"She had to have her stomach pumped and put on a drip and God knows what else. After your call, she was so upset. Crying the whole weekend. Then last night, she took a bunch of painkillers and sleeping tablets. Lucky thing her neighbor looked in on her this morning and found her with the empty bottles, else she'd be dead by now! They couldn't hardly wake her up." His voice choked up on the last words. "The doctors say she'll likely have liver damage now."

"I'm so sorry!"

"You should be. This is what comes from raking it all up again. And why'd you tell her about the insurance? You got her looking sideways at me now!"

"I was just trying to clarify things." A question burned on the tip of my tongue. I knew I shouldn't ask it when he was so upset, but on the other hand, he was so angry with me that I figured I'd blown any chance of getting further cooperation from him anyway. I had nothing to lose, and I might surprise an answer out of him. "Anthony, do you have life insurance on your sister?"

"You accusing me of trying to kill my own sister now?" he yelled furiously. "It's time for you to go home. Before someone makes you."

"Are you threatening me?" I said, but the line was already dead.

I plopped down on the bed beside my suitcase and glowered at my reflection in the mirror opposite. I'd accomplished nothing except to upset a bunch of people who wanted nothing more than to find a way to live with their unbearable losses. I'd even, apparently, planted the idea in Mrs. Cooper's mind that her own brother might've had a hand in her son's death. Worse, the thoughts of Jeron's death which I'd churned up were enough to make her want to "give up and die" — that's what she'd said, what she'd told me directly. And it hadn't even registered in my dumb brain that she might be hinting at suicide, hadn't occurred to me to alert Anthony to his sister's state of mind. Good thing I *hadn't* written the board exams and become a psychologist. I'd clearly be useless at that too.

Why had I ever agreed to stay and try to investigate? The answer came at once. I'd wanted to impress Ryan and, especially, Desirae, that's why. I'd wanted to prove myself, because I still didn't have faith — enough faith, consistent faith — in my own abilities. *Pathetic.*

Rubbing a hand behind my neck, digging my fingers hard into the tight muscles of my shoulder, I was startled to feel rough scabbed ridges beneath my fingertips. I lifted my shirt and turned around, angling myself to see my back in the mirror. Several long scratches crossed my back across my shoulders. Dammit. I'd been trying so hard not to scratch and pick at myself, been so vigilant about keeping my fingers out of my mouth, that I must've been scratching myself in my sleep. And now fresh beads of blood marked the spot where I'd torn off the scab at the end of one.

I grabbed a tissue from the complimentary box on the desk

and stuck it to the spot, then cursed when I saw that my shirt was flecked with blood. Was there nothing I could do right? Was there no situation I could make better instead of worse? Hot tears welled in my eyes, and I wiped them away at once. Self-pity was a disgusting thing.

I flushed the tear-damp and blood-spotted tissues down the toilet and went back to my packing, but my hands moved slower and slower. I couldn't stop thinking about poor Mrs. Cooper with her dead face and broken heart, now lying in the hospital. And about Jeron, so bright and alive in his graduation picture, now buried in the ground, his only legacy the grief and destruction he'd left in the wake of the murders. I saw again Camille's thin face above two halves of the same heart necklace. And Terry and Brittany — the holes in his chest, the holes in her face. I thought of the restaurant closing and all the jobs that had been lost; of the little girl who'd heard the shots; of Bashir's lost love, and of Melissa, outlived by her father and a tree in a garden. And most especially, I thought of Scott limping alone to sit in a bar and mourn his family, the photographs of his mother in his wallet, and of him collapsed and sobbing over her dead body on a cold kitchen floor.

Damn it. I'm not done here yet!

I couldn't leave things as they were. I needed to *do* something. Something else, something more. But what? Should I try to speak to Scott again, ask him more about the night, get permission to touch some of his family's belongings that were surely still in his house? Could I explore one of the other theories of the crime, try to perhaps chase down the organized-crime angle? Was there anyone else I could talk to? I replayed my memories of the interviews I'd conducted, racking my brains for any loose thread, any possible clue, and came up with one Hail Mary.

Grabbing my phone, I called Khurran Bashir. He, too, didn't sound pleased to hear from me again. Shocker.

"When we spoke yesterday," I said, "you mentioned an *interfering* interior decorator."

"What about it?"

"Was this decorator by any chance a female?"

– 35 –

I called Francesca DeMarco on the number Bashir tracked down for me, explained my interest in the Broussards, and begged to hear her story.

"I can spare ten minutes only," she said.

"That's perfect, thanks."

"Meet me at the cannon in Washington Artillery Park."

"Great. I'm wearing a red shirt."

Park, I discovered, was a misleading name for some pots of flowers set on a concrete platform at the top of a bunch of stairs. Still, the view of Jackson Square and St. Louis Cathedral to the west and the Mississippi to the east was unbeatable. As I waited, I amused myself by guessing which of the women coming up the stairs might be the decorator who'd sold Broussard the expensive chandeliers which had annoyed his partner so much.

The woman who took in my shirt with a disparaging eyebrow was in her mid-twenties, around five-two, with a curvy figure, olive skin, long curls of glossy black hair, chestnut eyes framed by sweeping fans of false eyelashes, and the sort of nails which would come in real handy for scratching someone's eyes out. She wore killer heels, skinny jeans, a low-cut blouse which showed her assets off to admirable advantage, and a glossy belt with a gold GG buckle. Gucci? I could tell it was meant to be impressive, but for all I knew, it could just as easily have been a knockoff from the market down the way as the real thing. The overall impression was expensive, not in the same effortless, high-class style Desirae had but in the *I'm going to wear high-end brand names so you know I mean business* kind of way.

She looked like a pampered, vicious kitten. Melissa Broussard, knowing her husband's wandering eye, would never have hired this pretty young thing as a server or hostess, but Melissa hadn't been in charge of hiring contractors for the restaurant, and somehow, Terry had happened upon Francesca.

"So," she said after we'd exchanged introductions, "you wanted to talk to me about Terry?"

"Yeah, how did you meet?"

"Let's walk while we talk. Get those steps in."

As she explained how Terry had hired her to jazz up the restaurant's dining area and the luxurious improvements she'd made to its lighting, seating, and general decor, we walked down a wide paved pathway called the Moonwalk and turned left onto the promenade that ran along the west bank of the river. A man in swimming trunks tried to hustle us with an offer to take a swim in the Mississippi.

"I'll do it for a dollar, ladies!"

The river looked neither clean nor warm. Anyone who took a dip in its muddy waters no doubt risked picking up *E. coli* or hepatitis, and that was if they didn't drown in the strong current sweeping plastic bags, straws, and bottles downriver, probably all the way to the Gulf of Mexico. I held up a *no thank you* hand, but Francesca was more direct.

"Fuck off," she told the man. "Honestly, you can't walk, like, ten steps in this town without someone trying to shake you down one way or another."

"You're not from here?"

"*I,*" she said like I'd gravely insulted her, "am from *Savannah!*"

"My bad." Glancing from the water on the right of the raised embankment we were walking along to the low-lying French Market to our left, I said, "Funny how the river is higher than the land."

"Yeah. In most cities, the river is the lowest point. Here, it's the highest." She gestured toward the French Quarter. "It used to be a swamp that sucked up floodwaters. Then people thought it might be a good idea to drain it and build an entire city of land below sea level." Long lashes fluttered as she rolled her eyes. "Savannah is safer. Prettier too."

"I'll be sure to visit it."

"Look, I don't have much time." She jiggled car keys between her talons to emphasize the point. "What exactly did you want to know?"

"Sure, uh, how did you and Terry Broussard get on?"

"Very well. I think he, like, valued my expertise."

"Look, I need to ask you something awkward, and there's no polite way to do it. So I'm just going to come out with it, okay? Were you having an affair with him?"

Francesca glanced out at the river, where a tourist steamboat with a giant red paddlewheel made its stately way up the river. "Define 'affair.'"

"Did you have a relationship with him that involved sex?" I said baldly.

"Well, if you put it that way," she said, making it clear by her tone of voice that she considered it an unreasonable way to define the word, "then yes, I suppose we did."

"How long did it last?"

"Around six months."

"So you must have known him fairly well?"

She shrugged her dainty shoulders.

"What was he like?" I asked.

"Bit of a prick, really. Like, a *real* narcissist. He never listened, Terry, like not to *anyone*. He was only ever interested in himself, what *he* wanted, what made *him* happy. But I'll give him this — he had a good eye for quality. And" — she gave me a mischievous grin — "he was real generous."

I could only imagine how that had gone down with his wife, and with Scott and Bashir struggling to get the restaurant profitable.

She flicked back her curls and ran an expert eye over my own straight locks. "You have very thick hair."

"Thank y—"

"I can recommend a stylist who could help you with that."

"Thanks. I guess. So, did Terry's wife know about him and you?"

"Don't know, don't care," Francesca said to the accompaniment of three long discordant blasts from the steamboat's whistle.

"I see," I said.

And I did. This creature took what she wanted without much concern about how it might impact others. She was a bold storm that breezed into lives, wrought havoc, and then departed.

"That was their business, not mine."

"What's that sound?" I said, looking around for the source of old-timey music that came to us in snatches on the breeze.

"The calliope on the steamboat. Look, are we done here? Only, I'm not, like, a tour guide or anything."

"Just a few more questions. How did the relationship with Terry end?" No answer. "Who ended it?"

"I did," she said too quickly.

"Had he started up with someone else?"

"How would I know? Didn't care, anyway — it was time to wind things up. It didn't worry me. There are plenty more men who're interested in me. Plenty. Besides, these things have a lifespan, like a best-before-it-gets-boring date, don't they?"

"Sure," I replied, despite having no personal experience of the natural lifespan of love affairs. Did Ryan and I have a best-before date stamped on our relationship, like gas station sushi?

Francesca turned her head away and looked down at her phone, thumbing through apps. Checking for an important message or hiding tears? I studied her for a long moment until she shoved the phone back in her bag, looked up at me, and demanded, "*What?*"

"You were really hurt when it ended, weren't you?"

It was like I'd pressed my foot on the accelerator of her emotions tank.

"I was *not!* Him? Hurt *me?* As if! It's not like I wanted him to put a ring on it." She stuck out her left hand, wiggling fingers bare save for their sharp claws. "Why would I want to get hitched to such an old, fat fuck? He was hopeless at business, didn't care for anyone except himself. *And*" — she gave a snort of laughter — "he was running out of money *and* hair." She turned to glare at me. Pink spots of color flushed her cheeks, and her lips were thinned. "He was an awful, awful man. Thought he could just toy with me while it suited him and then cut me loose. Well, I showed him."

She grinned, and the rage dissipated like the last notes of the calliope's melody on the air.

"How?" I said. "What did you do?"

She gave me an evaluating stare as though weighing up how much to share with me. "Well, for one thing, I called his wife to tell her all about what he'd been up to."

I nodded like I was impressed at this act of revenge. "How did she take the news?"

Francesca shrugged. "She hung up on me. But as my momma used to say, you can't unring a bell. She couldn't have been happy about it, right?" Francesca seemed pleased by the thought.

Was it possible that Melissa had gone on to confront Terry, that Francesca's misguided attempt to drive husband and wife apart had ironically led to some honest conversations, perhaps even an ultimatum that had gotten Terry to agree to the marriage counseling Walter Reed had spoken of?

"You think maybe Terry and Melissa might've been planning to patch things up?" I asked.

"I doubt it, but who knows? Those two were on again and off again like a flashing motel sign." She began jiggling her keys again, and I hurried to get in another question before she ended the interview.

"Can you think of anyone who might have wanted to harm the family?"

She shook her head. "Look, I really gotta go."

"Sure, let's head back."

"No, I'll just take a shortcut through the market."

I wasn't ready to part from her. I still wanted to see if I could get more, maybe even a reading off of her.

"I'll come with you," I said.

She made no effort to stifle an exasperated sigh and set off at a quick pace despite her heels. As we descended a flight of stairs off the embankment, I deliberately bumped into her, knocking the keys out of her hand.

"Hey! Watch it!" she snapped, but I was already bending to scoop up her keys.

The woman tosses her long hair over one shoulder, and her glossy lips break into a satisfied smile as she walks alongside a silver convertible.

One hand stretches out to caress its sleek body, but the car protests with a soft metallic screech. She circles it, dragging the key in her fingers along at hip height, circumnavigating the car with a deep, jagged scratch.

Someone was tugging at my arm and yelling, "Hey! *Hey!*" Francesca glared at me like I'd done something to personally offend her. "What's the *matter* with you?" She snatched her keys out of my hand.

"Sorry," I said. "Did Terry drive a silver Mercedes?"

"Yeah." She turned and walked away.

"Hey, Francesca?" I called after her.

Without breaking stride, she glanced back over her shoulder. "*What?*"

"You have a thing for anchovies, don't you?"

That stopped her. Her eyes widened, then narrowed. Face creasing in a fake smile, she said, "Well, bless your lil' heart — I just love them!"

– 36 –

I cut through the French Market, sidestepping pyramids of woven baskets in bright neon colors, ignoring vendors selling tacky tourist tat from all over the world, and hurrying past a stall advertising Hurricane mix and freshly grilled gator on a stick. I had an itch in my brain that demanded to be scratched. Something I'd seen or heard didn't fit, but I was damned if I knew what it was.

A call from Ryan interrupted my musings.

"I have a new suspect," I said.

"Who?"

"Francesca DeMarco. She was the interior decorator who revamped the restaurant, and she was also Terry's lover — until he dumped her, and she was inspired to take some very fishy revenge," I said in a rush.

"Whoa, back up. What, now?"

"Short version: Terry's spurned lover is a woman with a low tolerance for abandonment and rejection, a vindictive nature, and impaired impulse control. She could've hired someone — a dishwasher, say, that she met in her business visits to

Broussard's — to come and rob the place. She may even have hired him to shoot Melissa Broussard so that Terry was free to marry *her*."

"Wow, okay. So you're back on the case?"

"Yeah, it's a long story," I said, not telling him the part about Mrs. Cooper's suicide attempt and how half the town wanted me out of their hair. "It's just that I'd really like to find something that can ease these people's pain. And also" — I shook my head at a vendor offering me a dried alligator head souvenir — "I've been wondering about the organized-crime angle."

Perhaps it was something about that theory which was niggling at the back of my mind.

"But the NOPD ruled that out," Ryan reminded me.

"I know, but did they ever really follow up on it properly? I'm not sure how *I* could, though, to be honest. Do you think Agent Singh could help me? Or, better, Tyler Washington." Had either of the FBI special agents forgiven me yet for my interference in their last case? "Maybe they could contact their field office down here and check if there's anything worth investigating."

"You could try," Ryan said, sounding doubtful. "It sounds like you think this was all aimed at him, at Terry Broussard."

"Yeah. Maybe. I don't know. I've been thinking that someone might've wanted to scare him, give him some motivation to sell up and get out. It seems like there were lots of people who wanted him out of the area, and they could've hired an insider, and it went wrong."

"I don't know, Garnet. Why would they get an unknown

amateur to do a hit when they could've used one of their own professionals to do a guaranteed quick and clean job?"

He had a point, but …

"For all we know, Jeron wasn't unknown. He might've been in one of the gangs. He was getting drugs from *somewhere*."

"You said his uncle—"

"Yes, but I don't *know* that, not for sure. And he bragged to his girlfriend about an upcoming easy score — that might've been doing a job for someone who wanted Broussard out."

"Or he might just have wanted to steal a good night's earnings."

One of the city's ubiquitous jazz bands struck up nearby just then, and I headed for the exit. I'd go back to my calm, neutral hotel room and regroup. Figure out my next step.

"The thing is, the shrink in me just can't help thinking that Terry Broussard is at the heart of this."

"You think *he* engineered this?"

"No, that's not what I mean. What I'm trying to say is that it should've been only *him* who got shot. I mean, it seems like the guy pissed off just about everyone south of the Mason-Dixon Line. I truly don't want to victim-blame, but I keep circling back to him, like it's his character, his essential nature that kicked over the first domino in the chain of this whole tragedy."

"Victimology," Ryan said.

"What's that?"

"Part of getting to the root of a crime is understanding an individual's victim-proneness. What factors in their lives — where they live, what work they do, who they interact with, lifestyle factors, and, I guess, what they're like as personalities — make them more likely to be targeted."

"Right! And the thing that made Terry more prone to be targeted was his seeming inability to *listen*. Everyone I've spoken to makes mention of it. This guy just could not set himself aside for long enough to hear what anyone else was telling him. He wouldn't listen to advice from his wife or son or partner about how to save the restaurant, rejected the complaints of other restaurateurs in the area, ignored the unhappiness of his staff and suppliers, wouldn't even listen to his father-in-law in the inconsequential matter of catching a Fat Alfred."

"You've lost me again."

"It's a fish. *Not* a tuna," I said and, imagining his confusion, quickly added, "It doesn't matter. Point is that even in his last moments, when his very life depended on it, he didn't listen to his wife's pleas to cooperate or to Jeron's orders to go quietly into the cooler. And that refusal to listen is what ultimately set off the violence that got everyone killed. Terry Broussard simply never cared about what other people wanted. He was selfish. Greedy. Utterly focused on his own needs and pleasures. In a way, it was kind of inevitable that there was going to be a tragedy sooner or later."

Ryan was intrigued by my analysis and told me to stay in touch. I was still mulling my character-is-destiny theory when I noticed I was passing Madame Laveau's store and decided to pop in and get a new supply of candy for Henry. I grabbed a bag of the traditional pecan pralines and was debating whether Henry might also fancy the rum, chocolate, or peanut butter varieties when a screech behind me made me jump.

Spinning around, I discovered Madame Laveau standing behind me, staring at me with wide, shocked eyes.

"Damn, girl, you done pick up another one!"

"Another what?" I said.

"I told you so. I *warned* you more would be coming. Didn't I say they like roaches?" She shook her head, tutting in disgust. "You like a spirit *magnet*, girl."

Ignoring my protests that I wasn't interested, didn't believe her, had other things to be getting on with, the woman grabbed my arm in a surprisingly strong grip and dragged me into her dim, stuffy room. Muttering something unintelligible, she grabbed a small bag of worn brown leather on a long thong from a shelf and slung it around her neck.

"Sit yo'self down," she said in the tone of a dog trainer to a disobedient spaniel.

Reluctantly, I sank into the chair across the table from her and crossed my arms.

"Now how in the world did this happen?" Madame wagged her finger at the open air to the left and right of my head then held up a hand. "Don't tell me—"

"Wasn't going to."

"It came through the thinning. Am I right?"

"What did?" I said, determined to give her nothing she could use to conjure more creepiness. It hadn't escaped my notice that the marked French accent she'd had in our first visit had all but disappeared. Now she sounded merely Southern.

"I'll tell you what — this, this … beast here, by your right shoulder."

I flinched and glanced to my right. Saw nothing. Again, I wondered if she was a sensitive just reading *me,* somehow divining the horrible nightmare I'd had the night before.

"Any other funny business happen there?" she asked.

"Well, there was some knocking at the door, or maybe the window, but no one was there."

"How many knocks?"

"Three." I rapped the table in imitation of what I'd heard. "Like that."

"*Mon Dieu!*" She crossed herself. "Has anyone close to you died?"

"No!" I said, resisting the urge to check my phone.

"Then it is evil demanding admittance."

"What, the postman always rings twice, but the devil always knocks three times?"

"It is to mock the Holy Trinity," she said fiercely. "That's what comes from staying in that place. The warning's in the name, girl. Didn't you think maybe to go with the Best Western or the Hyatt? Now you stuck with this ugly entity." As though she heard a hiss or a growl in response, she shook the amulet threateningly at the space beside me. Then a look of revulsion rippled across her face. "Oh. It likes your hair."

I shuddered, feeling again the hot breath, the clawed stroke.

"And your golden boy don't like it none, either," she said.

"Colby's here too? I can't hear him."

"No, he's blocked by this one, stuck behind him."

"But—"

"Hush, now, let me listen. It's saying something."

– 37 –

"What's that?" Madame addressed the space to my right. "Uh? Uh-huh? Huh." Turning to me, she said, "It says it can help you. It *knows*."

"Knows what?"

Madame cocked her head, squinted at the spot beside me. "Knows what happened." She gave me a sharp look. "That mean something to you?"

I nodded slowly like I understood, but in truth, I felt dazed and confused. What was going on here? I didn't believe in gargoyles and ghouls. In my saner moments, I wasn't sure I even believed in ghosts.

As my grief for Colby had gentled, settling into a bittersweet bruise that hurt only when I poked it, I'd begun to wonder if there wasn't a more rational explanation for his "presence." Perhaps his voice simply came from within me. Maybe there was — had always been — a part of me that wasn't ready to let go of the grief but still wanted me to *live*, to be careful rather than reckless, to move on. And subconsciously, I'd felt guilty about it and split off that part of myself, allowing it to return only in the dissociated guise of Colby's voice.

Now I was confronted with this woman who claimed not only to see him but also to be interacting with the monster I'd seen — *dreamed!* — the night before and to know something of what he'd whispered to me.

"I know … I help." The gargoyle's rasped words came back to me.

I glared at Madame, not wanting to hear any more.

"Well?" She scowled at me. "It wants to know if you want its help."

Could it help? The thought came before I could stop it.

Silently, I groaned in frustration at myself, because I was again entertaining the possibility of something that was not, *could* not be possible. I felt torn in two. My rational, scientifically educated, and psychologically informed side scoffed at me. Told me to get up and go, before Madame scammed me out of another fifty dollars. That was my father's daughter — sensible, logical, sane. My mother's daughter, on the other hand, was stupidly superstitious and suggestible, too imaginative for her own good, and tempted to accept assistance from "beyond the veil" to help get at the truth of the murders. How was it possible for one person to have two such opposing sides at war within her? My mother would say it was because I was a Gemini, doomed to be divided against myself.

And right at that moment, the twin that wanted answers — answers for the here and now, from the wherever and whoever, was in the ascendant.

On the wall in the basement in my parents' house, above the workbench where my father stored his clutter of tools and fishing tackle, was a manual drill old enough to be an antique. He'd inherited it from his own father, who'd gotten it from his father before him. It was a thing of beauty, with a wooden body worn smooth by years of calloused hands and a crank handle which turned the drill attachment. Once, when I was around ten or eleven years old, I'd nagged my father to take it off its display perch and show me how it worked, and he'd even allowed me to have a turn trying to drill a hole into a plank of soft pine. I'd turned and turned that crank, but it was awkward to operate and made disappointingly slow progress. The drill bit kept slipping out of the notch in the wood.

I'd seen my father use his electric drill with its powerful motor and dazzling assortment of drill bits and thought it vastly superior to the disappointing vintage version.

"The old one's not very good," I'd informed my dad.

"It was state of the art in its day," he'd said.

"Why do you keep it?"

"For the heft of it in my hand and in my memories."

I hadn't understood what he meant. All I'd taken away from the encounter was the clear belief that power tools were the acme of DIY.

My investigations, using the tool of my gift, felt like grinding away with that hand drill — difficult to operate, too slow, and yielding rough results. Wouldn't it be nice to plug in to a supernatural power source where I could electrify my excavations, get useful pointers, or — even better — instant answers? Wouldn't it be grand to get help from a source that *knew*?

Colby — if he existed outside of my head and my heart — had never really been able to do that for me. Briefly, it crossed my mind that I knew Colby was a good guy, and he wasn't feeding me answers, which might mean that an entity offering to help me might not be righteous, but the thought was fleeting.

"Do you think it *does* know?" I asked Madame. "I mean, can it really help me?"

"Girl, those aren't the same question," she said darkly.

I wasn't really listening. I was toying with the pros and cons of another temptation, a stronger one. Apart from proving myself to others, wouldn't it be great to settle this argument with *myself* one way or another, once and for all? Even *if* Madame Laveau was merely some kind of super-intuitive mind reader, she wouldn't be able to pluck an answer to the Broussard murders out of my head, because I *had* no answers. So if she told me something that turned out to be true, then that would *have* to mean that she'd gotten it from a source other than me. It would open the door to believing in things I'd been determined to give no credence to, yes, but at least I'd *know*. I could stop this ridiculous, exhausting, endless shillyshallying about what was real and what was imaginary.

And really, what did I have to lose?

Nobody would know. I could predict all too well how my parents would react — my father with dismissive laughter, my mother with horror. So I simply wouldn't tell them. And for sure, I wouldn't tell Ryan, not ever. I couldn't say for certain how he'd react, but I was pretty sure he wouldn't look favorably on me doing a deal with the devil. Ryan Jackson literally sang in the church choir. I knew secrets weren't great for relationships, but how harmful could this one possibly be?

"Well?" Madame said.

"Ask it what it knows." The words spilled out before I'd consciously decided to utter them.

Madame Laveau muttered something under her breath. "You sure you want this? You be knock-knocking at the door of evil, girl. And what you going to do when it opens? There won't be no going back once you cross the threshold. Or when *it* does," she added with another glance at the spot beside me.

I was so tempted to cross this line. *Another* line, I realized, because I'd already crossed lines in bringing down the Button Man. I'd tapped into my shadow side, my own well of moral ambiguity that had allowed me to torture a psychologically damaged man, to neutralize the threat of him, at any cost. Had I always had that dark side? Had I been born with it? Or had it been born in me — a little seed planted in my time of darkest grief that flourished in the fertile soil of my despair? Or maybe something more than Colby's spirit had merged with me in the black sucking depths of Plover Pond, the place where the evil of his murder had happened, the spot where I'd drifted across into the land of the dead, even if only briefly.

*How*ever, *wherever* it had come from, there was a part of me that believed the end justified the means. Right now, it was telling me to go ahead and accept the offered help. Even just a little hint. A hint couldn't hurt, could it?

Madame thrust her chin forward and snapped her fingers in my face. "Evil is easy. But what comes easy? It don't come cheap. It costs you one way or another. You take a minute and think 'bout that."

I sat back in the chair, took a deep breath, and considered. My head, motivated by ego and reinforced with rationalizations, said,

"What's the harm?" But my heart beat quickly and in a rhythm fueled by fear, not excitement. My whole body felt heavy with dread. I stood at a crossroads. I'd never been religious and had renounced the very idea of a God when Colby was murdered, but now, listening to my deepest core, I discovered that I did at least believe in the existence of both good and evil. Never had I known how very thin the line between them was, how easily crossed.

I blew out a breath, placed both my hands palm down on the table between Madame Laveau and me, and said, "I'm sure."

– 38 –

"I'm sure that I *don't* want the entity's help," I told Madame Laveau. "I want it gone. You need to get rid of it for me."

Her body sagged in relief, but she roused herself sufficiently to say crossly, "*Me?* I ain't a spirit exterminator, girl. *You* called it—"

"I did not!"

"And you gotta send it back."

"Urgh!" My frustration had returned, but the fear and dread had lifted from my body. "And how the hell am I supposed to do that?"

"I got instructions for you right here." She rifled through a pile of papers on a shelf and handed me a faint photocopy titled "Spell to cast off unwanted attachments."

I scanned the list of ingredients.

"You can buy most of that right here in the store," Madame assured me.

"Why does that not surprise me?"

"You must do the ritual in a graveyard, and the best time is at twilight."

"Seriously? That's some Hollywood vampire bullshit right there. Besides, sunset is at, what — seven o'clock? Where am I going to find a cemetery that stays open so late?"

She glowered at me. "Fine, but not in the noonday sun, hear? And if you doing it in the daytime, you'll need *two* banishing candles and extra cayenne." We stood up, and she poked a bony finger into my sternum. "Then you go home, all the way north, you hear me? Do the ritual, then leave this town. There is nothing for you here except trouble. Trouble and temptation."

"Sounds like a good title for my autobiography." Tapping the spell sheet, I added, "It says I need something given to me by an older woman. And I don't think unsolicited advice counts, because how would I" — I read off the printed instructions — "place that 'diagonally on top of the tombstone?'"

She returned my expectant look with a dirty one of her own. "Here." She pulled a pin out of a pincushion and handed it to me. "Make sure the sharp end points east."

I threaded it carefully into the hem of my shirt and pulled aside the curtain that screened off her room.

"Best you add some of your hair to the vessel, too, since he like it so much," Madame said after me.

"Yeah, yeah."

Ten minutes later, I left with the paper clutched in one hand, a sack full of spell ingredients in the other, and the strong conviction that I'd just been well and truly fleeced. I felt like a naïve tourist in from the farm for the day. Worse, I'd forgotten Henry's candy and had to go back and spend even more in the store, where the assistant was now greeting me by name.

On my way back to the hotel, I detoured past Broussard's restaurant. A shopfitter's van was parked outside, and workers were dragging out rolls of old carpet and carrying in ladders and plastic shelving. The sound of banging and hammering drifted out from inside. I watched with a slight pang of something like regret as a woman in paint-splattered coveralls scraped the gold lettering of the restaurant's name off the window. In a day or two, there'd be nothing left of Broussard's except memories.

My stomach was empty and my nerves frayed, so I headed two doors up to the steampunk bar for a little something to mollify both. CJ's eyes lit up when he saw me, and Lisette, perched on a stool behind the counter, gave me a big smile of recognition.

"Garnet!"

"Shouldn't you be in school?" I asked her.

"I'm sick," she declared. She looked the picture of rosy-cheeked health.

I ordered a Diet Coke and some hot wings, and while I waited for my food, I attended to business. I sent Anthony Cooper a text, checking how his sister was doing, and Bashir one asking who had purchased the property at the auction.

The wings were spicy enough to bring a pleasant burn to my lips, and I gave CJ — who was being kept busy by a group clustered around a woman wearing a bride-to-be sash — the thumbs-up.

He grinned, and Lisette said, "I reminded him that you like it extra hot."

"Then you, young lady, get my thanks!"

She grinned. "You want to hear 'bout the gunshots again?"

"Sure," I said, licking my fingers.

"They went like this: pew … Pew. Pew … Pew-pew, pew-pew."

"Just like that, huh?" I said distractedly. Anthony's reply had just come through on my phone.

Duck off!

A second two-word text came in immediately after, making it clear Anthony didn't approve of AutoCorrect's version. I took it as a good sign, though, figuring that if his sister's condition had deteriorated — or worse — he would really have let me have it.

"*Just* like that," Lisette said.

I checked my phone again. No reply from Bashir.

I finished my meal, exchanging chitchat with my new BFF, and when I pulled cash out of my wallet to pay, the business card that I'd lifted from Jeron's room fell out. I'd completely forgotten I had it, but now, I wondered if it was the source of the niggle at the back of my mind.

"Cross your fingers for luck," I told Lisette and called the number. "You should've crossed your toes, too," I said, when I got an automated message that the number had been disconnected. I tapped my fingers on the countertop, thinking, then took a photograph of the reverse side of the card.

"Here goes nothing," I muttered, and sent the pic to Scott, Anthony, Francesca, and Bashir, each with the message:

> I know you don't want to
> hear from me, but do you

know whose number this is?
Do you recognize the
handwriting? Would
appreciate any help! Thanks,
Garnet (private investigator)

And while I was busy tying up loose ends …

Fishing the button I'd found in the cooler out of my jeans pocket, I sent a snap of it to Scott, Anthony, and Francesca — Bashir had already seen it and denied recognizing it — with the message:

And does this button belong
to you?

I wasn't seriously expecting a reply from any of them, so I was pleasantly surprised when Bashir called me back not two minutes later. Waving a goodbye to Lisette and her father, I answered and hurried outside.

Bashir sounded annoyed. "I cannot believe you're still asking questions about this, Miss McGee."

"Yeah, sorry to keep bugging you," I said, wondering why he hadn't just answered my questions in a text of his own. "I just—"

"The restaurant was bought by a Happily Asia After franchisee. They've been wanting to get a foothold in New Orleans for the last two years."

"Oh. Okay." I wasn't sure if I could do anything with that piece of information. "And the telephone number? It was on the back of a Broussard's business card."

"I don't recognize the number, but that handwriting is Melissa's."

"Melissa Broussard's? Are you sure?"

"I'd know it anywhere."

"Okay, thanks. And can I also just ask—"

"*Another* question?"

"Yeah, so I spoke to Melissa's father and—"

"I told you to call her sister."

"I did, but she wouldn't speak to me. Anyway, Walter Reed told me that Melissa and Terry weren't going to get divorced. In fact, he said they were reconciled and had been going to marriage counseling."

"Marriage counseling? Melissa and Terry?"

"Yeah."

"What else did he say?"

"That they were going to renew their marriage vows."

"That's not true!" Bashir insisted. "You can't believe what that man says. His memory is patchy; Melissa suspected that he had Alzheimer's."

"Can you be sure what she planned to do, though?"

"Yes. She was going to leave him and marry *me*."

It was impossible to know if he was telling the truth. And I really needed to know, because if Melissa had told her lover she planned on ending things with him and recommitting to her marriage, then that would've given Bashir another motive, in addition to the insurance payout, to want Terry dead. He could easily have contracted Jeron Cooper to kill her husband and set her free. But Terry had thrown a spanner into the works of that plan.

Then again, if Bashir had found out about the marital reconciliation, he might have plotted vengeance against the woman who'd broken his heart. Unlikely, I thought, but not impossible.

"What did he say about me?" Bashir asked.

"What's that?"

"What did Melissa's father tell you about me? Because if he said I threatened Terry, that's a lie, do you hear me? A lie!"

This was interesting.

"Want to tell me your side of that story?" I said. If I could just speak to him in person again, I was sure I'd be able to squeeze a few more details out of him.

"No, I do not. Goodbye, Miss—"

"He did tell me something about you!" I said quickly, before he could end the call. "Something very strange."

"What?" Bashir demanded.

"I'd prefer to talk in person. I'm in the French Quarter now if that suits you."

"It doesn't."

My phone buzzed with an incoming call holding, and in trying to send it to voicemail, I succeeded in disconnecting Bashir. I wasn't too bummed out, however, because it was Scott who was calling.

He didn't sound friendly, exactly, but he was at least polite. "I got your messages, Ms. McGee."

"Thank you for calling back." *Finally.*

"This investigation of yours — have you found out anything new?" he asked. "Or have you merely confirmed what the police found out?"

"There are some things that don't quite gel," I said, hoping to pique his curiosity. "I'd love to clarify a few things with you. Do you have a couple of minutes now? Or maybe we could meet up later for a quick chat?"

I was braced for him to hang up. So much so that when the line went quiet, I assumed he had. But then he spoke. "I can't talk now; I have a meeting starting."

"Later today? I go back home tomorrow."

"Well, I'll be visiting my family's grave at Metairie Cemetery later this afternoon. We could meet there."

How serendipitous was *this*? I could do the spell at the same time, killing two birds with one gravestone.

"Sure," I told him. "When and where exactly?"

"Let's say around five o'clock. The family tomb is in the northeast corner."

"Can we rather meet at the entrance or something?"

"I can't be sure of my times; it depends on how my afternoon goes. In fact, maybe we should scrap it — it would be rude to keep you hanging around, waiting for me."

"No, it's cool. I don't mind. I'll be in the northeast corner around five."

"How will I recognize you?" he asked.

Oh, crap. The moment he saw me, he'd recognize "Kimberley" from the bar at the golf club, but if I told him that now, explained how I'd pretended to be someone else, I stood no chance of getting to speak to him, so I merely said, "I have brown hair, and I'm wearing a red shirt."

"See you later."

I tried to call Bashir back, and when he didn't answer, I sent him a text:

I'll be at the entrance to
Metairie Cemetery at four
o'clock this afternoon if you
want to find out what I
know.

Three birds, one stone.

$$- 39 -$$

A quick internet search established that I'd be able to get to Metairie Cemetery on a streetcar from Canal Street, so I set out in a westerly direction, keeping my eyes open for the kind of store that might sell the one thing I hadn't been able to purchase at Madame Laveau's store. On the list of spell ingredients, between "a length of rope to bind the spirit" and "cayenne pepper to return negative energy to its source" was the item: "a heavy vessel of old metal, to hold the lure."

I'd spent enough time in the Quarter to know that most of its antiques stores were clustered around Royal and Chartres Streets, but I didn't want to double back — I'd spent the whole day crisscrossing the Quarter. Besides, that side of town was expensive, and I had no desire to waste money I could ill afford on some hocus pocus that was almost certainly pure baloney.

The deepening afternoon brought in a rising tide of tourists, touts called out happy-hour offers, and a twelve-man brass band ensconced on one corner blared out a quick-time version of "Camptown Races." I lingered to listen for a few minutes, my foot tapping in time to the doo-dah, doo-dah, then grinned as I spied a junk store down one of the quieter alleys.

Big Easy Bric-a-Brac and Treasures was located below street level, which meant, I realized with a little shock as I made my way down the narrow set of stairways into the store, that it was actually located below sea level. That might have been a fitting location if it truly housed treasures of the sort found on sunken pirate ships, but even by the dim light, it was clear that most of the stuff for sale was mere junk. The air was damp, and the smell of mildew and must caught in my throat. Coughing and wanting to get out as soon as possible, I walked straight up to the proprietor — a thin man wearing a beret of deep red velvet.

"Just browsing?" the man wheezed. The dank air in this place had clearly already taken its toll on his lungs. "Or can I help you with anything specific?"

"I need an old metal object." Would he think it rude if I pulled the neck of my shirt over my mouth and nose?

The man looked puzzled. "What kind of metal object?"

"Any kind." I checked the spell again, then folded it and returned it to my jeans pocket. "As long as it's old and heavy. And cheap."

"I have just the thing. Follow me." As he levered himself up out of his worn armchair, he was seized by a savage coughing fit.

Fearing any exertion might finish him off, I said, "Just point me in the right direction." Following his instructions, I weaved my way around stacked tables and between cluttered shelves to the far corner, where I found a large pewter beer tankard resting on a spindly-legged table.

"This is great!" I picked it up, appreciating the weight of it in my hand. Carrying it back to the man at the counter, I asked, "How much?"

"Twenty dollars." My face must've fallen, because he wheezed an asthmatic sigh and said, "I can let you have it for ten."

"Perfect!"

I handed over the cash and bolted up the stairs and out of the door, desperate to breathe in fresh air and rid my respiratory system of mold spores. I admired my purchase in the bright sunlight, turning it this way and that.

"Are you *kidding* me?" I said out loud.

"You talking to me?" a passing woman said aggressively.

"No!" I marched back down the stairs and handed the tankard back to the proprietor. "I don't want this."

"You just said it was perfect," he retorted.

"That was before I saw this." I pointed at the side of the mug, where some fool had engraved an image of a grinning gargoyle. "If I'd seen this, I wouldn't have bought it. But the light is so poor in here ..."

"*Caveat emptor.*"

"What's that mean?"

"It means I won't be giving you a refund."

"Okay," I said, exerting myself to keep my temper in check. "How about a trade-in, then? Do you have anything else? Old, heavy, metal receptacle. Cheap," I reminded him.

He sucked on an inhaler. "Sure, but you won't like it."

"Why? Does it also have a dumb gargoyle on it?" It wouldn't surprise me. I couldn't seem to get away from the horrible things.

"There, under that stool with the embroidered cushion."

I glanced to where he was pointing. "A potty? Seriously?"

"It's an iron chamber pot. I knew you wouldn't like it."

"It'll do." I marched over and dragged it out by its handle, sneezing at the puff of dust the movement sent into the air. The pot was enormous — just how large had the butt been that this had been made for? — and ugly, with peeling cobalt-blue paint and patches of rust. But it was indisputably both heavy *and* old. I lugged it over to the counter. "How much for this?"

"Twenty dollars."

"Seriously? It's junk. No one else will ever want it."

"One man's trash is another man's treasure."

"Fine. Good luck finding that man." I turned to go.

"I'll give you five dollars off for the tankard trade-in," the guy said quickly.

I stared at him, weighing the odds that I'd find something else that fit the bill before I'd need to catch the streetcar if I wanted to be at the cemetery gates by four o'clock.

"Take it or leave it," the man said.

I handed over my card. I was out of cash. "Charge it."

The man pointed to the sign above his head. *No credit card for purchases under twenty dollars.*

"Fine, then, twenty dollars!" I snarled, about ready to tear my hair out. "Want a pound of flesh to go with that?" I demanded as he put through the charge. "Maybe a pint of blood? A kidney?"

"You have a nice day now," he called after me as I trudged back up the stairs.

I dumped the plastic sack of spell ingredients into the potty and headed down the street, aware that I'd dropped twenty-five dollars in exchange for a piece of crap. It seemed oddly fitting, because all of it — the chamber pot; the herbs and candles and rope; the ridiculous ritual I'd purchased the stuff for — was nothing more than a great big pile of shit.

Was I really going to visit a graveyard at almost sunset, sprinkle salt and wave a sage bong around, and then pour whiskey into a pisspot?

Yes. Yes, I was. But not to rid me of a gargoyle attachment. At least not in the literal sense. For Madame, a "ritual" was some kind of magic spell, complete with exotic ingredients and mystical words to recite. But the truth was, we all performed rituals all the time: blowing out candles on a cake and singing a song on a child's birthday, bringing a tree indoors and decorating it every December, writing a list of resolutions every new year. And rituals had long held an important role in the field of psychotherapy. A psychologist might, for example, advise a client to complete a certain behavior — like writing an unposted letter, lighting a candle, or planting a tree — to celebrate an anniversary or consolidate a decision or symbolize closing a chapter in their life.

And that's why *I* would be doing the dumb spell — to mark the decision I'd made about what I was and wasn't prepared to do in my pursuit for justice. I'd drawn a line that I refused to cross, and the ritual, in its unforgettable silliness, would be a tangible way of cementing that so that I never forgot. So yes, I'd be performing Madame's ritual, but for sane and psychologically sound reasons. *And,* the silly, superstitious part of me interjected, *on the off chance that I did indeed have an entity attached to me, the ritual would put paid to it also.*

I shoved the intrusive thought aside. It was getting exhausting straddling two worlds.

– 40 –

Metairie Cemetery was a short walk around a corner and under the highway from the end of the streetcar line. I was waiting near the ornamental fountain at the front gates by a quarter to four, curious to see if Bashir would come. He'd sounded worried when I'd said Walter Reed had told me something odd about him. Why? What didn't he want me to know?

"Are you here for the tour?" a young woman with a buzz cut and a tattoo like an ivy vine climbing up her neck asked me.

I opened my mouth to tell her no then saw that her luminous orange T-shirt read "FREE walking tours."

"I'm supposed to be meeting someone here," I said. "Do you mind if I listen in while I wait?"

"No problem."

A group of around ten people had already gathered near her, and she began telling them about Metairie — that it had been founded in 1872, occupied a site of approximately one hundred and fifty acres of prime real estate, and that the land had originally been used as a racetrack.

Doo-dah, doo-dah, my "Camptown Races" earworm chimed in.

"The cemeteries of New Orleans," she pronounced it "New OR-linz," as I'd noticed most locals did, "are nicknamed the Cities of the Dead. Metairie alone has around seven thousand tombs, most of which house multiple occupants."

One of her group gave a low whistle. "That's a lot of dead people."

I checked my watch. Five to four. No Bashir.

"The burial vaults are monuments to some of the city's oldest families, and often, multiple generations of family members are interred in a single tomb," the guide continued.

"How does that work, then?" another of the tourists, a Brit by his accent, asked.

I'd been wondering the same thing, imagining piles of bodies being crammed inside and shuffled up to make room for new arrivals.

"In this city, we have above-ground tombs because of regular floods," the guide explained. "New bodies are interred in the upper chamber. These get very hot due to the climate here and the structure of the stone or brick vaults."

"Like an oven!" a kid in her group said.

His mom tittered about being respectful to the dead, but the guide didn't seem to take offense.

"Exactly," she said. "So biodegradation happens very quickly, and by the time the next person in the family dies, that first body has usually already decomposed."

The kid's sister made a gagging sound.

"The earlier remains are bagged and moved into a lower

vault. A normal-sized tomb could house dozens of people's remains over time."

Four o'clock came and went. I stepped up onto the low wall around the fountain to see better, but there was still no sign of Terry's former partner and Melissa's former lover. I climbed back down before someone made me and sent Bashir a text.

> Are you still coming?

Then, in case there was more than one entrance, I followed up with:

> I'm at the main entrance on Pontchartrain Blvd. At the water fountain.

"Scores of famous people lie interred here at Metairie," the guide said as a couple more visitors joined her group, "including ten state governors, eight New Orleans mayors, and many Civil War veterans, including P.G.T. Beauregard himself, the Confederate General who ordered the first shots of the Civil War fired at Fort Sumter in 1861."

Maybe Bashir hadn't caught the name of the cemetery. I sent him another message.

> Metairie Cemetery

"Inside, we'll visit the final resting places of many legends and a couple of scoundrels, including Calogero Minacore, crime boss and one-time head of the New Orleans mafia."

The guide made shooting gestures with her hands, and I thought again of Lisette and her "pew-pew" impression of the shots she'd heard on the night of July Fourth.

"But enough talking! Let's go inside, and I'll show you the resting places of many more of Nola's notables, including Eve Curie, daughter of the famous scientist Marie Curie, and in the so-called Millionaire's Row, the tomb which Anne Rice, author of *Interview With a Vampire,* built for her husband and where she will be interred when she passes away one day. If you get separated from the group, remember that the cemetery closes at 5:30 p.m. sharp, so you want to keep an eye on the time."

I checked my phone. Four fifteen. No messages. Damn. It looked like Bashir was going to be a no-show.

The visitors followed their guide down a curving pathway inside the cemetery and disappeared from sight. I paced up and down in front of the entrance, checking every car that passed. More people were leaving than entering Metairie now. I needed to get a move on if I wanted to finish the banishing ritual before meeting up with Scott. I gave it another few minutes, just to be sure, then called it quits. Checking the compass app on my phone to figure out which direction was northeast, I went inside, texting as I walked.

> If you don't want to come,
> fine. I'll just have to tell the
> cops what I learned about
> you.

There. If that didn't lure him out, I didn't know what would.

> But if you want a chance to explain your side of it, I'll be inside the cemetery, in the northeast corner. Wearing a red shirt.

The vast grounds of Metairie were magnificent, with enormous trees, rolling lawns, meandering pathways, and tombs spaced at generous intervals. Given its age, I'd expected the place to be more rundown, with crumbling bricks and flaking plasterwork. But this was clearly where the well-to-do laid their dearly departed, and it felt more like a well-maintained park than an old graveyard. I would never have thought that tombs could be beautiful, but there was a kind of haunting loveliness to the granite and marble mausoleums crowned with fierce griffins, drooping saints, or weeping angels and draped with fine floral scrollwork cut into the stone or adorned with stone crosses, orbs, and urns. Here and there, a smear of vivid color from more festive tributes — fresh flowers and strings of beads — caught the eye, and the low afternoon sun streamed through stained glass windows, setting rainbow lights to dancing on neat grass patches encircled by low iron fences.

Not even the vaults of questionable taste — family tombs that looked like miniature churches, complete with spires and steeples, and even one built in the shape of a pyramid with a stone sphinx standing guard outside — could disturb the peaceful atmosphere that lay over everything, like a funeral shroud made of fine gauze.

After my near-death experience, I'd informed my parents that if I died before them, I wanted to be cremated and have my ashes scattered in the mountains of Vermont. But looking around me, I figured this spot might be a wonderful place in which to lie for all eternity. Then I recollected that despite their fine vaulted ceilings and classical columns, these structures were nothing more than slow-working crematoriums for decomposing flesh. Shuddering, I resolved to leave my postmortem arrangements unchanged.

The sun tucked itself behind a cloud, and as I was passing a vault built to resemble the ruins of an ancient abbey, the skin on the back of my neck prickled a warning that someone was watching me. I glanced over my shoulder. No one was following me as far as I could tell, but in the tour guide's group — now clustered around a nearby tomb with a statue of a man playing a saxophone — a pale, beaky woman with the posture of a vulture stared at me blankly.

Okay, then, time to get moving.

– 41 –

Checking the compass again, I took off, walking quickly and softly singing the tune that had been looping around my brain like the bobtail nag on the five-mile-long racetrack of the song but this time with the words of the internet meme: "Off to do some sketchy shit; doo-dah, doo-dah. Hope I get away with it; oh, doo-dah-day!"

Once more, I felt eyes on me. Someone *was* watching me; I could feel it. Feigning nonchalance, I ambled around the corner of a tomb, out of the line of sight of anyone behind me, then quickly spun around and peered out past the edge of the cold stone. No one.

I huffed out a frustrated breath. I was just imagining things again. I stood still for a minute, listening with my ears for the sound of footsteps and with my heart and mind for a warning from Colby. Madame Laveau might've said he was blocked by the gargoyle, but the gargoyle had been a dream. All I heard was the susurrating hush of leaves ruffled by the breeze. It looked like a storm was building. Heavy clouds the color of ash veiled the sky, and the light was dimming. Hopefully, the rain would hold off until I'd finished the candle part of my banishing ceremony. Shivering, I made my way back to the path that headed mostly east.

Without warning, a giant of a man in a gray, flapping coat stepped out from behind a tree about twenty feet ahead and headed directly toward me with long strides. Anthony Cooper, my brain said, come to finish me off. He broke into a run. I needed to flee, but my feet stayed welded to the spot. As he closed the distance between us, my mouth opened wide, and I let out a high-pitched, wordless scream. The man's eyes boggled. He halted in his tracks and gave me a fearful glance like *I* was the dangerous one. Then, giving me a wide berth, he took off again, running down toward the route that led back toward the gates.

Not Anthony, just a young Black man hurrying home before the storm broke. I was tempted to run after him, stammering excuses that I wasn't crazy or racist, that I was just an easily spooked idiot set on edge by the lengthening shadows and increasingly creepy atmosphere. But the guy had already vanished from view.

Cursing loudly and vehemently, I decided two things: one, to get on with the ritual immediately and two, to vacate these deathly premises as soon as possible. And — okay, *three* things — if ever in the future I *was* faced with imminent attack, to fight back or run the hell away, rather than standing as still as a graveyard statue.

With twenty minutes to spare before I was due to meet Scott, I neared the deserted northeast corner of the cemetery. I wandered around for a minute, searching for a normal-sized tombstone, because sure as Southern tea was sweet, my piece of rope was not going to be long enough to wind around one of the huge vaults. Spotting a row of simple tombstones, each with their own flat, grass-covered plot, I chose the one that looked the most neglected — stained, mossy headstone, and no flowers — so as to minimize the risk of messing with a grave that someone still cared about. I emptied out my bag of ingredients on the grass, unfolded the printed spell, read through the steps one more time, and then began.

Setting the heavy chamber pot up against the headstone and, silently apologizing to Mildred Landry, who, according to the inscription had been a wife, mother, and lifelong teetotaler, I poured a generous glug from the old soda bottle filled with whiskey, which Madame Laveau had sold me under the counter.

"Liquor to welcome you," I said out loud, feeling like a complete fool.

Remembering Madame's extra instruction, I yanked out a few hairs from my head and added them to the potty to lure in the fiendish trichophiliac, and then I paced the perimeter of the small grave, sprinkling salt along its grassy border.

"Salt to hold you," I read from the spell.

Grabbing the coil of thick sisal rope, I wound it around the headstone and chamber pot, tying a loose knot.

"Rope to bind you."

I extracted the steel pin from the hem of my shirt and checked my compass before placing it in the correct orientation on the very top of the rounded tombstone. Glancing around to check nobody was nearby, witnessing this, and that Scott hadn't arrived, I lit the small bundle of sage tied with red cotton thread and waved the fragrant smoke all around myself.

"Sage to cast you off."

According to the instructions, cayenne pepper needed to be sprinkled at the toe end of the grave, but when I opened the bottle Madame had sold me, the spice was clumped together and refused to leave the bottle. Removing the lid entirely, I turned it upside down on the grass and hammered the base of the bottle with a small rock. The entire contents shot out, leaving a red heap of powder on the grass. Well, she *had* said to use extra. Flattening the heap with the toe of my boot, I set the two white banishing candles on top of it. The idea of the spell, as far as I could figure out, was to light the candles, which symbolized good, and then walk toward the tombstone while holding them, driving any evil or unwanted spiritual attachment back from the light toward the liquored-up darkness of the metal receptacle.

"Colby, if you're here, don't get between me and the headstone, or else you'll wind up trapped in the potty too," I said out loud.

I opened the baggie of frankincense resin and dusted the tops of the candles with the brown powder. It was time to light the candles. The wind picked up around me, sweeping dry leaves, flower petals, and scraps of paper along the ground. It was as dark as the twilight Madame had recommended. I was alone and feeling increasingly unnerved. Movement in my peripheral vision had me snapping my head to the right, but it was just the boughs of a cedar moving in a gust of air. My imagination was running riot; next thing, I'd be hearing the howl of a werewolf.

But instead, what I heard as I flicked the lighter on was a man's voice.

$$- 42 -$$

"Ms. McGee? Is that you?"

I spun around. Scott Broussard was limping toward me.

"I saw the red shirt and thought it might be you," he said. "What are you doing there?"

"Nothing, nothing," I said quickly.

"What in the Sam Hill?" he exclaimed as he drew close enough to see my face in the low light. "It's you! Balloon girl, from the club."

"Yup, it's me."

"What the hell? Who *are* you?"

"I'm Garnet McGee, the private investigator."

"How *dare* you? I trusted—"

"Look, I'm really sorry about not fully introducing myself at the club, but—"

"Not fully introducing yourself?" He crossed his arms and glared at me. "You out-and-out pretended to be someone else."

"No! I mean yes, sure. But not entirely. The bit about my boyfriend being murdered was true, and I *was* in town for a romantic weekend. I just also … you know … happen to be a private investigator."

"Leaving messages on my phone," Scott grumbled. "Ringing the bell at my house, following me to the club."

"I wasn't the only one hiding the truth and pretending to be someone else, though, was I?" I interjected.

"What do you mean?"

"Playing at being your own butler? What's that about?"

For a moment, he looked stunned, then he surprised me by bursting into laughter. "Busted! What gave me away?"

"Nothing. You were a very plausible Jeeves. I just recognized your voice when you spoke at the club."

"I didn't recognize yours."

"I disguised it a little."

"You sure had me fooled," he said, sounding less angry.

"Look, I'm sorry I did it, but I really wanted to hear what happened from someone who was *there*."

He stared down to where his toe stubbed a small hollow into the dirt.

"I won't take up much of your time," I said. "I just wanted to ask a couple of questions, straighten out a few details in my mind. Please."

He looked away as though considering, then back at me. "No more lies, okay?"

"Sure, of course."

"Then let's sit down. I've been on my feet all day, and my leg's killing me."

"Sorry. Yeah, just not right here." I indicated the grave where I'd been going about my silly business.

"Seriously, though, what *are* you doing, with the rope and the …" He gestured toward the chamber pot.

"Oh, just a bit of tourist fun." Noticing that I was still holding the lighter, I shoved it into my pocket. "You know, trying to get into the spooky spirit of this town. How about right over here?"

Scott whipped out a large handkerchief and spread it on the damp grass for me like a real gentleman, and we both sat down, backs against the double headstone of the grave adjacent to Mildred's. Then he retrieved a silver hip flask from an inner jacket pocket and held it out to me.

"Can I offer you a drink?"

"As old metal receptacles go," I said, "that's a mighty fine one."

"Want a sip?"

"As it happens, I have my own private bottle." I leaned across to snag the old soda bottle, which still had a good few inches of whiskey sloshing around inside, and tapped it against his swanky flask. "Cheers!"

"To life," Scott said solemnly.

"To life."

The first sip went down my throat like liquid razorblades — Madame Laveau hadn't wasted good liquor to fill the bottles she sold for spells. I screwed up my face and shuddered.

Scott laughed softly beside me. "What did you want to ask me? You said there were some details that didn't gel. Were they about the business card?"

"Yeah. Bashir confirmed it's your mother's handwriting."

"Uh-huh."

"But he didn't recognize the number."

"Can I see it again?"

I extracted the card from my pocket and handed it over.

Scott studied the front and back. "I think it's the number she used when she hired new staff and didn't want them to have her personal number."

"Right, okay, that makes sense." I risked another sip. "But can you think of any reason why Jeron would've hung onto her card? I mean, he would've seen her at the restaurant all the time if he needed to speak to her, right?"

"I guess."

"So why keep the card?"

Scott shrugged. "You've got me there." He sipped from his flask. I was willing to bet it contained a better grade of booze than mine did.

"Can I have the card back?"

"What? Oh, sure. Here you go."

I shoved it back into my pocket. "I have another question, but it's … delicate."

"Oh, yeah?"

"Were you aware that your mother and Khurran Bashir …" I let my voice trail off.

"Were having an affair? Yeah, I knew." He looked down at his flask, and I couldn't see his expression.

"How did you feel about that?"

"I guess no one *wants* to think of their mother in that capacity, but I didn't begrudge her a chance at some fun and happiness. Not when my father was a serial offender."

"So you knew about that, too?"

"*Everyone* knew about that. He was hardly discreet."

A twig snapped behind us. "What was that?" I said, peering over the top of the tombstone.

"What?"

"Nothing, I guess." More whiskey. It had numbed my mouth and gullet, and was going down smoother with every sip. "And 'some fun and happiness' — that's how their relationship struck you? I mean, you didn't think she'd finally met the great love of her life?"

"I don't think the words 'Khurran Bashir' and 'great' go together. Look, he's a nice guy, okay? Honest, kind, patient. But he's not …"

"Charismatic?" I said, thinking of how Scott's grandfather had described Terry.

"Exactly."

"So you don't think your mother was planning to leave your father for Bashir?"

Scott gave me a sharp look. "That's what you're thinking? That Bashir tried to get rid of my father so he could have my mother?"

"And the money," I said. "Don't forget the money."

"The money? You mean from selling the restaurant?"

"Yup. And also the life insurance."

"Right! Wow. Can you prove it, though? Because the police have closed the case."

"I can't prove a damn thing. But if karma's real, he'll get what's coming, one way or another." I swirled the remains of the rotgut around in the base of the bottle. I could feel the alcohol softening my edges. "You believe in karma, Scott?"

"Me?" He smiled. "No. I believe we create our own fate." He tilted his hip flask to drink the last sip, then screwed the lid back on. "Well, that's me done."

"Before you go," I said as he made to rise, "can I ask just one more thing?"

"Yeah."

"Can you take me through that night again, but just the shooting bits."

"Why?"

"I'm not sure."

He gave me a doubtful look.

"I just … I have a niggle at the back of my brain, and I can't quite put my finger on it."

"Okay," he said slowly. "In the kitchen, when my father grabbed Jeron, the gun went off and …" Scott paused, swallowing hard. "And the shot hit my mother."

"*Pew*," I said softly.

"What's that?"

"Nothing. The next one?"

"He shot my father and sister in the cooler."

"Two shots each?"

Scott nodded.

"*Pew-pew, pew-pew.* Then next, he shot you when you tackled him outside the office?"

"Yeah. We wrestled for the gun. He shot me, then I shot him."

"*Pew. Pew.*" I gave a frustrated sigh. "It doesn't fit."

"What doesn't fit?"

"There was another witness that night."

"*What?*"

"An earwitness — if that's a thing. Someone heard the gunshots."

"Who?"

"A kid who was nearby. But she heard a different pattern. *Pew ... Pew. Pew ... Pew-pew, pew-pew.* It doesn't match up, see? The rhythm doesn't match."

"Maybe she remembered wrong? Or even heard wrong? There were fireworks all night."

"Yeah, you're probably right. Occam's Razor, right? The simplest explanation is probably the correct one."

Maybe, when Lisette had said, "Just like that," she hadn't meant that exact pattern and rhythm, she'd merely been reinforcing the *pew-pew* rather than the *bang-bang* sound. Ten to one I'd misunderstood her. So why did I feel like something was still nagging at me?

"It usually is," Scott said. "We should go. I don't want to get locked in here overnight."

"Scared of ghosts?"

He gave me a fleeting smile. "Can I ask *you* a question before I go?"

"Shoot," I said, then winced at my choice of words.

"Did you ... see ... anything about that night? In a vision or something? I mean, are you really a psychic, or is that just some bullshit patter to get people interested enough so they'll talk to you?"

"It's real." The cynical, disbelieving smile on his face was one I knew all too well, and it goaded me into saying, "Want proof? Give me something of yours to touch. That hip flask will do."

It began as soon as my fingers touched the smooth metal.

– 43 –

An electric thrill rippled over my scalp, my chest swelled, my breath paused. I closed my hands around the hip flask and shut my eyes against the clouds and graves and Scott's skeptical expression. Then I sank into the images that were already flickering into being inside of me.

"What are we gonna do, man? This wasn't supposed to happen!" The young man, the one with the gun, pulls off the ski mask, wipes his sweaty face with it, and drops it to the ground.

The man in the blue shirt pulls a hip flask out of his jacket and takes several swallows. His eyes move from side to side as he walks down the narrow hallway. He's thinking hard.

The younger man gives an agonized groan. "Your mother, man! I had no beef with her. Why'd your old man come at me like that? Nobody was supposed to die! What the fuck we gonna do now?"

"We stick to the plan. We stay calm. We do what we planned."

"Are you kidding me?" He moves from one foot to the other, his voice rising in agitation. "That plan's already gone sideways, in case you didn't notice, bro."

"Garnet!"

I opened my eyes and stared open-mouthed at Scott.

"Are you okay?" he said.

"Yeah. Yeah." I took a gulp from my bottle, coughed, and cleared my throat. "Oh, Scott, what did you do?" The words were out before I could bite them back.

"What do you mean?" He wasn't looking incredulous anymore, no sir, no ma'am. He was looking worried.

All day, I'd been standing at different crossroads, choosing between paths. Stay or go. Back out or head in. Stay strong or give in. And here I was again, needing to choose which road to take. I could duck out of this exchange — pacify him with a lie about some random thing I'd "seen" him do and walk out of this cemetery right now. I could go home, hug Ryan, give Henry his candy, and find missing dogs. It was the safer option, the more sensible path.

But the thing about dying was that it had dulled my fear of danger, because what is the fear of danger but a fear of death? And having died once, dying again didn't seem so bad to me. Not that I was in any kind of hurry, but I was prepared to risk things I never would've before. A foreshortened sense of future was a symptom of posttraumatic stress disorder. I knew that. Knew that individuals who'd had a close brush with death tended afterwards to believe that they'd die young and were inclined to take stupid risks because of that fatalistic attitude. I was no exception.

"I saw," I told Scott. "I saw Jeron in that stretch of hallway between the kitchen and the back office. Panicking, sweating. Taking off the ski mask and dropping it. You must've gone back afterwards and placed it in the kitchen. Clever, because losing the mask would've given Jeron his supposed motivation to kill you and your excuse to shoot him. And how would anyone know it hadn't come off in the tussle with your father except me? In my vision before, I saw that he was still wearing it in the kitchen, even after the scuffle, but it didn't click. *That* was what was bothering me. *That* was the itch."

"What are you talking about?" His voice was breathy with unease.

"Oh, Scott, don't." I shook my head sadly. "I know what happened. I *saw* it."

For several long moments, he sat silently, eyes flicking from side to side, considering the options, calculating the odds, recalibrating his course of action, just as he had that night. Then, he cursed softly and said, "You're the real deal, then? You actually are psychic?"

Finally, the validation I'd been looking for.

"Yeah," I said. "Yeah, I am."

"I'm going to need more alcohol."

I handed him my bottle. He took a long slug, winced, and then slumped back against the headstone.

"Tell me what you saw, what you know," he said.

"I didn't see everything, but what I don't know for sure, I can guess."

Scott glanced at me with an evaluating stare, and I sat upright. "You should know that I told my boyfriend I was meeting you here this afternoon. He's a cop. A police chief to be exact," I warned him, though honestly, Scott didn't feel like a threat. He seemed perfectly calm and relaxed — resigned even — and there was no whisper of a warning of danger from Colby.

"Garnet, I have no intention of harming you. You can't imagine how complicated, how deeply sad and utterly exhausting these last few months have been. What went down that night? It wasn't supposed to work out like that. I can't even express how much I regret what happened. None of those deaths were supposed to happen."

"I believe you. I mean, that's the reason why Jeron wore a ski mask in the first place, right? You didn't want anyone to recognize him. You didn't plan for anyone to get shot."

"*No.* Hand on my heart, no," Scott said earnestly. "We just wanted to give my father a little fright."

Hah, I'd been right about someone wanting to shake Terry Broussard up enough to get out of the restaurant trade. But it had been his son, not some faceless gangster, who'd wanted to scare him.

"You wanted him to sell the restaurant," I said.

"It had to be done. We were up to our eyeballs in debt, and we needed to settle up before we lost absolutely everything. But he wouldn't listen to reason," Scott said and added bitterly, "He never did."

"So, you came up with the idea of an armed robbery?" I prompted.

"*She* did."

"Brittany?" Had her I-adore-my-father attitude just been an act, then?

"No, my mother."

"Your *mother* had the idea? Wow. So you were in it together, then?"

Of course they were, the pair who'd been so close, bound by their love and mutual common sense. And their contempt for Terry's libertine lifestyle and spendthrift ways.

"We had such fun planning it. It was like a prank, a trick we'd be playing on him." Scott wiped the back of a hand across his eyes.

"If it was just a prank, why was the gun loaded?"

"It was Jeron's job to get a gun. I didn't tell him to put bullets in it!"

Why had he done it? I wondered. Was he just playing gangster, or had he imagined a circumstance when he'd need to fire it, to give a warning shot, perhaps?

"Your mother was the one who dealt with Jeron," I said. "That's why he had that business card, so he could call and make arrangements." I thought a moment. "It was a burner phone, so no calls could be traced back to her or you." That's why Bashir hadn't recognized the number. Then I gasped as another piece of the puzzle slotted into place. "And you got rid of it afterwards. That was your hand dropping it into a bucket of soaking dishtowels." The glimpse had been so brief — swamped by other unimportant impressions, and displaced by the raw screams and intense images of the gun — that I hadn't noted the shirt.

Scott stared at me wide-eyed and gave a little "huh" of a laugh. "You saw all that too?"

"Maybe it was even your button in the cooler? The card and

the button — my messages are what brought you here tonight? You wanted to find out what I knew?"

He sighed, leaning back against the headstone. "I had to check. I had to be sure."

Ahead of us, something dark fluttered in the dim light between the trees. An owl? A bat?

"So," I said, "you and your mom hired Jeron. He was supposed to come in—"

"To come out from the storeroom, where he'd been hiding since we locked up. We were all gathered in the dining room to celebrate my birthday with a late dinner."

"I'm curious," I said. "Was your father going to buy you a Porsche too? And bring you into more of a management role, like he did with your sister on her twenty-fifth."

Scott swung his head from side to side. "He said the time wasn't right."

And Scott had realized that it might never be.

"So Jeron came out, waved the gun around, made some threats. Then he was supposed to lock your family in the cooler and take you to the office, where he'd rough you up a little in full view of the security camera."

"I had to take one for the team," Scott explained, "to make it look convincing. To make my father feel bad and worried about all our safety. To give him some incentive to sell."

"Jeron told his girlfriend he had an easy-money gig coming up."

"We told him not to tell anyone anything."

"Good help is so hard to find these days, isn't it?" I said, and Scott's lips twitched. "He was supposed to leave you behind to 'rescue' your family while he got away with the bag of takings?"

"That was his cut."

"I don't think so. He bragged to his girl about *big* money."

"We planned to give him a top-up afterwards, and a promotion."

"Only it didn't pan out that way."

"No, because my asshole father had to go and fuck things up, just like he always did!" Scott played with the plastic lid of the soda bottle, squeezing and turning it between his fingers. "Your father still around?"

"*Mine*? Yeah, he is."

"What's he like?" Scott sounded mildly curious.

"He's a good guy. Kind, smart. He's in my corner."

"That's so cool. It must be amazing to have a dad like that. *My* father, on the other hand, was the worst dickwad you can imagine." He crushed the bottle in his fist. "God, I *hated* him."

"Did you hate your sister too?" I asked, thinking of the bullets straight to her face, right into her eye.

"Well, I didn't *love* her. There wasn't really any 'her' *to* love. She was just a satellite to my father, moving in his orbit, following his orders, pandering to his vanity, spouting his opinions. He could've told her the moon was made of cheese, and she would've insisted it was true. Fancy dying before you've ever lived."

"Yeah," I said, though what I was thinking was, *She didn't "die," though, did she? She was murdered.*

$$-\ 44\ -$$

"Where'd you learn to handle a gun?" I asked Scott.

"My grandfather took Brittany and me shooting when I turned eighteen. I don't own my own weapon, but I've kept my hand in at the range over the years."

"Your grandfather on your mother's side? I spoke to him, you know? About your family." I sighed. "If I'd *listened* better, I would've suspected you sooner."

"Why's that? Did old Walter describe me as the murderous type?"

"No, nothing like that. He told me an interesting story, but I understood it all wrong. I thought it meant you were kindhearted, merciful enough to want to spare an innocent creature's life. But really, you were just pragmatic, like Walter said. Quick thinking and coolheaded. Able to quickly assess a situation, come to a decision, and do what needed to be done. Prepared to get your hands dirty if necessary. And that's what you did that night, isn't it? You kept your head, told Jeron not to panic, and recalibrated when your father ruined the plan."

"I was an idiot for ever expecting he'd do what he was told. He was such an arrogant egotist that he couldn't allow another man to have the upper hand, even when there was a gun pointed at him, even when his family was in danger. And he *always* overestimated his own abilities."

"And then your mom got shot."

"I blame *him!*" Scott almost shouted. "He as good as killed her!"

"Scott—"

"Why didn't he just *listen*? He's screwed things up for me my whole life. I hate him! I loved my mother, *loved* her! My life without her is hollow. Empty!"

I wasn't sure how to react. I felt like he needed to be held and comforted, but I had no inclination to do so, so I sat still and quiet as the outburst spilled from him.

"And he took her away, spoiled everything," he raged. "And for what? So afterwards he could brag to everyone that he'd been the big hero? He wasn't a hero. He was a conceited, selfish, stupid prick!" He drew in a ragged breath, clearly trying to regain control of himself, and said bitterly, "Look at what he made me do!"

"Yeah, suddenly, the whole plan had gone to hell," I said, picturing the events of that night. "Your mother was dead, and that changed everything. Without her there to rein in his excesses, your father would be free to do what he wanted with the restaurant. He and Brittany would be in charge — in charge of the business *and* in charge of you. In seconds, your position had gone from bad to worse. You were thinking fast, and you knew they had to go too."

"Yeah, you can see that, can't you?" Scott said, sounding grateful that I understood.

"But you knew Jeron would never agree to do the shooting?"

"No. He was freaking out completely. All he wanted was to get away. It had taken some work to persuade him to do the fake robbery in the first place; no way was he going to do what needed to be done."

"He wasn't a killer," I said.

I'd share that with Anthony and Mrs. Cooper. Hopefully, it would comfort them to know they hadn't been wrong about the young man's essential nature.

"*I* wasn't a killer, either," Scott said resentfully. "My father forced my hand. It wasn't my fault, not really. If he'd just done as he was told for once in his miserable life ..."

"Okay," I said in a soothing tone, not challenging the massive self-delusion and denial. "So your father and sister were locked in the cooler as planned, and you went with Jeron to the office?"

"I told him to stick to the plan. But—"

"You knew you couldn't leave a witness?"

"He had to go. He'd shown he wasn't the sort of guy who could keep his cool under pressure. If the cops came around came asking questions, he'd have told them everything."

Scott, on the other hand, was exactly the sort of guy to keep his cool when the cops came calling.

"So you pushed Jeron out of the camera's range, grabbed the gun and shot him."

Scott nodded.

"Then you shot yourself?"

"I knew I'd be suspected, so it had to look like I'd been in genuine danger." He barked a short, harsh laugh. "I did *not* know that shooting myself in the leg could've been fatal. I don't know anything about anatomy." He rubbed the heel of his hand over his thigh like the wound still ached. "Fortunately, it wound up looking good to the cops. No killer would risk killing themselves, right?"

"Yeah, luckily, that worked out well for you," I admitted.

"It hurt so bad — like *fire* — and I was bleeding like crazy."

"Same as you would've if Jeron had shot you, and there would only be your word that he hadn't been the one who fired first. Then you headed back to the kitchen. You'd explain the blood trail by saying you went to check whether your father and sister might still be alive. That was a normal, caring response. But really, what you needed to do was make sure that they were dead."

"None of it was supposed to happen," Scott repeated, clearly determined to hang on to the rationalization, wanting or needing to believe that the murder of his father and sister had somehow been accidental or inevitable rather than cold-bloodedly mercenary.

"You went into the cooler and shot them. First him, then her, each with a double tap. *Pew-pew, pew-pew.* Efficient and pragmatic. There was no one to say it hadn't been Jeron who shot them ten minutes earlier; he already had gunshot residue on his hands from when the gun went off, and the residue on yours could be explained by your shooting him."

Scott said nothing, merely stared out into the growing darkness where the tree limbs bowed and dipped in the wind, scattering leaf confetti on top of the dead.

"You didn't think of separating them, just getting rid of *him*?" I asked.

"Now how would I have done that? Excuse me, Brittany, would you mind closing your eyes and ears while I take Dad aside and shoot him? Besides, I was running out of time, bleeding way more than I'd figured I would."

It had been quicker and easier to kill them both there and then, leaving no inconvenient witnesses behind and no one with whom he'd have to share the inheritance.

"You got your mother's burner phone — she would've kept it on her — and dropped it in the bucket. And then you went to go call 911 from one of the phones on the table in the dining room."

"I didn't think I'd make it. I was cold and shivery, nearly passed out a couple of times. I couldn't walk anymore — I crawled. First on my hands and knees, then on my belly like a gator. And it took forever. It was the longest journey of my life, like those phones were moving away down a tunnel and I'd never get to them. I was this close to dying." He held up a thumb and forefinger half an inch apart.

"But you made it."

"I did." He sounded almost proud of the accomplishment. "Well, this has been ... surprisingly good," he said, getting to his feet and dusting off the seat of his pants. "It's been a relief to finally tell someone, to get it all off my chest."

"I get that," I said, standing up. "Keeping secrets takes a lot more energy and effort than most people realize. You must've been so lonely, because it's got to be utterly isolating, right? To have done this massive thing — so terrifying and yet also so clever — and not be able to share it with *anyone*. You can never, ever allow anyone to get truly close. You can never share the real you."

"Yes!" he said, clasping my hands and staring deep into my eyes. "You really understand."

"In killing them, you lost your life too — the life you had. Because from that moment on, you've had to live a fake life, guarding every word you say, minding your face and faking your body language, careful never to slip up and reveal what surely matters most, what the most significant event in your entire life was. And no one really knows what you've been through, what you've had to live with ever since."

"Evil is easy," Madame Laveau had told me earlier. But it wasn't always, not for everyone.

Making decisions in the heat of that July moment *had* been easy for Scott. As his grandfather had said, he was good in an emergency. But afterward — living with what he'd done — that hadn't been easy at all.

Scott stood in front of me, shoulders relaxed now that a weight had been taken off of them, face calm and peaceful. He breathed out a long deep sigh. "Thank you, Garnet," he said. "Truly, I can't thank you enough for this."

"Sure," I said, feeling gratified. I picked up my bag and slung it over my shoulder. "Come on, I'll go with you."

He blinked at me. "Go where?"

"To the police station. Where else? Or I guess if you prefer, we could call them to come out here?"

Scott threw back his head and let out a peal of laughter. In that moment, in that place, the sound of it was shocking.

"I'm not going to speak to the police, Garnet. I'm not going to *confess.*"

"But, but you admitted it!"

"To *you.* Not to them." He gave an amused snort. "I have no intention of telling *them* what really happened."

"What you *did,*" I corrected, nettled by his passive language, his lack of accountability. "Fine, then. *I'll* tell them." Immediately, I wanted to take back the stupid declaration, but Scott didn't seem at all bothered or threatened.

"Sure. Whatever, lady. You just run along and tell them everything," he said pleasantly. "About how you were tying rope around a headstone and sacrificing God only knows what in a graveyard when I just happened along and confessed. How you're a *psychic*" — his fingers sketched quotation marks around the word — "who saw me killing my family. Oh, no, scratch that. You didn't even actually see me doing that, did you? Else you would've known before tonight. You just guessed that part."

Scott retrieved his handkerchief, flapped it out twice, and tucked it into his pocket, while I stood gaping at him like a complete dupe.

"And be sure to tell them how you put this whole absurd story together based on your visions, the character judgments of an old man with dementia, and a little kid who thinks she heard gunshots on an evening of fireworks. Go on, do it! Who are they going to believe — the only survivor of all those murders, the last remaining member of one of New Orleans's oldest families, the poor young man who tragically lost his entire family and came so close to losing his own life? Or the kid, the old-timer, and the kook?" He placed his forefinger under my chin and closed my sagging jaw. "Good luck with Inspector Dupre. Man, she's a peach, isn't she?"

And with that, he pushed past me and walked off into the darkness.

– 45 –

Well, *shit.*

I stood on the spot, watching Scott disappear between tombs and gravestones, at a loss for what to do next.

Should I chase after him and try to stop him? How exactly would I manage that? I could call 911, but it wasn't exactly an emergency, and besides, I didn't want cops coming to *me*, I wanted them going after him. I was uncomfortably aware of the truth of his take on my situation. I *couldn't* imagine cops setting off to arrest Scott purely on my say-so.

Damnit, why hadn't I thought to hit record on my phone at the start of our little chat? Because I hadn't suspected Scott at all, that's why. I hadn't seen through his pleasant charm, his real grief, his lingering limp, and his poor-little-orphaned-me act to see the toxic narcissist beneath. Because I was an idiot.

He'd played me like a harp, just as he had at the country club. His performance had been pitch-perfect and polished, because it was so practiced. He must've put it on for scores of people — cops, relatives, friends — and they'd probably all been taken in just like I had.

What a fool I was. He'd been so relaxed and cooperative, I'd assumed he'd stick around to be arrested, that he'd repeat everything he'd confessed to me to the police. But he'd had no intention of being caught, just the same as on that fateful night when he'd covered his tracks so thoroughly. I knew I should feel relieved he'd left me unharmed. Scott was capable of anything, but like his child self who'd tossed the useless fish back into the ocean, he'd let me go. I should count myself lucky.

But instead, what I mostly felt was irritated and humiliated. I, too, had been fishing. And Scott was the big one who'd gotten away.

I wanted to call Ryan, growl out my frustration, and get some sympathy. And advice, because I sure needed advice. What would Ryan do in this situation? I kicked the chamber pot in frustration. Ryan would never have gotten himself into such a stupid situation in the first place. What would he advise me to do now if he were here? The answer was clear. I took out my phone, thumbed my way through to where I'd saved Detective Dupre's cell number, and hit the call button.

"Caroline Dupre."

"Hi, Detective, this is Garnet McGee. We met at your police station yesterday morning? And—"

"Is this the crackpot psychic?" she snapped.

"I—"

"Get off my tail, will you?"

"I'm sorry?"

"I'm on the road. Son of a bitch behind me is way too close."

"Right. I hate it when they do that," I said, ingratiatingly.

"How did you get this number?" Dupre demanded. She was about to hang up. I could hear it coming.

"Scott Broussard just confessed to me that he killed his father, sister, and Jeron Cooper!" I said quickly.

"*What* did you just say?"

I had her attention now.

"Scott and Melissa Broussard hired Jeron Cooper to rob the restaurant. Melissa was killed when the gun went off accidentally, but then Scott killed Cooper so there would be no comeback, and then he shot his father and sister so he could get full control of the business and the whole inheritance."

"And he just told you this?"

"Well, I'd seen some of it, in my visions, you know? And that got him talking, and he confessed everything."

"It's a *red light,* asshole! What d'ya want me to do?" Dupre yelled. I imagined her dispensing curses and middle fingers while she drove, stealing parking spots, and going for the gap. She was the polar opposite of courteous, considerate Desirae, and I liked her the better for it. "Any witnesses to this confession?"

"No. Well, I mean, we were alone in Metairie Cemetery, so it's not like anyone was around to hear us."

"Metairie *Cemetery?*"

"Yeah, he was coming to visit his family tomb, or at least that's what he *said.* And I came here to— Um, I'm still here. He just left. He's headed for the gates and then home, in all likelihood, if you wanted to pick him up."

Dupre mumbled something that may have been, "For fuck's sake." Then she asked, "Have you been drinking?"

"No! Well, yeah, but just a few sips. I'm not drunk! Or crazy."

"And apart from your so-called visions, do you happen to have any real evidence?"

"Umm …"

"Any facts that I could verify? *Anything* solid?

I thought for a moment. "Yes!" I punched the air in victory. "I do. I have a business card for Broussard's restaurant, with a cell number written on the back. The handwriting is Melissa Broussard's, and the number is for a burner phone. If you get the records for that number, you'll find a bunch of calls and probably texts between her, Scott, and Jeron. And all activity will have ceased around midnight on the night of July Fourth, when Scott killed the phone."

There was a moment of silence then a sniff. "Okay, leave this with me. I'll contact you later." She didn't sound enthusiastic about the prospect, nor did she sound in any great hurry to pursue Scott.

"So you'll go question Scott Broussard?"

"We'll do what needs doing, Miss McGee," she said crossly. "Get out of my way, fool!" I hoped the last was intended for someone on the road.

"Okay, so, I can go back home to Vermont?"

"No, not yet. But you undoubtedly should leave the cemetery."

"I think I'm probably already locked in," I admitted. "But the gates didn't look too high to climb."

"I'm not far away from Metairie; I'll come get you. Wait for me at the gates on Pontchartrain."

"Thanks. See you in a while."

"Wait— Did you tell Scott Broussard you were going to tell the cops about all this?"

"I didn't have to. He already assumed I would. And he didn't care — he said you would never believe me."

"I'm still not sure I do," she said and ended the call.

I sighed in satisfaction. I'd persuaded doubting Detective Dupre to investigate, and I'd scored a ride back to the hotel — unless she planned on taking me straight to the police station or to the local mental hospital. I glanced at my watch, wondering if I had time to complete the wretched banishing ritual. It surely wouldn't take more than a minute or two, and I'd feel better if it was done.

Wind whipped at my hair, and tiny drops of cold rain kissed my face. The deserted cemetery was a whole lot less peaceful and a whole lot more spooky now. It felt like the keys to the place had been handed over to the dead, and it was almost dark.

"Good," I said out loud. "All the better for banishing attachments."

Quickly, I moved to the foot of Mildred's grave. I lit the two candles and, holding one in each hand, walked slowly toward the headstone, reading the prescribed words on the spell as I paced.

"Leave me now, unquiet spirit," I said firmly. "I reject your attachment. I order you to leave me be and to remain in this place when I depart."

I repeated the commands three times, as instructed, then placed the candles on the ground in front of the iron potty, crouched down, and blew them out. Immediately, a faint, whining buzz started in my ears, and I felt a whooshing sensation in my head. Had I done it all wrong? Because it felt like a presence was flooding back *in* rather than going away.

Shaking my head to clear the growing whine, I stood up and dusted off my hands. "Well, that's that," I muttered to myself and gasped when I got a reply.

Two replies, from two different male voices.

Inside my head, I heard Colby. *Run! Get away!*

Behind me, a familiar voice asked, "You all done now?"

– 46 –

I yelped in shock and spun around.

Scott Broussard. He'd crept up behind me while I'd been distracted with the ritual; my voice must've masked the sound of his footsteps.

"Scott! What—"

Go! Run! Colby warned, his voice louder.

"I was already at the gates when I realized I had to come back," Scott said calmly. "No choice, really."

"Why?" My voice was high and breathy. The smell of cola was strong in my nostrils.

"I'm sorry. I *like* you, I do. But I can't allow a loose end, Garnet. Not even a kookie one."

I began edging backward, away from him, but came up short as my heels reached the side of the large potty.

"C'mon, Scott. You don't want to do anything you'll regret."

Run! Run run run!

But I couldn't. I was wedged between the gravestone and Scott.

"What I'll *really* regret is leaving a potential witness. I've come so far, done so much. And to lose it all now because of you? Nope, no can do. Sorry."

He lunged at me, knocking me over.

"No!" I yelled, landing hard on the grass. "NO!"

Before I could roll away and get to my feet, he was on top of me, pinning me in place with his hips.

"Help!" I screamed.

One of his arms batted away the blows I aimed at his head and chest. The other reached across to tug the rope free from the tombstone.

"Help! HELP!"

I thrashed on the ground beneath him, trying to throw off his weight. When I lifted my head and screamed louder, he wrapped the rope around my neck. Tightened it. Above me, his eyes glinted with stone-cold determination.

He pulled the rope tighter, crushing my throat. I couldn't breathe.

They say that in your last moments, your life flashes before your eyes, but what I saw was flashes of what would happen *after* — Ryan's reaction to seeing crime-scene pics of me strangled to death; my mother and father getting the dreadful knock at the door, being felled by the news of my death; the headline on the front page of the *Pitchford Bugle:* "Psychic private eye throttled at scene of dark magic ritual"; Desirae rushing to Ryan's side to console him.

Screw that.

I stopped tugging at the rope that choked off my air, stopped trying to scratch Scott's face. I let my right arm fall sideways, felt around for the chamber pot, and seized the handle. Spots of light burst behind my eyes, and the darkness of unconsciousness closed in. Bringing my arm upright, I knocked it against Scott's head as hard as I could. It *boinged* like a struck gong, and he collapsed on top of me.

"Get *OFF!*" I shoved him to the side and got to my knees, head drooping, gasping for breath.

"Garnet McGee!" someone yelled from off in the distance.

I turned to the voice and saw Detective Dupre running toward me, leaping over urns of flowers, and hurdling gravestones. I collapsed onto the grass. Thank God, the cavalry had arrived.

Scott stirred and groaned feebly, so I hoisted the potty once more and slammed it down onto his back, knocking the wind out of him. Then I sagged back down onto the ground, still clutching my makeshift weapon.

As old metal receptacles went, mine might not have been pretty, but it was very heavy. And dead useful.

– Epilogue –

"**S**omething to drink?" the flight attendant offered.

What I *wanted* was a birdbath-sized margarita. But the thought of anything acidic or alcoholic burning my throat — which was still raw from all the screaming and strangling — made me wince. Hot drinks were likewise out. I shook my head sadly.

"Snacks?"

I eyed the salted peanuts and sighed.

"Just water for us both, please," Ryan said.

A good woman would've told her partner to go ahead and eat and drink whatever he fancied. But I wasn't a good woman; I was a piteous one. That it should come to this: nothing to eat and water to drink. It felt like penance for my lifetime of gluttony.

Ryan tapped his little bottle of sparkling against my bottle of still, reminding me of the toast Scott and I had shared in the cemetery. "Cheer up. The doc said you'll be all better in no time."

"Hmph." I ran a finger under the silk scarf wound around

my neck. I reckoned the rope burn and bruises Scott Broussard had left there would take at least a couple of weeks to fade.

"I think I should consider another line of work," I told Ryan hoarsely.

"That would make the most sense," he replied, but something in his tone told me he didn't think I'd make big decisions based purely on logic, no matter how admirably rational my intentions might be.

I sipped my water — surprisingly good for something tasteless — and rested my head on his shoulder. He'd flown down on the first available flight after getting my call, and he'd stayed by my side through the two days of police questioning that followed. He'd kept apologizing for allowing me to stay on alone and investigate until I'd had to tell him sternly, "You don't 'allow' me to do anything, Chief. I'm an adult. What I chose to do is on me."

He'd called Desirae to update her, and I'd glowed with pride when he'd praised both my second sight and my detecting abilities. Now he took my hand — every single nail chewed down to the quick on the night I'd spent at the police station — and held it firmly in his.

I closed my eyes and rested. The flight back to Burlington was only half full and blessedly quiet — no chanting sports fans and an empty seat to my left where I could dump my purse and bags of last-minute airport shopping — a box of beignet mix which would no doubt lurk in the back of my grocery cupboard until it inched past its expiration date, three bags of extra-hot Gator's Kick chips to be devoured as soon as I could handle spice again, and pralines for Henry. No Roman candy, though, which was probably a good thing — it would give him something other than my horticultural skills to grumble about.

Back in the Eighth District, Detective Dupre was spending her days building a solid case against Scott and probably spending her nights lying awake, wondering how I could testify in front of a jury without any mention of my visions and intuitions. For now, at least, my part was done. Was I glad I'd made the trip? I wasn't sure. I'd nearly been taken out — again — and I'd been left with more horrible memories to add to the collection already stored in the bowels of my damaged brain. Plus, now, I had another trial sometime in my future at which I'd have to testify. It was becoming a habit.

However, I *had* accomplished what Ryan and I had set out to do: figure out exactly what happened that Fourth of July night. It made a difference to me, knowing that I'd stopped a murderer from getting away with taking the lives of his family and of a young man who might have been coming off the rails but who was a long way from being beyond redemption. I'd been able to reassure Anthony that his nephew hadn't murdered anyone, that while he bore some culpability for Melissa Broussard's death, it had ultimately been an accident. I'd been able to tell Mrs. Cooper that Jeron had been killed precisely because he *wasn't* a murderer. I figured knowing what had happened would bring her some comfort and maybe ease a little of Anthony's guilt.

I didn't think Khurran Bashir would care either way exactly how Melissa had died or why. His love for her would blind him to the fault of her involvement, and he'd steadfastly cling to the belief that she'd planned to leave her husband and spend the rest of her life with him. Ah, well, his heart would heal in time. Hearts do.

The restauranters in the French Quarter had some juicy gossip to feed on for a week or three, and CJ and Lisette would have a fine tale to tell the customers who lingered at their bar counter, quaffing cocktails and oysters. Francesca DeMarco — not the sweetest orange in the pocket to start with — would be unaffected by the details of the story, I reckoned. Then again, knowing firsthand what it was like to be on the receiving end of Terry Broussard's selfishness, maybe she'd have a little more sympathy than most for Scott.

I'd once read that history is written by the victors. For a while, that had been Scott Broussard, but now, it would be truth and the justice system that had the final say. Always assuming, of course, that some high-priced lawyer didn't get him acquitted.

I felt a little like a victor myself. Partly, this was due to what I'd uncovered, as well as to winning the fight in the graveyard. But it was also because I hadn't given in to the temptation to accept help from "the dark side." Whether or not there actually had been a gargoyle with a hair fetish, keen to dish some hot tips about the Broussard murders, I'd resisted the *true* temptation, the urge to abandon my scientific, rational self and surrender to mushy, mystical woo. Of course, the truly scary part was that I'd wavered at all. I'd knocked at the door of either evil or stupidity, and I'd been so determined to prove I *could*, that I almost didn't stop to ask if I should.

My mother, predictably, had been thoroughly overexcited to hear about the entity and the graveyard ritual. I hadn't meant to tell her but hadn't been able to come up with a good excuse as to why I'd been in a cemetery after closing hours.

"Didn't I tell you to beware of the interfering woman?" my mother said when I called her. "That was Madame Laveau!" She was clearly delighted at her own perspicacity. "This ritual, now, what exactly did you have to do? Did it involve blood? Bones?"

"Of course not." Not unless you included old Mildred a-moldering in the grave.

"And black magic? You have to be careful with that, you know."

"It involved salt and candles and frankincense."

"*Frankincense!*" she said, sounding awed. "Fancy that! And you never sensed that you were in danger?"

Ryan had asked me the same thing when he'd finally finished hugging me and inspecting my injuries. His face had been tight with anger, fear, and guilt.

"No," I'd had to tell both him and my mother.

The admission pained me, because it proved I was a rotten judge of character.

"Tell me more about the attachment," my mother had demanded.

"I'd rather not."

"It was evil? Of course it was — didn't I deal the devil card? I can hardly wait to tell your father all about this. You know how he always pooh-poohs anything beyond the material world. Just wait until he hears I have proof!"

"It's hardly proof, Mom. The woman could just as well be a complete scammer," I said, though I didn't believe it myself.

"How can you say that after everything that happened?" my

mother demanded. "The only thing that didn't materialize was a whirling wind — the storm that the cards foretold."

For a moment, I considered telling her about the rainstorm that had been blowing up in the cemetery and, before that, the eddy of cold air in the dark corner of the gargoyle hotel, but I was saved from having to add fuel to my mother's fire when she said, "We'll discuss it all in detail when you get back. Your father wants a word with you now." She lowered her voice. "I think he's a little shocked, to be honest. What do you do when you're a nonbeliever and then suddenly, you're confronted with the undeniable *fact* that the world you can see and touch and measure is not all that exists?"

Good question.

"What in the world have you been telling your mother?" my father said when he came on the line. "She's jumping around like a hungry flea on a dog."

"Just the bare basics, honest." I could just about hear his eyes rolling. "I thought she'd get a kick out of hearing about it."

"Did you consider me, kiddo? Because you know I'll be hearing about this nonsense nonstop now. It'll go on for weeks!"

"Sorry, Dad," I said, laughing. "Maybe it's a good time to get away on a fishing trip?"

"Seriously, kiddo," he said, all trace of humor gone. "Are you okay?"

The concern in his voice made me choke up, which was painful, given the rough state of my throat.

"I'm fine, Dad, really. Please don't worry."

"I love you."

"Love you too, Pops. Bye."

"Wait— Your mother wants another word with you."

"Hello?" she said. "Still there, Garnet?"

"For my sins," I muttered.

"I forgot to ask the most important question: did it work? The ritual, I mean. Did it banish the attachment?"

"Yes, definitely," I'd told her, though at the time, I hadn't been certain.

Now, however, I was pretty sure it had. For the past couple of nights, I'd slept like the dead. Or rather, like the dead are supposed to sleep. There'd been no bad dreams, no phantom knocking, no sense that I was being watched. Whether that meant the ritual — mystical or psychological — had worked, or whether it was because I'd dealt with my real demons — the inner ones of doubt and approval seeking — was anyone's guess. My mother would surely go with the former explanation, which automatically made me a believer in the second.

Inner monsters weren't the sort you could banish by burning sage and reciting words, but I'd done battle with my jealousy and my need to have my worth validated, my gift vindicated. I'd solved the puzzle using my brains and my gift, and that made me feel proud. Also, in seeing my own petty issues contrasted with the real pain of those who'd lost loved ones, I'd matured a little. That counted as a victory too.

I snuggled closer into Ryan's shoulder, enjoying the warmth of his hand holding mine, the touch of his lips when he kissed the top of my head. It had been so good to have him by my side, supporting and protecting me these last few days. Being able to call him and knowing, *knowing* that he would rush to me, had made all the difference. Not to be alone, not to feel adrift in the world, fighting battles on my own like some feral cat — it had meant more to me than I'd been able to express to Ryan.

If anyone had asked me — just a year ago — about falling in love again and trusting myself to a real, deep relationship, I would've scoffed. To lose your heart was to risk losing yourself — that's what I would've told them. Loving someone opens you up to being ripped open and left hollowed out when they leave you. Now, close enough to feel the steady thud of Ryan's heart under my cheek, I was ready to risk it all again.

"I love you, Chief," I told him softly.

"I love you more," he replied, holding me tighter.

I loved you first. Always and forever, came the faintest echo of Colby's words. I told myself that they were more a fond memory than an actual message from him. Perhaps I was at last completely free of any and all attachments, I thought with a bittersweet pang.

The flight attendant was talking to a passenger in a row ahead and across the aisle from us. He wanted a window seat. It was his first time ever flying, and he wanted to see the clouds. Could he move to a window seat? I grabbed my bags off the seat beside me, expecting the attendant to direct him there. But her eyes passed over the empty spot as though someone was already sitting there, and she pointed to a seat several rows back.

I stretched out my left hand and let it lie on the seat beside me. My lips curved into a smile. I had one hand in each world, and it felt good.

Better than good, it felt like the best of *bon temp.*

Dear Reader,

If you enjoyed this book, I'd really appreciate it if you'd leave a review, no matter how short, on your favorite online store or on Goodreads. Every review is valuable in helping other readers discover the series.

Visit https://dl.bookfunnel.com/4groclo2pv to join my VIP Readers' Group and get my monthly newsletter, which includes advance notice of my latest releases, competitions, giveaways and offers for free review copies, as well as a behind-the-scenes peek at my writing process. I won't clutter your inbox or spam you, and I will never share your email address with anyone.

I'd love to hear from you! Come say hi on Facebook, Twitter or Instagram, or reach out to me via my website, and I'll do my best to get back to you.

– Jo Macgregor

Other books for adults by this author

The First Time I Died
The First Time I Fell
The First Time I Hunted
Dark Whispers

Acknowledgements

Thank you to my fabulous beta and expert readers: Emily Macgregor, Nicola Long, Edyth Bulbring, Chase Night and Heather Gordon, without whom these books would be much the poorer! I deeply appreciate each one of you.